Readers love
JAIME SAMMS

Off Stage: In the Wings

"Reading this well-written, intense story was all-consuming, but quite emotionally satisfying…. Thanks, Jaime, for a thought provoking, intense reading experience."

—Rainbow Book Reviews

"The story flowed so smoothly and you were never jarred out of the story. The author gave such a quality story with wonderful characters. It was a wonderful and powerful read and I'm really glad that I got the opportunity to read this book. Take the chance and fall into this wonderful story. You'll be very glad that you did."

—Love Bytes Reviews

The Foster Family

"A wonderful, deeply engaging book that I won't soon forget."

—My Fiction Nook

"It has the perfect mix of inner struggles, angst, friendship, humour and love."

—Sinfully Sexy Book Reviews

By JAIME SAMMS

Better
The Foster Family
Grand Adventures (Dreamspinner Anthology)
My Rugby-playing Twink
New Linen
Not As Easy As It Looks
Paying the Piper
Renegade
Stained Glass
Still Life
Wishing on a Blue Star (Dreamspinner Anthology)

OFF STAGE
Off Stage: Right • Off Stage: In the Wings

WINGS OF FAITH
Angel Elegy
Angel Requiem

Published by DREAMSPINNER PRESS
http://www.dreamspinnerpress.com

scars
on his
heart

Jaime Samms

Dreamspinner Press

Published by
DREAMSPINNER PRESS

5032 Capital Circle SW, Suite 2, PMB# 279, Tallahassee, FL 32305-7886 USA
http://www.dreamspinnerpress.com/

Scars on His Heart
© 2014 Jaime Samms.

Cover Art
© 2014 Photo by Ethan James Photography.
ethanjamesphotography.com
Design by Paul Richmond.
Cover content is for illustrative purposes only and any person depicted on the cover is a model.

ISBN: 978-1-63216-179-6
Digital ISBN: 978-1-63216-180-2
Library of Congress Control Number: 2014943219
First Edition August 2014

Printed in the United States of America
∞
This paper meets the requirements of
ANSI/NISO Z39.48-1992 (Permanence of Paper).

This one is for E, because there is nothing like sitting in front of your publisher reading brand new unedited material when you've never read your stuff to an audience before. You make it safe to be brave, so thanks, Elizabeth. For everything.

one

AWKWARD. THAT'S what this was. Awkward and silent and slightly terrifying. As Joe walked, he listened for the crunch of Cam's boots behind him on the path. They progressed in silence toward the pond where they had swum together as teenagers and to the beach covered in flat, smooth river stones. Those stones were the goal. They had been sent to collect some for the centerpieces for the reception tables for his cousin Katie's wedding. He suspected the task had been his aunt's way of thrusting him and Cam together. Alone. To talk. As they hadn't done since Joe had left the farm five years ago. So far, there had been no talking.

Joe spent the walk from house to pond remembering what a spring breeze felt like on parts of him that had no business being bare to it. Old thoughts of wind and sun on his ass only made him wonder if today was going to be a replay of That Day. Not that he had been thinking it might be. Certainly every moment of That Day came back to his mind with sparkling clarity the instant Cam walked into Aunt Marie's kitchen this morning and eyed Joe over the rim of his coffee mug.

Joe was home for his second-youngest cousin's wedding. His aunt Marie had picked him up at the bus station and brought him back to the farm the night before. When they arrived, just after midnight, Cam had already gone up to bed and Joe had crashed out on the couch. He'd been grateful for the quiet homecoming. So much swam through his head, he'd felt he'd needed the time to himself before confronting Cam.

"You're thinking again." Cam's voice cut through the cheerful nature sounds of the spring morning. He drew Joe to a stop long before they got to the clearing. "You've always been the thinker, huh?"

Joe shoved his hands into his jeans pockets. "So?" He wanted to pull free of the gentle graze of Cam's fingers in the crook of his elbow. He wanted to pull free because the grip wasn't powerful enough, and if he couldn't have it all, he'd rather have nothing. He remained still, a deer under Cam's bright, knowing gaze.

"So stop thinking," Cam teased. "Just tell me what's on your mind or—"

"You remember Maggie's wedding day?" Joe asked, failing to block the events from his own mind. Not the wedding. That had been incidental to what had happened after the wedding, in the clearing just around the next bend in the path.

Cam studied him, stoic expression giving him nothing. "I remember soggy grass."

So not what Joe remembered. Cam's gaze remained steady and impossible to read.

"Come on." Cam let his hand fall back to his side as he turned to follow the path. "We're going to be late and your aunt needs those rocks."

Joe watched Cam's back for a count of ten but the calming mantra had no effect.

"Soggy grass?" All of a sudden it mattered. He didn't want to let it go, because for whatever reason he'd thought they had come out here together, Cam was obviously only headed down to the pond to get the stones as he'd said. Nothing more. Joe's memory of That Day was of something Cam either didn't remember or chose to forget.

A breeze blew up, picking strands of silky hair from Cam's ponytail. That had tickled, Joe remembered, and stuck in his sweat when Cam pulled him closer, draping over his back. He shivered.

"If you'd just hurry the fuck up, you wouldn't be so cold!" Cam called to him.

"I'm not cold."

The clearing was in sight now, and it kind of surprised him to see it wasn't much different from his recollection of it, even years later. The grass was as green as in his memory and as soggy as Cam apparently remembered. It squished underfoot as they crossed. Around the edges, bright green moss climbed the trunks of the poplars. The scent of new growth, peculiar to the new buds of the balm of Gilead that made up this glade, filled his senses. His uncle had planted the fast-growing trees all through the farm's back acres, and the smell was home to Joe. He breathed it in.

"Cam." He stopped in the center of the open space. "Is that really all you remember?"

Cam had made it across the clearing. He thought his friend might just keep walking, disappear down the winding path through the trees on the other side, and pretend he hadn't heard.

But he didn't. He stopped, free hand in his pocket and the other tightening and loosening on the handle of the pail he carried. The clench and release made a rhythmic sound of the pail's squeaking handle, as steady and unchangeable as Cam himself. His golden eyes fixed on the path, gaze following it into the shade of the new leaves as though he wished he could too. Something held him back.

"What do you want, Joe?" he asked. "To know I remember exactly how soft your skin is? How tight you are? How fucking perfect we should have been?" He turned around. "You want to relive a five-year-old dream like it's something you can keep locked away in your head for a rainy day, and you don't even get that for me it doesn't work that way."

"Then how does it work for you?"

For a number of heartbeats, Cam said nothing at all.

"Cam?"

"Do you know how pale you are in the sunshine, Joe?" Finally, he actually lifted his gaze enough to look Joe in the eye. "How very white and pasty your ass is—"

"Fuck you."

Cam grinned. "I remember. The difference between your hairy chest and your smooth back, and the noises you make. Oh yeah. I remember it. And, I remember the soggy grass because it left green smudges on your knees and a wiggly pattern of dents in your skin, and I always think...." He grinned wider. "Wouldn't all those marks look better on your really pasty white ass."

"God, you're such a prick!"

But Cam only shook his head and sighed. "I'm honest, Joe. Which is a hell of a lot more than I can say for you."

When he turned this time, there was no looking back. No slowing. No questioning or waiting to see if Joe followed. He was just walking away.

AUNT MARIE was pleased with the collection of river stones they brought back and much to Cam's dismay, had cheerfully enlisted them both to help her arrange the sixty-odd centerpieces for Katie's reception tables.

"You know, Auntie," Cam said, "just because I'm gay doesn't mean I have any sense of style. I could make the ugliest centerpieces poor Katie-girl ever laid eyes on."

She tsked at him. "You'll do just fine, sweetheart. Here." She indicated a finished example. "Just do that."

"Just do that," he muttered with an indulgent grin.

"You too, sugar. Snap, snap." Aunt Marie literally snapped her fingers in Joe's face. "Pay attention."

Joe had been paying attention. To Cam. Cam knew because he could feel the heat of Joe's gaze on him as he joked with Aunt Marie. And he'd been acutely aware that no matter what he told Joe about That Day and what he might or might not remember, the thing that stood out most in his mind, always, was that Joe had left. They'd done what they had done—and Cam had really thought it meant something—and then Joe had run off to school and never come back.

Now, Joe blinked at his aunt, and Cam watched him fumble a thin smile onto his delicate features. Five years might have passed since that ill-fated Day of Disaster, but he could still read Joe's expressions. That much hadn't changed. He knew his friend was wondering if Aunt Marie had noticed his fascination. Difficult to believe she could have missed it but all she did was start on the next decoration and begin to hum "YMCA." Cam grinned.

Joe scowled.

Cam refused to read anything into the expression.

It took them hours to get the pieces done. Cam's back ached and his fingers were pricked raw from the wires in the ribbons, but he was pleased to see that his clumsy attempts weren't terribly different from Aunt Marie's or Joe's, with his nimble fingers and confidence in his ability to get the bows just right.

It was so unfair that he was right there and so far away just on the other side of the table. It was doubly unfair that Cam had to watch him work and be reminded once again of how perfect his hands were. How delicate his wrists and fingers were and how very fucking strong he was even though he didn't look it. And ironic that the candleholders he arranged were clearly the best of the bunch. As if that didn't give him away. But no. No one in his family even suspected who he really was.

Cam shook his head. That was just sad.

"Cam, honey, be a dear and start on the flower arrangements," Marie said. "I'll get Joe to help with loading these into the boxes, and then I'll be back to help you."

There it was again. Joe was straight, so he got to do the easy shit. Cam was gay, so he had to figure out how the hell to make roses and daisies look right together in the same vase. Fan-fucking-tastic.

"You do know I'm a stableboy, right?" he asked her.

She smiled at him. "You know you're much more than that, honey. Now"—she waved at the flowers and vases—"arrange."

She left him to it and began directing the loading of the candle arrangements into the boxes for the short ride over to the tables set up in the barn.

She was back before long, though, and they worked together in silence.

"You're not as bad at this as you seem to think you are." She examined his first attempt, shifted a single bloom, and nodded approval. "Katie will be pleased."

Cam gave a small nod and a smaller smile. "That's all that matters."

"What's wrong, honey?" She came around the table, wiping her hands on her tan walking shorts. "You've had that long face on all day. What is it?"

"It's nothing, Auntie. Not yours to worry about." He smiled down at her, and it struck him that her eyes were the same changeable greeny-brown as Joe's. Right now, they were clear and light—filled with happiness. Almost green to match the moss-colored golf shirt she had on. He envied Joe, suddenly, to have that family resemblance in common with her. With anyone, really. There was no one in the world whom Cam could look at and say, there, that's where my gold eyes come from. Or his thick, ringlet-tight tan curls or his height or oddly crooked pinkie fingers and big toes.

She tsked again and slapped his arm. "You might not be blood, young man, but you've been mine to worry about for a long time."

"Since the very first shovelful of horse shit I ever tossed out of your barn," he agreed.

"Since before then, Cameron. Your daddy made sure of that. Now out with it."

"Honestly. It's nothing." He hated the dark aura that clouded her gaze whenever anyone mentioned Cam's vanished father. The man had left Cam, five years old, alone on the farm after working there for a season. Only a note, pleading with Aunt Marie and Uncle Albert to look after him, and the few clothes Cam had owned were left with him. No one had ever heard from him again. Uncle Albert tried for years to find out what happened to him, or who Cam's mother might have been, but never had any success. Eventually, they'd stopped trying, and when legally allowed to, they had adopted Cam. They were his family now. He, one of their many strays.

"Don't you lie to me, boy," Marie admonished gently. "I know nothing, and this isn't it. Talk."

She never could let sleeping dogs alone. He offered her a pale smile, then sighed. "You don't think he's acting strange?" Cam asked, his gaze shifting from flowers to Joe's back as he hefted a box onto the wagon.

"How did you expect him to act? Gone for years like he has been"—she shook her head, a quick motion of perplexed annoyance—"he's no more strange now than he was when he came home for Albert's funeral."

But Cam wasn't convinced. Joe had always been the quiet one. He brooded. Still, he wasn't as happy to be home for his cousin's perfect day as he should be. This was a wedding, not a funeral, and he was acting like something in his world had ended.

"He just seems so… sad. You think it's just me?" Maybe it was. Maybe he was projecting what he was feeling onto Joe because he'd wanted his old friend, his almost ex-lover, to be more enthused about this reunion. He watched, frustrated and silent, as Joe loaded the last box and waved the hand on the tractor off toward the barn. Joe turned without a word and disappeared into the house.

"It's the wedding," Marie decided, letting the dark shadow pass. "You'll get yours soon enough. You just have to find the right boy."

That made him smile. The right boy. What would she say if she knew? "I suppose so."

"I know so. Now, here come the girls. You go inside, get yourself a sandwich, and get yourself back to work."

"Always more shit to shovel." He kissed her cheek and took the opportunity to flee. He loved Joe's family like he imagined he might love his own if he had one. The endless stream of female cousins had always been a reliable source of entertainment, hugs, and food. They'd also been shameless in their flirting, even knowing he was gay. He'd never made a secret of it, and it didn't faze them in the least. Today, with thoughts of Joe so prevalent, hell, with Joe so very *there*, he was not in the mood to fend them all off.

Accepting Auntie's offered escape, he made his run for the kitchen.

NOW THAT his gaggle of female cousins had gone outside, the house was very quiet, and Joe liked it that way. In his memory, the place was a hub of activity and chaos, but at the moment, with the women all out in the yard, gathered around the picnic tables to arrange flowers, inside, it was cool, quiet, and serene. He'd missed both sides of this place.

Closing his eyes, he ran his palm along the banister as he mounted the steps. Three on the right, two on the left, the sixth in the middle and skip the last. Only way to sneak up the stairs without making them creak. Many misadventures of his youth had taught him how to get from the door to his bedroom without making a sound. He could still literally do it with his eyes closed.

At the top he turned sharply right and followed the galley hallway to the end, keeping close to the railing until he got to the blue-painted door of his old room. For a second, he hesitated. The last time he'd been in there....

"You okay?" Cam pushed the door open and entered, closing it behind him.

"Funerals suck." Joe kept his back to the room and his eyes on the pastures.

"Yeah. I'm sorry, man."

Joe shrugged. "Why?" He wrapped his arms around himself. "You didn't do anything."

"I'm just sorry you're hurting."

He shouldn't have allowed it, but when Cam circled his bulky arms around him, he didn't move away. He didn't protest. Every cousin and aunt had given him hugs, full ones, perfumed ones, soft, or bony ones. His uncles had patted his shoulder or done that weird guy handshake and half hug, pounding him on the back and mumbling something appropriately sympathetic.

Cam's arms went around his waist, his chin rested on his shoulder, and good God, but it felt nice to have the strength there to hold him up if he felt like collapsing into it. He didn't, but it was nice just the same.

The very best thing was that he didn't say any of the kindly meant platitudes. No speech about how his uncle was better off after his long sickness, or how everyone could get on with things now, or how much he would be missed. Yes, all those things were true. It didn't change the fact that now both his parents were dead, his sister too, and now Uncle Albert. No matter how many aunts and uncles, how many cousins, he was alone in the world. His blood family was gone, and he was all that was left. All there might ever be.

"Hey."

Joe about jumped out of his skin. Cam's voice leapt out of his head to fill the room. He almost turned, but resisted. Because he didn't want to look at Cam? Or because he wished with all his being for that same feeling of safety and belonging he'd felt with Cam's heavily muscled arms holding almost too tight around his ribs?

"You okay?"

Joe marveled at how the man could fill all the empty space around him by just standing there.

"Joe?"

"I'm fine."

"Hiding out?"

He crossed his arms over his chest, thought better of the motion because it was a poor substitute, and pushed his hands into his pockets. "Maybe." Immediately, the pull of tender skin on his back eased.

"From?"

Honestly? He wasn't sure, so he didn't say anything. Behind him, the door latch snicked softly.

"What are you doing?" The way Joe's heart pounded wasn't right. The sweat suddenly dampening his palms and stinging his back brought a regretful lump to his throat.

A soft chuckle rolled through the room on the back of Cam's sweet hay-and-horse barn scent. "Honestly?" The word sent a shiver up Joe's spine. "I think I'm stalking you."

"That's awesome." And in an unsettling sort of way, it was. Because it was Cam, and because he wanted it to mean something.

"You only have yourself to blame, you know. You're the one who brought up That Day, and now I can't get that image of you out of my head."

"So...." Joe turned away from the window to look at his old friend. "I mentioned sex we had years ago and that means... what to you, exactly?"

"You want...." Cam lifted a shoulder and let it fall, sidling a little closer.

"No, I don't."

Cam snickered. "Right. Because you're not gay. I forgot. Sometime when you were kneeling in the grass with your pants around your ankles and your ass in the air, I forgot the line about you being straight."

"Who's mad now?" Joe asked, edging toward the door.

"Don't know why you think I shouldn't be. You let me fuck you, then you ran away."

"I went to school. Different thing."

"Yes. Right. Went to college and in five years, only came home when someone died."

Joe flinched because hearing truth, especially couched in nastiness, didn't make it any less true. Just made its already sharp edges jagged as Cam pulled it out and plunged it in again with more barbs.

"And you spent all that time dating girls and what? Pretending what we did was an experiment?"

"For your information I happen to like dating girls."

"But fucking boys."

"Fuck you!"

"You keep saying that but I don't think you really mean it." Cam stalked closer to him, and somehow without his noticing, he'd been backed up until the window frame dug against his thighs.

"What are you doing?" he asked again, enunciating, because he still needed an answer and he was pretty sure Cam was being dense on purpose. He intended to shove Cam off, but Cam kiboshed that plan, grabbing him by the wrist and advancing that last step that left Joe's shoulder blades pressed against the window. Cool glass countered the sharp sting of pain, and he managed not to flinch, but barely. "What are you doing?" His breath came faster now, and he arched to keep the tops of his shoulders against the glass and spare the rest of his back.

"What does it look like I'm doing?"

Joe should say something. Stop what was going on. Do something. But Cam lifted his arm, his knuckles impacted the window, and once again, the contrast of cold glass against the warmth of Cam's grip distracted him for that critical heartbeat in which *no* would have been possible.

"Caveman," Joe muttered, staring up into the intense, glittering gold of Cam's eyes, unable to look anywhere else.

Cam grunted and pressed forward.

Joe's head told him he should stop this, but a lot of the rest of him wanted to give in. "Cam."

Cam smiled, a slow sort of expression that left the hairs on the back of Joe's neck on end.

"What are you doing?" He put his free hand on Cam's chest with some vague notion of pushing him away. And still, his friend said nothing.

Experimentally, he did push. He wasn't sure what he expected to happen or if he was surprised when that hand joined the other against the glass. Not being surprised was maybe not the same as wanting it to continue. And yet he didn't stop it.

And Cam didn't say anything. He just stared, big, not-quite-brown eyes clear, focused, and demanding.

"What do you want?" A different question might get him an answer.

Cam smiled, but didn't speak.

There went every little hair on Joe's body, standing on end, making his skin tingle, keeping his focus on Cam completely.

"You know"—Joe had to swallow before he could continue—"when a person asks a question, it's generally because they want an answer."

"What am I doing? I'm getting you where I want you. What do I want?" He leaned so close Joe could smell turkey and mustard on his breath. "I should think that's pretty obvious."

It wasn't as though the kiss could be a surprise at this point. Still, Joe gasped, and that parting of lips gave Cam the opening to push his tongue into Joe's mouth. The pressure of Cam's taking forced Joe's head back against the window. He felt like a bug, pinned there, wrists, head, back cold against the glass, thighs aching with a pleasant throb where the lip of the windowsill dug in. His skin complained at the stretch over ribs and the bunching of muscles under its still raw surface. Cam trapped him where he wanted him and Joe did nothing. He let him, and despite the discomfort, he liked it.

It wasn't as though Cam was taking what Joe didn't want to give. Only that he was taking what he wanted. Nothing short of an outright refusal to go to this place would stop him, and maybe Cam knew it, but Joe wasn't ready to make anything that final.

Some part of him knew anyone passing through the yard or pasture could easily look up and see him like this. The thought should have spurred him to push Cam away. It only made him groan because getting caught would be… final. A relief, maybe. A way to get out of the impossible situation. Out of his life.

Cam's free hand that had been resting on one of Joe's hips slid up until calloused fingers traveled along his throat, calling him back to the immediate sensations of his body, coaxing out another moan. Thick thighs pressed against Joe's. Surely he'd have indelible marks on the backs of his legs where they were clamped to the windowsill. The pain was just enough to make his brain melt. Not so much he wanted it to stop.

If he twisted and squirmed, the pain would become real. The hold would become real. Or it would be let go. Either way was a step toward solid ground of one sort or another. Joe hung by Cam's grip, suspended over the swampy mess of his own emotional wasteland and reveled in the fact he felt anything at all.

Cam glided his thumb along under Joe's chin, fingers up under his hair, tightening, holding his head where he couldn't get out of the kiss.

Not that he tried, but now Cam had him immobile, exposed, and helpless, and something about being that much under another's control freed him. He gave. Everything Cam wanted in that moment, Joe gave. As in the grass That Day, everywhere Cam had led, Joe followed. Nothing between them had changed.

Joe squirmed. Cam's grip tightened, the kiss deepened. He thrust his tongue farther past Joe's teeth, and the squirming to get away turned to rubbing and grinding and then stillness as the silky power of Cam's tongue in his mouth and the rough pressure of his hands on Joe's skin overtook everything else, and all he knew was that Cam owned him.

He had no idea how that happened. But it was done, and just when he'd decided it was good, Cam moved away.

"The question isn't really what I want at all, is it, Joe?" Cam asked. And he walked out, closing the door behind him.

Joe slumped, resting his ass on the windowsill, trying to find his brain cells that seemed to have flowed south, along with every ounce of blood in his body, straight to his traitorous dick. He palmed it once, twice, cursed, then popped open the top button of his jeans. Just for some relief.

Yeah, right. Relief came only when he slipped his hand inside, yanked his cock out, and began to stroke. He pushed his jeans down far enough for what he needed, and his ass contacting the window was a reminder of the contrast, cold to hot, Joe's reluctance to Cam's insistence. He didn't need fantasies or have to close his eyes to call up images. All he needed was the knowledge that Cam could take away his autonomy with a kiss and a grip like iron, and Joe would let him.

Part of the arousal was in the terror of that thought, and he groaned, pushed his entire back against the window, just to feel the reminders of why it was a bad idea. Still, Cam's possession sizzled through his memory, and the pain in his back faded to unimportant. Or, at least it was less important than even the memory of Cam. He jacked off in record time.

He found tissues to clean himself up, and when he passed the window again on the way out, Cam waved up at him from where he was leaning on the pasture fence facing the house. One of the yearlings nibbled at his hair, and he patted the horse, turning his back on Joe.

"You have got to be fucking kidding me," Joe muttered, moving out of Cam's line of sight. He rolled his shoulders and felt his T-shirt resist, sticking to his skin, then popping free. "Shit." He reached around to feel the spot and felt dampness. "Goddammit." He peeled the shirt off over his head and examined the fabric. A streak of red dots adorned it in a slanting line.

"Joe?" A sharp knock on the door accompanied the soft female voice saying his name. It made him jump, and he hastily balled the shirt up and crammed it into the trash bin.

"Be right out, Aunt Marie."

"I need a few things in town, Joe. Do you think you can make a run?"

"Of course! Yes. I'll be right down."

The doorknob rattled, and for an unhinged moment, Joe was sure his aunt was about to walk in on him in the ultimate adolescent nightmare. And he was well past adolescence.

"It's for dinner, Joe, so I'll need you to hurry." Her footsteps padded away toward the stairs, and he breathed out a sigh of relief. It really was as if he was back in that summer between high school and college. Because being eighteen apparently hadn't been brutal enough the first time.

Gritting his teeth, he grabbed a new shirt, pulled it on, and hurried across the hall to the bathroom where he could examine the damage. The cuts weren't that bad, but a day and a half was not enough for them to heal, and he'd aggravated the scabbing-over process so that they were bleeding again. Not profusely, but enough that if he didn't cover them, he'd ruin another shirt. He went back to his room, retrieved the bloodied shirt and put it on under the good one, and hurried out to his truck. He could go to the clinic in town and have them bandaged.

If he wore a flannel overshirt, no one would notice the bulges. No one would ask him to explain.

two

MAYBE IT was wrong of him to enjoy that show so much, Cam thought. But the sight of Joe's ass, still as pale as he remembered, plastered against the glass, the fast pumping of his arm, was a heady vision. Sure, it left Cam with a boner and wanting relief, but it was a kind of proof Joe couldn't deny. That was why Cam had been sure to let Joe know he'd seen.

Joe couldn't pretend it hadn't happened if he had a witness.

Next to him, the horse huffed gently, and Cam patted her neck. "You saw that too, right, girl?" he asked with a small smile. "Equine witness. No one can argue with that." She whickered softly in response and nuzzled at his pockets.

More than the proof that Joe wasn't impervious to their past, Cam enjoyed the feeling of the control he had. The control Joe gave him. Later, they'd talk about the shape of the control and of Joe's surrender. Later, once Cam managed to convince him to give it up again.

"Come on." Cam took the horse by her halter and led her toward the barn. "You need to get cleaned up and ready for the big day. You have an important part to play."

For the next hour, he hosed, scrubbed, lathered, and rinsed the big horse, and took his time brushing water and knots from her shaggy coat. When she was dry and clean, he fed her and left her in her stall. She'd need prettying up, but that wasn't his department. He'd mention to Aunt Marie that maybe Joe would make a good candidate, with those supple fingers of his, to braid the mare's mane and tail.

He'd had plenty of practice making his mounts pretty for his dressage competitions. Cam had once thought he should find such an activity entirely too girly to take seriously. But Joe had never skimped on the care of his horses or the attention to detail in making them presentable for tournaments. It took a long time for Cam to get that it wasn't about how pretty the animal looked. One of the worst arguments he'd ever had with Joe had taught him the truth behind the pampering.

Joe's hands were no less supple and talented twisting bits of mane into plaits than Cam had noticed they were on the reins, guiding the horse through his paces. He had to stand on a stool to reach the animal's fetlock, and Cam could see in the horse's eyes there was no way he was lowering his head for something as petty as getting his hair done.

Cam didn't blame him. It was demeaning.

"You know, you really should look at show jumping or—"

"Shut up." Joe didn't even look at him, but kept his eyes on his task. The wine-colored ribbon he was braiding into the horse's mane blended well with the russet and contrasted with the coal black strands in his mane. It also matched the jacket Joe would be wearing, and Cam hated just a little bit that he was gay enough to notice these things.

Or maybe he hated that he was gay enough to notice Joe, to see everything *about him, and know Joe noticed nothing about him in return. Joe didn't care to notice, because Joe wasn't gay.*

Except if Cam got close enough, he'd see Joe shake, watch the braid go a little askew, and feel the sigh come out of his friend as he pulled the work out and started again.

"Did you want something?" Joe asked. Irritation edged his voice.

"I just came to clean the stalls. But you're using this one."

"Only this one."

Cam remained where he was, watching, fascinated by the quick movements of Joe's fingers, the way the ribbon was slowly eaten up inside the twists of hair. The stillness that surrounded this small space while the whole rest of the barn hummed with activity fascinated him. This particular horse, Blue Reign, he was called, exuded a kind of regal calm most of the time. Here and now, it was as if that steady, unflinching demeanor was amplified, throwing out a shield that kept the rest of the world out.

"This is the one I need to clean," Cam said.

"So wait."

"I am waiting."

"Somewhere else."

"What?" Cam took a step forward and leaned on the low door near the horse's head. "Am I throwing you off your game?"

Joe let out a sharp breath but said nothing.

"I am."

"You could not throw me off anything," Joe told him.

Then why are your hands still shaking? *Cam wondered. But he didn't dare ask. That might, in fact, ruin his friend's concentration. He patted the horse's nose instead, and the animal tossed his head high, nearly knocking Joe off his stool and ripping the almost finished braid from his fingers.*

"I don't have time to do all these braids twice. Do you mind?"

"Sorry." Cam felt a little bad, but at the same time, he couldn't help himself. Getting under Joe's skin had become a favorite pastime. "Here. Let me do some. I can make them pretty enough for the ring."

"Don't touch him!"

"I just want to help."

"You don't help! You fuck everything up."

For a moment Cam was dumbfounded. "I what?*"*

"Just... go away. I don't need you here." Joe soothed the horse to stillness again and began undoing the ruined braid.

"You already forget you're the one who asked me to come along?"

"I asked for a stable hand. I didn't ask for you."

"Well, excuse the fuck out of me for wanting to help."

"You don't help," Joe said again.

"Because you don't let me! I can manage a few braids, Joe."

"Don't touch my horse!" Joe slapped Cam's hands away. "I can do it myself. Go wait outside. I'll let you know when I'm done in here."

"You know what?" Cam tossed his pitchfork against the stall wall. "Toss your own shit, asshole. Next time, trust me, I'll stay as far away as I can fucking get."

"Good!"

The horse danced restlessly, tossing his head and nickering at the raised voices and the clatter of Cam's tools as he flung them into a corner.

"Shhh. Sh." Joe stroked and cooed and whispered softly to the animal for a long time. Cam, listening, watching through the open doorway from where he leaned on the fence in the yard and chewed mercilessly on his lip. Because he damn well was gay enough to know he wanted that kind of tender caress on his face, his neck. He followed the path of Joe's lovely hands down Blue Reign's shoulder and let a shudder travel through him, just as it did the horse.

"You lucky son of a bitch," he whispered.

Nearly an hour passed as he watched. Joe said nothing as he led the horse down the staging area toward the gate and his turn in the dressage rink. His mount gleamed in the sunshine. Every braid fell in a neat, perfect line, terminated with a precise red knot. His own jacket and black pants and boots were brushed and polished to immaculate exactitude.

As they passed, Blue Reign lowered his head just enough to brush his nose along the curve of Joe's neck. Joe's soft laughter trailed after them, and Cam's chest caved in.

"Fucking lucky bastard."

They'd won that tournament. Horse and beautiful young Joe were in perfect synch, not one hoof or hair out of place despite Cam's interference in their preshow ritual. And Cam didn't watch because he was too busy shoveling shit.

If only he could have anything approaching that kind of connection with the man now. He'd fallen completely that day and he knew it. Nothing he'd had or done since then had compared to just being around Joe on a daily basis. It hadn't stopped him trying to bury the feelings in other men's asses, in learning to tie them up and command them, but none of it ever approached the serenity of knowing he was, like that horse, completely in Joe's hands. Somehow, he had to make Joe understand that.

THE JINGLE of harnesses ringing through the barn made Joe think of the wind chimes on his mother's balcony, and he smiled. It barely made him sad anymore to think about the apartment he'd grown up in. Or the people who'd raised him. His quiet, distracted father and his practical, dependable mother had created a safe haven for a boy who never managed to fit his square peg into any of society's round holes. Didn't mean he didn't miss them every day, but at least he could manage a smile for them now, fifteen years later.

Here, on his aunt and uncle's farm, he'd managed to carve out an ill-fitting, but still safe place for himself after his parents' deaths. It had taken time and more patience from his guardians than he would have thought anyone had, but he'd finally molded himself into their family alongside his riotous cousins and the melee of farmhands. It had been a good place to recover from the shattering of his life. He'd always loved the sanctuary of the barn and the stoic horses the best, and he'd retreated there now, hoping for some solitude and time to get his head screwed back on after Cam's display in the upstairs bedroom. It had worked for a while too. But eventually, the dust and the smell of warmth, clean hay and not-so-clean hay reminded him of a summer he should try not to dwell on.

"You look happy." Cam came up close and patted the shaggy yearling's neck.

Joe shrugged and picked up a hank of mane to braid. "Just remembering."

Cam groaned and made a face. "Soggy grass," he muttered, and Joe shook his head.

"You're a bit of a jerk, you know?" Joe said after a minute.

There was a moment of silence, then Cam's caress ceased and he sighed. "Yeah, I know."

"Did you want something?" Joe tied off the braid and started on the next.

He was using cream-colored ribbons this time, because they blended with the cream and gray of the horse's mane and coat. He had attached clear glass beads and tiny silver bells to each braid as he went.

The white collar and harness had already been polished, and the horse's tail was intricately braided about halfway to the tips, also interspersed with the beads and bells until the whole thing looked like an elaborate net of knots and twisted hair that flowed into a fan of loose waves and elegant ribbons. Since this wasn't dressage, there were no rules, and Joe took advantage of the fact he could do whatever he wanted with the horse. Make the animal look however he wanted, to suit the occasion.

It had been a miracle of quiet and calm working out here away from the rest of the day's hubbub. Yesterday's flower arranging had been bad. He'd had to be "on" for so long, and after his basically solitary existence of the past five years, that much company for that long a stretch had begun to wear on his nerves.

Thus the escape to the upstairs bedroom, which had been pleasant enough until he'd found himself not alone. Cam's all-too-brief interruption of Joe's solitude had made the room that much emptier when he'd left again. He feared his peace in the barn might meet with the same taint if he didn't get Cam away before he fell under the man's spell again.

"She looks good. You do the bride's hair too?" Cam joked.

Joe glanced at him over the horse's shoulder. Cam looked so…. Joe didn't even know what that look was about. As though he was forcing himself to bite down on a toothache and take the pain. "I don't *do* people," Joe growled, and focused his attention back on the braiding. What was with this man and his ability to say just the thing that got under Joe's skin and made him itch and squirm until he couldn't keep his irritation inside?

"No. I know," Cam amended. "I just meant that the horse looks good."

"Good enough to be people?"

Cam chewed on his lip. "Just good. Pretty. Katie-girl will be thrilled."

"And if she hears you call her Katie-girl on her wedding day, she'll give you a fat lip, so you'd better watch it."

"Wouldn't be the first time I said something to piss someone off."

Joe made a noise in his throat but didn't say anything tangible. What could he say? Cam was so right about that.

"You mad at me for the bedroom thing?" Cam asked.

The question knocked Joe on his heels. Mad at him? There were just too many ways in which what Cam had done was wrong for Joe to begin to make him see. And then there was the fact that Joe had felt so right when it was happening. He didn't understand that part of it himself. How the hell would he explain it to Cam?

"I'm here to see Katie marry her farmer, Cam. Nothing else."

Cam nodded. "Yeah. I know."

More silence as Joe braided, and after a few minutes he could feel that skin-tingling sensation of being watched. He could imagine Cam's clear, brown-flecked golden eyes fixed on him, and it brought back all those times in the rink when he knew Cam had been watching him. He'd never said anything then, either.

"So what do you want?" Joe asked at last, figuring Cam had totally missed the question being asked the first time. It was a dangerous question. Cam's answer could be as perfectly innocent as "Aunt Marie sent me to tell you lunch is ready," or as greedy and lascivious as "I want you on your knees."

Joe knew he wasn't hungry. Not even for Aunt Marie's cooking. But for the other?

That watchfulness continued, only now it was laden with a million things Cam wasn't saying. Joe pulled in a breath and let it out again with a strained "whatever" falling through the silence after it.

"God, you just gave me the perfect opening, didn't you?" Cam said at last.

"Well, I thought so, but you know, whatever." He began a new braid.

"You're really good with your fingers." Cam's spontaneous observation made Joe laugh.

"Even better with my mouth is what you're thinking."

Cam shrugged. "Are you?" Because he'd never had the opportunity to find that out, Joe knew. Something about kneeling and sucking Cam off was far too intimate. Kneeling and presenting his ass, somehow less so. He didn't understand it, but that was how he rolled. And Cam seemed to think there was something odd about it. Something more to the fucking than a physical act they'd both wanted.

"Maybe that's just what you want me to be thinking about," Cam cut into his thoughts.

Joe shrugged and purposefully turned his mind away from the implications of using sex to distract Cam from… what?

"I was just thinking that you have nice hands. Strong." He ran his own fingers over the back of one of Joe's as Joe worked. It slowed Joe's movements, but he didn't dare stop. If he did, he might as well flash a neon "fuck me" sign for Cam, and he didn't want that to be what they did now.

"Can we be a little bit more obvious?" he said instead. "Because I think even the horse knows we want to fuck, and no one wants to be the first to admit we completely screwed it up the first time."

"Horses are not that smart."

"Fucking smarter than either one of us," Joe snapped.

"You don't have to get mad."

"I'm not mad. I'm frustrated, and you standing that close is fucking torture."

A slow smile spread over Cam's face. "Torture, huh?" He held something up that Joe hadn't noticed he'd been holding. It was a bit of horse tack with buckles, and Joe realized it was what had made that faint jingling. Suddenly he wasn't thinking about his mother's wind chimes anymore.

"What's that?" No way to pretend his voice didn't shake, but he could at least pretend he didn't understand the significance of the straps.

"Something I hope you'll like."

Joe raised an eyebrow and kept braiding, though this particular braid came out looking more like a dreadlock.

"Gimme your wrist."

Joe shook his head, but without thought, he'd stopped moving, fingers tangled in the horse's mane.

"That'll do." Cam slipped the leather over both Joe's wrists and slowly began to wrap it around. And around. And a third time.

"How does this work?" Joe asked, swallowing a lump of nerves. "We go from dancing that I-don't-want-you dance straight to bondage?"

Cam smiled. "You've never been tied up before?"

Joe rested his forehead against the furry neck. "Oh fuck."

"Relax." Cam turned him around, but Joe dropped his head and stared at his own boots. No way he could look Cam in the eyes now. Not like this.

"Have you been tied up before, Joe?" Cam asked again. The teasing was absent from the question.

Joe almost looked up. Almost looked into Cam's eyes, but caught himself just in time. If he didn't look into his eyes, then he couldn't fall. He'd figured that much out about this whole scene. Eye contact was connection. No eye contact, no connection. No connection, no guilt.

"Joseph Andrew Conner, I asked you a question. Have you ever been tied up?"

"Yes," Joe snapped. He tugged at his bonds, not really to get free. Just to get Cam's attention back on them. On the physical. On the here and now and off the fact that this was different from anything he'd done over the five years of college, because this man knew him. His middle name. His favorite drink. That he couldn't swim, was allergic to strawberries, and that the fuzz on peaches made his lips tickle. Cam knew he liked to read and had no interest in video games. He knew the little things: all those details that made one man different from any other. And now Cam knew he'd been tied up for sex, and that was not such a little thing to know about a person.

"Did you like it?" Cam asked. His voice was crooning, but also firm and no-nonsense. He was asking a question he expected an answer to.

In Joe's experience, Doms who knew what they were doing had that tone. There was a subtle difference in the way they asked a question, like "Is this too tight?" or "Are you doing okay?" that they needed answered, and answered truthfully, from the type of question they already knew the answer to. That kind, the "You like that, don't you, boy?" that they asked when they had their cocks buried deep, were not ones that required an actual response. The answer was in the deed, and Joe was by now honest enough not to deny that yes, he did like that. Quite a bit.

"Yes," he whispered, still not looking Cam in the eye.

"Hmm." Cam cupped his chin, and in that instant, Joe knew he *couldn't* look the man in the eye. And if anything was a deal breaker in the world where men found pleasure in what Joe liked, the inability to look each other in the face was one any Dom worth the title heeded.

Cam brought Joe's arms up to where the binding leather around his wrists was in his field of vision. He bent and kissed Joe's tightly crooked knuckles, then straightened. "Now I see. Some anyway." He cupped his big hands around Joe's finer ones. "This changes everything."

Joe nodded.

Cam gripped the back of Joe's neck and pulled him forward, kissed his forehead, and let a small sigh whisper across the heated skin. "Okay. Finish braiding your horse's hair. Then you should eat something before you get ready for the ceremony. You're getting too thin."

Joe snorted and was about to ask if that was an order, *Sir* in the most sarcastic voice he could muster, when Cam stepped back and released him with a few deft flicks of his wrists. The leather snapped and whirred through the air as it spun out and away from Joe's wrists. The sound made him flinch, then fidget as his cock swelled slightly.

"No arguments," Cam said flatly. "Auntie's worried about you, so I'll make sure she doesn't have to. I'll make you a sandwich. Kitchen. One hour."

In that heartbeat, Joe knew he should say something, do something, and he did. He screwed up his nerve to look at his friend, but by the time he'd managed to lift his gaze, Cam had turned his back and was exiting the barn.

It took Joe more than a few attempts to get the next few braids as straight and uniform as those he'd done before. He didn't have the heart to undo the completely crooked one he'd finished earlier. He trembled as he held it, at the last, ready to undo and fix it. But he had a flash of Cam's gaze, brown and gold and searching, and he couldn't bring himself to negate the moment even in that small way.

"No one will notice, honey," he told the horse.

The horse flicked an ear and dropped her head to pick a mouthful of oats out of her bucket.

"Guess you're ready," he told her. "Someone will come get you harnessed." He glanced at his watch for about the eighth time and sighed. "I have to go shower." Stroking her shaggy neck, he toyed with the idea of remaining with her until the hour had passed. He had about twenty minutes left before Cam would come looking for him.

"I have to go shower," he said again. He could always stay under the hot water past the appointed sandwich date. Cam wouldn't dare come searching him out in the bathroom. Probably.

But a faint smiled played over Joe's lips. Of course Cam would barge into the bathroom if Joe didn't meet him in the kitchen. That was how Cam did things. But what would he do once he was there? Before the leather around his wrists, he would have bet his remaining meager bank account that Cam would have taken advantage of his naked ass and finally done what they were both dancing around.

Now, he wasn't so sure. Now there was a chance Cam would do something more like reprimand him for not keeping the appointment, and Joe wasn't sure he wanted to put either of them in that position.

Not for the first time, Joe cursed the day he'd ever discovered this thing in him that longed for the bonds and everything they implied. It did, as Cam had pointed out, change everything.

three

Cam set out sandwich fixings. Joe like toasted tomato, but Cam added cheese to his pile of ingredients, real mayonnaise, and placed a few chunks of pickled herring on the plate. How anyone could stand the stuff was beyond him, but it happened to be one of Joe's favorites. He also spooned Greek yogurt into two bowls. One for himself and one for Joe. The smaller man needed protein. College life hadn't agreed with him so well, Cam thought. Although Joe wasn't offering information for free, his shrinking physique was a dead giveaway that something wasn't right.

More than half an hour after Cam had left the barn, the back screen door to the house squealed and banged. A pair of heavy boots hit the floor as if dropped from a height. Licking the last of his yogurt off his spoon, Cam leaned back on his stool to peer around the wall. He caught a glimpse of Joe's tight ass as his friend disappeared up the stairs. His boots were sprawled on the floor near the boot rack, and Cam thought about calling him back to pick them up, but decided against it.

Tidiness was his thing. It had never been Joe's. And he certainly wasn't going to pick fights over that. He had already spooked Joe enough. It wasn't his fault if he couldn't keep his thoughts or his hands to himself. Well, okay, it was totally his fault, but he'd managed to pry himself off the other man this time and take a step back.

Unbidden, the memory of Joe's skin in the sunshine came back. Again. His long back and willowy, muscled thighs had made Cam's mouth water back then, and even still, dimmed as they were by a five-year-old memory, the images of him like that made Cam's breath catch. He was ashamed to admit how often That Day featured in his wank sessions. He just couldn't deny that Joe offering himself like that, giving Cam what he claimed he'd not given anyone before, still did it for Cam.

Almost directly over his head, a door slammed, and Cam jumped, yanked from his memory by the sound. A moment later, he heard the shower come on and he glanced at the clock over the stove. Fifteen minutes left before the hour he'd given Joe was up. He had no idea what he'd do if Joe didn't appear for his lunch in that time. He hadn't thought this through at all.

"Dammit." He let out a sigh and moved to the sink to rinse his bowl.

"Cam, honey, what are you doing in here? I thought you were getting the carriage ready for the ceremony." Aunt Marie's voice was slightly sharper than normal, and Cam turned. Tiny lines etched paths around the tight corners of her eyes.

"Yeah, I know. I asked Mindy to do that. She and Abby have it under control." Abby was the farm's resident mechanic and general all-round handylady. She and Mindy, Marie's youngest daughter, were fast friends as well, and coconspirators in the campaign to divest Marie of her ingrained gender politics.

"She is supposed to be changing, Cam."

Cam snorted. "If you get that girl into a dress, Auntie, I'll wear one too, I swear to God."

Aunt Marie sighed. "You're not helping." But those little lines eased a bit, at least, even if she didn't laugh.

Cam made a soothing gesture and reminded himself that her daughter's wedding was no doubt a source of stress for Marie. "Do you think Katie will care if her little sister shows up at her side in a flow of pink taffeta or a pair of grubby jeans and cowboy boots, Auntie?" Cam asked. "Or do you think she'll be too busy making moon eyes at Jerrod to even notice if Mindy's there at all?"

Marie's eyes narrowed again, and the green in them glinted through the slits. "Not helping," she muttered.

Cam smiled at her irritation, but a part of him twisted inside. "You have got to let this go, Auntie. Mindy is who she is. She's not going to put that dress on without a shotgun prompt. You have got to let them be who they're going to be."

Her head tilted slightly to one side. "Them."

Cam took a small step back. There he'd gone and put his foot in it. He'd said too much, and perceptive as she was, Aunt Marie was not going to let the slip pass without explanation.

"What's all this, then?" she asked, tone still crisp as she indicated the sandwich fixings.

"Lunch," Cam stated. "For Joe. He's been hiding in the barn all morning. Didn't eat breakfast, either."

"You noticed." Marie wasn't asking, and so Cam nodded without elaborating. "That boy will be the death of me, I swear. If he would just get his head out of the horse ring and his books for one minute, I'm sure a nice girl would spot him and snap him up in a heartbeat. He needs looking after, that one. Just like his dad." She smiled fondly. "And his uncle. The lot of the men in that family need looking after."

And I'm the one to look after Joe, Auntie. Cam nodded again and gestured to the sandwiches. "Well, he hasn't even stepped foot in a ring in years. And as for the books, he must have finished that course by now."

She sighed. "He is. He told me on the ride home the other night that he was." She looked devastated. "I would have liked to see him graduate."

"What?" Cam frowned. "Why didn't he tell us?"

"That's one answer I couldn't get out of him, Cameron." She looked to him hopefully. "Maybe you'll have more luck."

Maybe. Doubtful, though. "In the meantime, I've got his back, Auntie."

She turned her smile on Cam. "You're a good friend to him, Cam. Don't think I don't know that."

He couldn't resist an answering grin. "I do my best, Auntie."

She studied him carefully as he took a few slices of bread from the bag and dropped them into the toaster. Her gaze on him felt like what he thought a mother's gaze should be, and he wondered bemusedly if it should feel odd that she was, essentially, the only mother he'd really ever had, and the one who had mothered Joe after his had died.

They could be like brothers. But they weren't. It was weird. It didn't stop the attraction he felt or make that attraction feel wrong. Maybe because he knew they weren't brothers. From the moment a somber, sad twelve-year-old Joe had stepped foot on his uncle Albert and aunt Marie's farm, fifteen-year-old Cameron O'Grady had been head over heels. Nearly eight years of growing together, arguing and sniping and working side by side had only cemented the feelings. To Cam's chagrin, they hadn't dimmed in the slightest when Joe left for college and stayed gone for the past five years, either.

"Let them be who they are," Aunt Marie said softly. "It's very good advice, Cameron."

Cam kept his attention on slicing the cheese. "Yes."

"Is he—is my Joe—" Marie sighed.

"Gay?" Cam was very careful not to let the knife slip.

Marie only let out another monumental sigh.

"Would it matter if he was?" Cam asked. The question left him suspended slightly, in a limbo of his own making because the answer mattered. Not just to Joe, but to him. She *was* the only mother he knew. If being gay mattered, then it changed everything.

"I love my boys," Marie said at last, patting his arm. "I wouldn't want either of you to walk away from this house with a broken heart, Cam. I know you love him."

"Of course I do," Cam said, turning to her. "He's my—"

She placed her fingers over his lips. "I know you love him. I want you to be happy. I want him to be happy. I have never judged you for who you are, Cam. You know that."

He nodded. She hadn't. It was true. He'd never been secretive about his orientation because it had never occurred to him to doubt the security of his chosen home and family. He'd never known anything but the safety of a home where he was accepted and cared for. It didn't matter he had no idea who he was or if he had blood family out in the world. This was his home. Whatever had happened to him before he could remember, he'd been on this farm since he was five, and he had never questioned that he belonged.

The story he knew was that a drifting ranch worker claiming to be his father had worked and lived on Uncle Albert's farm for just under a year, and Cam had lived there with him. Then one night, the man had left. No explanation, no communication. He'd gone and Cam had remained, waking in the bunkhouse with the other farm workers one morning to find he'd been left behind. He'd been five. By summer's end, he barely remembered that there had ever been anyone but the farm's foreman, Cassidy, their regular employee, Seán, and Aunt Marie and Uncle Albert to look after him.

When the state had suggested putting him in a group home until foster parents could be found, Marie had held on to him fiercely and said no. She'd kept him, and Cam had been happy with that. He'd been a kid who loved horses and farm life, and had barely noticed that his father had gone away without him. He didn't remember the man and had long ago decided it didn't matter. Aunt Marie had kept him, and that was all he needed to know.

"You've got some herring on his plate." Marie smiled, but followed it up with a shiver. "Lord only knows why he loves that stuff." She patted Cam's cheek. "You take good care of him. Make sure he eats."

"I will, Auntie."

"You're a good boy, Cam."

He chuckled. Hardly a boy anymore, but he suspected that would never change in her eyes. In the same way, Joe would always be the son she never had, the heir. The one who would carry on the family now that Uncle Albert and Joe's own father had both passed.

Cam flipped the butter knife over and over as he waited for the toast to pop. He couldn't give Joe the life his aunt wanted him to have. He couldn't offer kids. Family. He didn't want to hurt either of them, but more and more, he knew in his heart that he had the key to the life Joe wanted. Needed, even. Except that living that life could break Marie's heart. And hurting her was not something he, or Joe, could ever do.

By the time the toast popped a few seconds later, Marie had left the room, and Cam realized the shower upstairs had ceased its soft patter. He pulled the toast from the toaster and focused on assembling sandwiches for Joe. He had them stacked neatly on the plate next to the fish, and the plate sat on the table with the yogurt and a glass of juice when he heard footsteps descending.

"What am I?" Joe asked. "Six?" He stood in the kitchen doorway in his tuxedo pants, chest and feet bare. His hair was mussed and wet, and a towel draped over his shoulders and back caught the drips. Soft curls of auburn hair—more than Cam remembered—covered Joe's pecs and trailed down the center of his pale abdomen to disappear behind belt and pants.

Cam forced his attention back to Joe's face. "If you were six, I'd have given you cookies too. Sit down and eat." Cam pulled out the chair next to the food and motioned Joe toward it. He sounded exactly like he was ordering a recalcitrant six-year-old around. He couldn't help it. The conversation with Marie had reminded him of all the reasons he'd not protested Joe's leaving to go to college in the first place.

Joe gazed at him, something he'd been utterly unable to do in the barn. His chest rose and fell too heavily. His lips were slightly parted, and spots of pink flushed his cheeks.

That was from the heat of the shower, Cam told himself. There wasn't a defiant glint in Joe's eyes, challenging Cam to make him sit. There wasn't a determined set to the smaller man's shoulders. Not any more than there ever had been, all Joe's life. Determined not to be the runt, the incapable one, the disappointment.

"I'm not hungry," Joe said quietly.

Should Cam pretend he didn't hear the desperate plea in Joe's tone for Cam to insist? He looked Joe in the eye. "Sit."

Nerves danced a familiar jig over Joe's body as he tugged at the hair at his nape, scraped a hand over his neck, then his chin, and stuffed the offending hand into his pocket. He took a small step into the kitchen.

"It's going to be at least six hours until the reception, Joe. Katie-girl will never forgive you if you pass out getting her to the altar because you decided to dig your heels in over eating a goddamned sandwich. Plant your ass in this chair and do as you're told for once in your life, and just eat the damn sandwich."

"For Katie," Joe said.

Cam rolled his eyes. "Heaven forbid you should do it because I told you to." He pulled out a chair and motioned for Joe to use it.

Joe's eyes narrowed and his lips twitched. He clenched and unclenched his fist at his side, but he moved at last. Instead of entering the kitchen, however, he first pulled a dark shirt over his head and tossed the towel onto the steps behind him. He shuffled forward then and gripped the back of the chair. "Maybe just because you made it," he conceded, then yanked the chair from Cam's grip to pull it in toward the table.

Cam gaped. It took a heartbeat to lower his empty hand. How the hell had control been snatched from his fingers without him seeing it coming? "You're a fucking pain in the ass," he snarled as he began to clear up the mess from the sandwich assembly.

Joe's only answer was to bite into his sandwich and close his eyes as he chewed.

four

JOE NEEDED to close his eyes and shut out the view of the yellow wallpaper with the pink roses covering the wall where the phone hung. He needed to shut out the long, cushioned bench where he'd sat his whole life, between Cam and Katie for every meal. If he didn't see the bench to his left, he didn't have to acknowledge he was sitting in his uncle's empty chair. He wasn't the head of the family. He wasn't in charge.

His whole being had leaned toward the command Cam exhibited, yearning to do as he was told. He wanted it so bad it made him ache all over. Because Cam was good, and safe and real. Cam was comfort. Familiar. Cam was the most dangerous thing in the universe because he could be perfect.

Joe took another bite of the sandwich. Beyond his own chewing he listened to the slamming and clunking of dishes and the refrigerator as Cam cleaned up. He'd pissed his friend off. He'd had to. He couldn't let Cam control him. He'd already given in to his desire for the man once. That had been five years ago, and everything was as messed up now. As it had been That Day.

Joe snorted at his own thoughts. Everything was a mess, but it wasn't Cam's fault. It was Joe's own doing, and he had no idea how to fix it.

"You should hurry up and finish," Cam said softly.

Joe swallowed and opened his eyes to find Cam standing in the doorway.

"Forty-five minutes until Katie's ready for the ride to the church. You need to be there before her. Jerrod will be waiting for you to make sure everything goes smoothly."

Joe smiled. "Waiting for me to hand my little cousin off to him, you mean. Are you sure this is the right thing?" He'd known Jerrod Campbell his whole life. He didn't dislike the man, but he was a lot older than Katie. He had his own ranch, and he was successful. There was no reason to think the match was anything other than love, though. Katie loved him, of that Joe had no doubt. And he'd already had the talk with Jarrod over his intentions back when Katie had called him to tell him Jarrod had proposed. The whole courtship had been very old-fashioned and decidedly decent.

"You're joking, right?" Cam asked. "You're questioning it now? On the day of *I do*?"

Joe shook his head. "Not really. But…." He drew in a breath and let it out in a long sigh. "You ever wonder what she sees in him? He's…."

Cam grinned. "Old?"

"She's twenty-five. And he's, what? Sixty?"

Cam laughed. "Asshole. He's forty-one. And he worships her. She is mad for him. They're perfect together, and you know it."

Joe nodded. Try as he might, though, he couldn't imagine himself marrying anyone that old. He'd been with guys as old as Jarrod. He'd been in their beds and under their rules, even if only for a night at a time. He couldn't fathom anyone that old ever getting what it was really like to be his age. To need the things he needed. To understand. Or maybe he just couldn't imagine anyone that old respecting the wishes of someone as young as he and Katie.

Cam's eyes were narrowed at him again. He imagined his friend was looking into him, seeing the things he wasn't about to show anyone in this world. He'd let the other world, the one of college and bills and stress, leak over if he allowed Cam to see inside. Quickly, he looked away from Cam's scrutiny.

"Never mind. You're right. I guess I'm just seeing everyone grow up and its… weird."

"Normal. People do. Look at you. You went away to college and here you are, back all sophisticated and world-weary. And it's only been five years."

"World-weary?" Joe frowned and almost managed to look at Cam again. "Really?"

"Just eat your sandwich. I'm going to get into the monkey suit."

"Sure." Joe settled on the out Cam had given him and focused on his meal. He tried not to let the longing get to him when he was alone in the kitchen. He tried not to wish for Cam to return quickly so he didn't have to feel the world-weariness close in on him.

THE WEDDING itself, of course, was beautiful. Katie had planned everything perfectly, and Aunt Marie had seen that all Katie's plans had been executed to perfection. Thanks to Cam's sandwich, Joe didn't pass out while pictures were taken, or as he walked Katie down the aisle to her husband-to-be. Now, with the ceremony over and the couple grinning like mad fools, Joe knew his part was done. He wasn't his uncle—not Katie's father—so there was no pressure on him to give a speech. He was just an extra cousin who happened to be available to awkwardly fill Albert's shoes for a few steps down the aisle. He was barely even older than Katie, so the whole thing was more as if he had accompanied his sister to the front and offered an older, wiser man the chance to take care of everything.

After the vows and tears and kisses, Katie and Jerrod had climbed back into the waiting carriage for the ride back to the farm. The reception tables would have been set up on the old farmhouse's front lawn. Joe had seen to it himself that all the fairy lights had been hung in the barn and the DJ booth set up in readiness for the dance after dinner. God himself made the sun shine and the birds sing. The spring breeze was warmer than normal for the time of year. It couldn't have been a more perfect day.

"You doing okay?" Cam asked, appearing from nowhere at Joe's shoulder. Joe had been watching the carriage roll away from the bottom step of the church. People around him waved and laughed, grins and happiness shining through the late afternoon brighter than the sunshine.

Joe fidgeted, lifting a hand to the back of his neck to hide his start. "Of course. Why wouldn't I be?" He let the hand drop again, irritated at himself for the flinch.

"Don't know, but you've barely cracked a smile since we left the house."

"You should be watching the bride," Joe admonished. "It's her day, after all."

"She's had a million eyes on her. She didn't miss mine. And she doesn't see anything but Jerrod anyway."

Joe glanced at Cam. "That's what a person in love does, isn't it? Gaze besotted at the object of their affection."

Cam's eyes widened a fraction, then narrowed. His lips pulled tight, but before he could say anything, Joe turned and hurried away.

He wanted to feel a surge of satisfaction at getting the dig in. He only felt hollow. Jumping into his truck, he forced the feeling away. He forced away the memory of the feel of grass under his knees, so long ago, and cold glass against his back—was it just the day before? Carefully, he took all those thoughts and stored them in a place where they couldn't haunt him.

It took a moment to calm himself enough to get the key into the ignition, but once the truck roared to life, he felt steady enough to drive. The truck, at least, responded exactly as he expected it to and pulled smoothly away from the curb. Joe pointed it toward the farm and turned the music up loud. For a short while, the racket of heavy rock drowned out the small voice in his head that told him he was being a complete idiot.

He barely lasted through the meal, and didn't manage to eat anything from his plate. This wasn't his aunt's cooking anyway. Hell, it wasn't even a toasted cheese-and-tomato sandwich. It was sawdust and lumpy gravy. Not appealing.

"Yes," Cam said when he plopped down in a chair next to Joe.

They were sitting just outside the barn door, watching as Seán directed a couple of the farm's workers to carry chairs from the tables into the barn. They placed them around the edges of the dance floor for the elderly family members to sit and watch the party. There was plenty of room in the open space for them to be comfortable.

"What?" Joe asked. He didn't turn his head to look at Cam. It didn't mean he couldn't feel the other man's eyes on him, or the heat radiating from Cam's body. But then maybe that last bit was his imagination. There was no way to be inconspicuous about the way Joe shifted his weight to ease a little farther from Cam.

"Yes," Cam repeated. "That is what people in love do. They watch the ones they care about. They pay attention." He held out a small plate of cheese, grapes, and two Oreo cookies. "Eat something."

Joe glared at the plate. "This is going to get old fast."

"Uh-huh." Cam joggled the plate. "Eat."

Reluctant, Joe accepted the offering. "I thought I pushed the food around enough to make it look like I'd at least eaten some of it."

"Would have been more convincing if you'd put the fork to your lips even once."

Joe had picked up a cookie and was about to take a bite. Now he held it before his mouth and looked over it a Cam. "You watched me the entire meal?"

"That's what people do," Cam said softly. "Please eat."

This wasn't a surprise. Not really. Was it? Joe slowly bit into an Oreo and chewed, barely tasting the sweet cream and dark chocolate. He couldn't look away from Cam's gaze, though, nor could he deny the man this one, small thing.

While Cam hummed the Oreo jingle—"wonder if I gave an Oreo to you"—Joe ate everything on the plate. "Happy?" he asked, returning it to Cam.

Cam smiled, but it was sad and a bit confused. "For now."

They sat and watched as the first few dances of the evening progressed. The bride was as beautiful as she should be, and Joe was more than grateful that Cam took Albert's place for the duty of the father-bride dance. When it was over and Cam looked from the dance floor to Joe, still slouched in his seat just outside, Joe rose and stomped off into the darkening evening.

Strings of lights had been hung in the trees leading down to the pond, but the narrow path was deserted. The small clearing was ringed with citronella torches, and more lights led off from the far side. Between the trees, Joe could see the water glinting. The place seemed deserted. Just the way he liked it.

They had lucked out with the warmer-than-average weather. It was too early for mosquitoes, and just a bit past blackfly season. The music from the barn was only a faint sound in the distance, barely heard over the songs of the mating bullfrogs. More torches lined the water's edge, throwing their flickering gold light out across the expanse.

An occasional splash sounded out beyond the reach of the light. In the near dark, the gurgle of the small creek that fed the pond seemed louder than Joe remembered. His boots dislodged the stones of the shore and they clacked together, a quiet counterpoint to the rest of nature's music.

Joe bent to pick up a few of the smoother, flatter ones. He fitted one into the crook of his index finger and twisted his arm out and around. The stone sailed out over the water in a low arch. He lost sight of it in the darkness, but he heard it splash once. He tried another and a third, but each stone only hit the water with a plop and sank.

"Never were very good at that." Cam's voice drifted from the head of the path. He hadn't ventured out onto the stones, so Joe hadn't heard his approach. Still, his voice didn't send a shockwave through Joe. It was as if he had expected the other man to come eventually.

"My dad tried to teach me. We used to come here all the time when I was a kid."

"I remember."

"You do?" Joe turned to watch Cam saunter across the beach.

Cam's broad shoulders filled out his suit nicely. He had his hands buried in his pockets, and the jacket was hitched up around them. His tie hung loose around his neck. Joe eyed that tie and a slow slide of want slithered through him.

"Course I do," Cam said. "I've lived on this farm my whole life, remember?"

Joe nodded, because of course he knew that. And he remembered Cam from the years before he had come to live with Aunt Marie and Uncle Albert. Cam had been a farmhand by then. Well, he always had been a farmhand, but Joe had never paid any attention at that young age. It was only when he'd moved into the farmhouse after his parents' deaths that he'd realized Cam was more than *just* a regular worker....

Very shortly after Joe had moved here, Cam had proven to be so much more. He'd quickly become Joe's confidant. His best friend. A lot of things Joe didn't understand until he began to understand Cam wasn't the only boy who fascinated him. He was just the one who fascinated Joe the most.

"The lights out here are nice," Cam said.

"Yeah. Katie thought of everything."

"I thought more people would be out here enjoying it."

Joe shrugged. "Dancing is still going strong. Give them time. They'll start slipping away in pairs soon enough."

"Hmm." Cam nodded sagely.

They watched each other in silence for a while. Finally, Cam bent and scooped a few stones from the ground. He flung them, one after the other in quick succession, and they could be heard skipping across the water far into the dark.

"Yeah, well." Joe kicked at the ground. "Never did get the hang of it."

Tossing the rocks had brought Cam closer to the shore and closer to Joe. "We all have our different strengths."

"Sure." Joe watched as Cam tugged on the loose ends of his tie. The blood rushed in his veins at the thoughts of what Cam could do with that tie. It made his mouth water and his palms sweat. He swallowed that reaction down.

"I rushed you earlier," Cam said softly.

Joe kept his gaze riveted on the fingers curled tight around the strip of silk.

"Joe?"

Joe licked his lips.

"I've always been rushing you."

"No."

"Oh?" Cam let go of one end of the tie and pulled it from his neck. He passed it to Joe. "You hang on to this. I can't be trusted."

Joe almost smiled. The thing was, Joe knew a lot of men who couldn't—or shouldn't have been—trusted. Cam was not on that list. It was Joe and his inability to say no that was the problem. He took the tie anyway.

As if it was some sort of cue, Joe suddenly found he could lift his gaze farther than Cam's chest. He stared into his friend's face and found a sweet, longing expression there. That was enough to break down something in Joe that had kept him at a distance.

He took a step, all that was needed to put him inside Cam's personal space, and tilted his chin up. He didn't say anything. He didn't think he had to. A heartbeat later, Cam caressed Joe's jaw with a touch both firm and gentle.

Cam bent his head. "Joe."

"Shh." Joe had to lift up onto his toes to reach. He pressed his lips to Cam's and tilted his head slightly. It was as though Cam was holding his breath. Waiting. As though he was being extra cautious and still. As though he thought if he moved or breathed, Joe would bolt. Joe pressed forward, pushing his mouth over Cam's, parting his lips and darting his tongue out to lick lightly.

"Kiss me, idiot," Joe whispered against his lips. "Kiss me before I start to think again."

Cam's fingers grew resolute, traveling farther back to tangle in Joe's hair. He pulled Joe to him and turned so their mouths slanted over each other and their lips locked. He took control of the hesitant kiss so fast Joe's head spun.

Grabbing handfuls of Cam's suit jacket was the only thing keeping Joe grounded. He moaned softly and pushed his tongue past Cam's lips. The kiss went from tentative to true to tangled in a matter of seconds, and Joe knew if he let go, or if Cam did, he would be lost. He *would* bolt. He needed the contact, the feel of Cam holding on to him to be brave.

When Cam's tongue swept into Joe's mouth, it was over. His will evaporated, and he pressed his body against Cam. He would have burrowed right into him if he could. Cam's arm went around his waist, and Joe groaned. He could feel Cam's cock, as solid as his own, digging into his hip.

"I want to fuck you," Cam growled against his mouth. "I want to lay you out and fuck you 'til I'm all you know, Joe."

Joe moaned and attempted to crawl up Cam's body.

"Oh God." Cam tightened his grip in Joe's hair, pulling painfully. "Come to bed."

Joe would have agreed to spread out right there on the unyielding stones if Cam demanded it. He nodded even as Cam took another kiss, another breath, another bit of him.

When they finally parted, Cam dragged him back toward the path that lead to the barn. They branched off at the clearing, though, and took a narrower, unlighted track that came out in the backyard of the house. There were fewer lights there, and no people. The party had been carefully contained to the public, front half of the property.

Cam led Joe inside. He dropped his boots by the welcome mat, stopped, and pinned Joe against the door for another implacable kiss. The door rattled and complained, being bounced against the wall with the force, but Joe couldn't have cared less. In that moment, he wanted only the reality of Cam claiming him. Even the twinges of feeling in his back couldn't distract him from what he longed for.

"Upstairs," Cam demanded, removing his lips from Joe's long enough to say the word. He crashed them back down once more, a short, sharp kiss that stole Joe's breath. He stumbled when Cam propelled him toward the back stairs. His slippery shoes slid from under him, and he caught himself with a slap of his palms against the polished wood steps.

The sting made him wince, but he righted himself and hurried ahead of Cam to the top.

Cam's room was closest and Joe slipped inside. He barely had time to turn before Cam was on him.

"Outta these," Cam muttered as he tugged at Joe's clothes.

Joe didn't complain. He squirmed and twisted to get his arms free of his jacket, his shirt open, then helped with his belt and pants. Cam shoved the fabric roughly down and pushed Joe onto the bed. Landing with a plop, Joe gazed up at his friend, almost fearful even this slight moment of separation would bring one of them to their senses.

It didn't. Cam dropped to his knees at Joe's feet and yanked at the pants and shoes holding them tangled in place around his ankles.

"Leave them," Joe said. "Just leave them."

Cam narrowed his eyes. "You sure?"

Joe nodded and reached for Cam, but the big man shook his head slightly and grabbed his wrists. He planted both of Joe's hands on the edge of the mattress and smiled at him. "You leave those there." The butter-colored silk of Cam's tie contrasted with the dark wood of the floor as its ends dangled from Joe's grip. He would not let that lifeline go. He couldn't.

Anticipation dropped through Joe to tingle in his balls. He swallowed and stared into Cam's eyes.

He waited, implacably calm and still, until Joe finally managed a small nod.

"Good." Cam's smile turned sharper, and he splayed a palm over Joe's chest under the thin white cotton of his undershirt. His fingers brushed through the hair there, and Joe pushed into the too light caress. When Cam's fingers ghosted over his nipple, he gasped, but Cam moved on without pause.

"Sensitive," Cam mused, studying his face. Slowly, he retraced the path his hand had taken and pinched when his fingers found the tight nub.

Joe clamped teeth down on his bottom lip.

"Hurt?" Cam asked.

"No. Fuck!" Joe thrust his chest into the sharper sensation. He shifted his hips forward until his ass was close to the edge of the bed. "Cam...."

Cam released his other wrist to tickle the hair along the inside of Joe's thigh. "Spread," he instructed softly. "Let me see you."

That was when Joe registered his debauchery. Mostly naked with his pants down and his shirt rucked up, his every transgression rose so close to the surface. He caught his breath. He was revealed; sin stretched too tightly over bone, sinew, and soul. He was layers of half-truths, slippery compliance, and moral ambiguity patched over his need for forgiveness. Cam would see if he looked close enough.

Still fully clothed, Cam lifted his head, dragged his gaze like white flames over Joe's transparent layers. That stare was benediction.

Joe watched him, unable to ignore the command or the gentle flicking of fingers encouraging his legs wide. He dropped his knees open.

"That's it," Cam approved in a soft, gravelly voice. He dropped his gaze to Joe's crotch and his smile widened. "Oh yeah." Without another word, he shifted and took Joe's length deep into his mouth.

Joe bucked into the heat. He couldn't help it. He'd been without any comfort for too long.

The wet slide of lips, the pressure of tongue, and finally, the careful caress of teeth made Joe squirm in agony. He tightened his fingers over the edge of the mattress and fought to hold in the sounds clawing at his throat. He didn't dare make a noise anyone coming in the back door might hear.

Cam worked his cock expertly, though, and in a moment, his calloused fingers teasing Joe's balls added to the torment.

"Cam." Joe barely grunted his name. He wasn't going to last long. God, this was going to end too fast, and he couldn't form words to warn Cam.

Then Cam's mouth stopped, lifted, and he wrapped those merciless fingers around the base of Joe's cock. "I said I was going to fuck you." He looked up from his crouch and caught Joe's eye. "Get on the bed properly."

Joe nodded through the sweat haze and fumbled to toe off his shoes. The pants didn't fall neatly away as he hoped, but Cam fixed that. He wrenched them off as Joe scrambled up and spread out in the middle of the bed. The cool sheets cradled his ass. His shirts still hid the bandages, now loose and pulling at the fine hairs of his back, almost too sensitive in spots. Joe sucked in a breath and wiggled upward, trying to ignore the discomfort crisscrossing his skin.

"On your hands and knees," Cam instructed. "You seemed to like that—"

"No." Joe shook his head, a sharp jerk to the side that also flipped his hair out of his eyes. "Like this."

Once more, Cam's eyes narrowed as if he was looking through what Joe said to what he wasn't saying, but he didn't argue. Instead, he reached past Joe and pulled open the drawer beside his bed.

"You know I haven't been with anyone but you," Cam said.

Joe stared up at him. That Day, with Cam in the clearing, had been his first time. Cam had said then that he'd never fucked anyone, either. But in the five years since, Cam had never?

"I mean," Cam clarified, "I've never fucked anyone else. Been with some in other ways. Used toys on them, done other things, but not that."

Joe nodded slowly. Was this the condom talk, then? "In five years?" It was hard to believe.

Cam shook his head as he squeezed the lube. A tiny amount of liquid squirted out over his fingers and dripped onto Joe's belly.

"Never?"

Another shake of Cam's head.

Joe tried to push himself to sitting, to be level with Cam where he was kneeling over him, but Cam placed his clean hand on Joe's chest. "That surprise you?" he asked.

Frankly, it sort of did. Cam wasn't shy about his sexuality, and according to Joe's cousins, he didn't hide that he went into town on a fairly regular basis. If it wasn't to get laid, then why?

"I guess my first time, bareback with you, sort of spoiled me." His slicked fingers disappeared from Joe's view. They made themselves known again as Cam kneaded the soft skin just behind Joe's balls.

Joe dropped back onto the mattress and groaned, squirming once more as Cam played with him, teased, without offering even a modicum of relief or satisfaction for the torment he used to build Joe's momentum.

Cam smiled. "Wouldn't mind doing that again."

It was the condom talk. Joe slumped. "No," he said, voice flat. He didn't realize he'd pulled away from Cam's touch until he felt the cool air on the damp skin under his balls.

A shadow flickered through Cam's eyes, but was gone again in a flash. "Okay," was his only response, and he reached into the bedside table again and took out a fresh box of condoms.

Joe closed his eyes on all of the implications inherent in Cam having an unopened box of condoms when he claimed he didn't screw around.

"Should I stop?" Cam asked. God, he had to be so gentle about it too.

Joe shifted slightly, letting his legs fall open. The movement reminded him why he wasn't turning his back to a lover, not even Cam. He didn't know what to tell his friend.

Yes, stop, because you have no idea what you're getting yourself into. And god, no, please don't stop. Let this be exactly what happened in that clearing all over again. Let me go back to That Day and start over.

"Joe?"

Joe moved his feet so that he could spread his legs wide and offer Cam every part of him. Anything the other man could want, the choice was his to take or not to take. Joe was the one practically naked on the bed. He'd already made his choice. Some things just couldn't be taken back. Gripping the backs of his thighs, tie still wrapped around his fingers, nearly forgotten until it impeded his hold and his hand slipped, still, he held himself open to Cam, keeping his gaze steady. There could be no mistaking his intent.

He watched in silence as Cam finally shed his clothes, stripping off his jacket and shirt to toss on the bed. He slipped his belt from its loops to join the shirt and peeled away his pants. He was glorious. Joe hadn't imagined a thing wrong when he'd fantasized about what was hidden under Cam's faded jeans and flannel the past few days, or under the new, crisp suit he'd just tossed aside. He was toned and broad, hairy, perfectly formed, and it caught Joe's breath in his throat to see it.

"You like that?" Cam asked, stroking his own rampant cock and continuing up his abdomen. He stopped over a nipple to flick it.

Joe was fascinated, watching the brown little bud stiffen and goose flesh pepper the smooth skin of Cam's upper arm.

Joe reached for him, but Cam shook his head and wagged a finger at him. "Ah-ah. Did I say you could touch?"

Joe had no words. He let his hands drop back to his own body and roam over his chest, a poor substitute for Cam's broad, calloused ones.

"Don't make me tie you down, Joe," Cam said sweetly.

"What if I want—"

But Cam placed a finger over his mouth and shook his head. "Not this time."

Joe tightened his lips and clamped his teeth around his protests. He wasn't going to beg.

As forceful as he'd been before, now Cam was all gentle contact and calm demeanor. There was neither force nor tentativeness as he readied Joe. His fingers, always strong and sure, traveled everywhere, and he was tender as he slid them over and into Joe, preparing him. The kindness, the methodical care, was more than Joe could stand.

"God, *fuck* me already," he snarled.

Cam frowned at him. "Not so fast," he said quietly.

"Why do you think you need the condoms, Cam? I've done this before. You don't have to be careful." Joe pushed his lover's hands away from him to snatch up the foil packet Cam had removed from the box and laid on the bed. He ripped it open and would have tried to put it on Cam himself if Cam hadn't seized it from him.

"What's your hurry?"

Joe growled and rocked his hips. "Just want you in me." He flicked a look over Cam's face and fixed his attention on the condom. "Please." He didn't want to beg.

Cam slowly rolled the latex over his cock. "It isn't always going to be like this," he warned, giving Joe a stern look that made Joe's blood boil more. "You aren't always going to be in charge."

Joe growled again, knowing Cam had no idea what he was suggesting. His friend wasn't prepared for what Joe turned into when a scenario like that happened. For a guy who hadn't had much more experience than their one fateful encounter, he couldn't know. And Joe wasn't at all certain he wanted to even give Cam a hint.

"Just fuck me."

Cam curled a lip and let out a sharp little laugh. "As you wish." He had the condom on now, and he gripped one of Joe's ankles, lifting his leg and shuffling forward.

Joe tried to move with him, but Cam manhandled Joe into position, bending him in half and positioning his cock. He glared down at Joe and a wicked smile tilted his lips. "You want to be fucked? I'll fuck."

The stretch as he steadily pushed into Joe was mind-numbing. Joe caught his breath, tried to pull in air, couldn't. Couldn't move. Couldn't protest. Couldn't look away from Cam as he was taken over.

"Oh Godohgodohgod," he finally gasped when Cam had stopped moving.

"Too much?" Cam asked. Concern flickered in his eyes, but he didn't move, retreat, or release Joe's ankle. If Joe didn't know him as well as he did, he would have thought Cam had no care for the burning pain flashing through Joe's body, making him sweat and swear.

"I'm fine," Joe ground out. It wasn't just the stretch of allowing Cam's entrance into his body, but the press of his back into the mattress, and the renewed sting of scabs loosening and raw skin rubbing against loose coverings.

"Fucking liar." Cam snapped his hips sharply. There was very little movement of his cock, but it was enough to remind Joe who was in control.

Joe whimpered and squeezed his eyes shut. "Wait!" he whispered.

Cam's grip on his ankle shifted, lessened, but remained firm. He smoothed his other hand over Joe's other thigh but remained still.

It took Joe a few attempts to get a full lungful of air, but the burn diminished, and slowly, he began to rock his own hips as the sensations changed from pain to pleasure. He could ignore the rest. At least for now.

Cam clamped down on Joe's hip, leaned to prevent him moving, and that sharp, cutting grin crossed his features again. "I'm fucking you, remember?"

"Oh God." Joe whimpered from desperation now instead of pain. "Please." He swore he wasn't going to beg. But Cam had all the right instincts, holding him open, holding him down, taking what he wanted. Joe struggled to move, to feel the slide of a cock in his hole, the satisfaction of being the one this man, of all men, used to get off.

"Please." He tried not to let the word squeak out. He tried. So hard.

Cam shifted, slowly moving, taking what he wanted at his own slow, torturing pace. It was exactly what Joe dreaded; he took his time. He did what he wanted, and Joe was left to languish and accept what was given. Just exactly how Joe liked it.

five

CAM WATCHED Joe. Some part of him wondered if he was going too far, taking too much, too soon. But the way Joe's head thrashed back and forth on the pillow, the tight squeeze of his eyes, the panting. It all told Cam Joe was into what was happening. In a strange way, he was fighting the very thing he wanted. Cam took his time. He watched carefully. He should stop. He should refuse. Any other man he did this with, he would have.

This was too uncertain to be a real scene, but he knew Joe like he knew himself. He would know if there was real distress. Real reason to stop other than Joe's stubbornness. Under him, Joe struggled to get more, faster, harder, and Cam held him tighter. He'd give what he thought Joe could take. And he'd torture him with the anticipation of pleasure for as long as he thought his friend could stand it.

It didn't do his own racing heart any harm to watch Joe's struggle. Knowing he was solidly in control of how much, or how little, Joe got out of the encounter, was what did it for him. He knew he'd please Joe in the end. There was no way he couldn't give this man anything he asked for. Anything he needed. But Joe didn't need to know that as he danced along the very edge of the precipice and tried to throw himself over.

Watching the desperation play across Joe's features ramped Cam's own pleasure to heights he rarely reached when he played with others. Maybe because with them it was a game. It didn't mean anything more than some pleasure for both parties. Here was something infinitely more real. More desirable. More dangerous. And so, more exciting.

It wasn't long before Cam's slow rocking wasn't enough for him, either, and he sped up, shooting his hips forward with more vehemence with each stroke.

Joe jolted under him with every impact, grunting and moaning with the force, spreading his legs, fighting Cam's grip to join in the momentum. Cam held him down and fucked mercilessly until Joe's voice was loud and constant, out of control.

"You're making a lot of noise," Cam whispered in his ear. "I like that."

Joe clamped his lips shut, but it only lasted a few strokes before he was whimpering, groaning, and once more calling out in need. The door at the back of the house slammed, and they both froze. Joe's eyes flew wide. He pushed at Cam, struggling to get up, but Cam pulled out of him, knelt, and caught his wrists. Quick as he'd ever roped a calf, Cam had Joe's wrists trussed up in the tie and the free end wrapped around the bedpost, hauling Joe's arms over his head. He glared down at Joe, daring him to struggle more.

Joe groaned and squirmed, and Cam plastered a hand over his mouth, careful to keep his nostrils clear. They listened as slow footsteps climbed the stairs. The sound of heels, solid and practical, and the soft sigh as Aunt Marie reached the landing.

"I'm going to start this again," Cam whispered. "Hold on to this." He tucked the end of the tie into Joe's fingers, effectively making him keep his own hands out of the way. "Not a sound," he warned as he uncovered Joe's mouth.

Joe remained still and silent, watching him.

"Okay?" Cam asked, holding his gaze.

Joe nodded and moved his leg enough to indicate he wasn't done yet, either. Cam managed to get his cock back inside Joe's body, and Joe opened his mouth to say something as the footsteps resumed their tread up the stairs.

Cam shielded Joe's mouth, reminding him with the gentle rock of his hips that he wasn't finished with him. They stared at each other.

Joe looked more panicked than Cam had ever seen him.

"Shhh," Cam whispered. He rocked his hips slightly and Joe moaned. "She's just going to bed. Keep quiet." He fucked a little more emphatically.

Joe stared up at him, desperate, frightened, but still, there was that lust and need in his eyes, and he didn't try to stop Cam taking what had already been offered. He didn't let go of the tie. He was bound and by his own choice, remained that way.

"Cameron?" Marie's soft knock on the door made Joe go preternaturally still under Cam. "Honey, are you all right? I saw your boots. Are you in there?"

"Dodgy tummy, Auntie," Cam called. "How's the party?"

"Winding down. Can I get you anything?"

"No. Just sleep. See you in the morning?"

"All right, dear. Good night."

"Night."

He kept thrusting into Joe, almost gently as they listened to her footsteps clomp softly off down the hallway toward the front of the house where her room was. After a few minutes, her door thumped closed and silence returned to the house.

Cam pulled back and thrust into Joe, hard.

Joe groaned under his palm.

"You can breathe?" Cam asked.

Joe nodded, gaze locked on his, no longer defiant. Just needy. Wanting.

"Good."

Joe whimpered. His nostrils flared, and he begged, silently, with his eyes, for Cam to do something.

"You want to keep going?"

Joe closed his eyes softly and shifted his legs far apart. If he'd asked Cam to take him, it wouldn't have been clearer. So Cam did, fucking for real after that, keeping Joe's mouth covered firmly.

Joe stared up at him, accepting that along with everything else.

Cam couldn't hear his sounds, but he did get a sense of Joe's quickening breath and tensing muscles, and he knew from the deep plea in his eyes when he was close to coming. When he was sure there was no stopping the inevitable, Cam released Joe's mouth and leaned down to take it with his own instead.

He kissed and fucked the orgasm out of Joe, and the tightening of his body around Cam brought Cam's along in its wake. When he had eased out to dispose of the condom, Cam noticed Joe had managed to keep his death grip on the tie throughout his climax.

Gently, Cam caressed his stiff fingers and encouraged them open a little at a time. Joe groaned and cradled his hands to his chest, ignoring the tie still circling his wrists.

"Sore?" Cam asked.

Joe moaned and wiggled closer to where Cam was now lying, facing him on the mattress. Joe never really looked up at him again. He snuggled in, allowing Cam to release the tie after a few minutes. Once freed, he coiled tightly, as close to Cam's chest as he could get. In minutes, he'd fallen into a sound sleep, and Cam leaned his head on one hand to watch him.

Not all of Joe's skin was that incredible pale white Cam remembered. Joe took a tan beautifully, and that was the first thing Cam could remember of this man he'd known since, what? Ninth grade? That he was beautiful. Not that he'd ever known to put it that way back when he was a teenager. But it had been the truth that lit up his world. Joe was beautiful, and that fact had made everything else fall away. Or fall into place.

It had been the riding lessons and the rink practice that brought it to his attention. Joe sat a horse wonderfully, but the magic had always been in his hands, his wrists, and the delicate twists and turns that didn't give away the strength they held. Even knowing most of the action was in the legs when a person rode a horse, Cam had admired the power in those hands and the supple way his wrists moved.

He ran a finger over the pulse point in one now, and Joe made a soft sound. He didn't wake or move as Cam opened the buttons on the cuffs of his dress shirt. He didn't have the heart to wake Joe and get him to take it off. He suspected along with food, sleep was something Joe had long been deprived of lately. Cam wished he would share his problems.

Faint red lines marked the tan around bones and over blue veins of Joe's wrists. A tiny black-ink horseshoe throbbed with every beat of Joe's heart as he slept. Cam covered the tattoo with his thumb.

"Tell me I didn't screw it up this time," he whispered.

Joe slept.

Unable to tear his gaze from the marks he'd left on his friend—his lover—he settled on the pillow next to him and caressed the skin from knuckle to wristbone.

"Don't think I don't know. This doesn't really make you mine." He traced the marks, drew small circles in the hair where the wrinkle of palm met the smoothness of arm. "But I know I didn't screw us up this time."

And he would figure out all the things Joe was holding back. He'd find out what happened while he was away. He'd fix everything wrong in Joe's world. He would make this beautiful man his. He'd waited long enough.

Of course when he woke, Joe was long gone. Cam's bed was cold and too big. He tried not to be surprised. Well, he didn't have to try. He wasn't surprised. He couldn't say he wasn't hurt, though, even knowing it was bound to happen and bracing himself for it.

Joe wasn't out. It would be difficult to explain what he was doing in a gay man's bedroom all night without the subject coming up. Cam punched his pillow and swore softly, more angry with himself for being angry than he was with Joe for sneaking away. Resigned, he rose and began to strip the bed. If Joe was going to stay in the closet, Cam wasn't going to force him out through carelessness.

So he yanked the soiled sheets from the bed, hung his suit, and gathered his laundry. It didn't escape his notice that his tie was missing from the rumpled pile of clothes. A small smile crept over his face and—despite his best efforts—into his heart. The last time Joe had run out after they'd had sex, he'd been gone for five years, and he certainly hadn't tethered himself.

six

HIS SHAKING was beginning to aggravate the horse, Joe knew. Every time his hands jerked, they yanked on the curry comb and tugged at the animal's mane. She was stoic enough not to kick him in the balls, but her tail was a wicked whip as she swished it in irritation. The ends of it bit, a thousand tiny whip cracks over his knuckles and through the thin material of his long-sleeved T-shirt. It was the only shirt he'd found with cuffs long enough to stretch over the marks around his wrists.

His cock throbbed at the memory. "Fuck me," he muttered, more resignation in his voice now than there had been last night, for sure. After a quick glance around, he peeled back one cuff and ran a forefinger over a swath of skin, redder than the rest. It was totally wrong to feel this glow inside just looking at the marks, knowing who had put them there, remembering....

"Imagine finding you out here before breakfast."

Cam's voice made him jump, and he hastily shoved at the sleeve. He was too slow, and Cam's thick index finger hooked under the fabric and hauled it farther up his arm.

"Damn, boy-o, but that looks good on you."

"Shut up!" Joe stumbled out from between Cam and the horse, who shifted nervously at the sudden charge of emotion arching through the air.

Cam reached calmly and took the horse's halter. She quieted almost immediately, and Joe wished that would work on him too. Maybe it would if he wore a halter for Cam....

His heart thundered at the idea. He could imagine the straps of leather crossing his chest and back; it made his dick shift in his jeans. He barely resisted the urge to glance around the barn to see if any of the men clearing away the remains of the wedding dance had noticed them.

"None of them even saw me come in," Cam said quietly. "Relax."

As if he could relax with the ache of want his giddy imagination left behind in his balls. Joe found himself clasping his wrist to his chest, fingers of his other hand painful around the bones and sinews. He let his arms fall. "Don't you have work to do?"

"Playing lord of the manor, Joe?" A stony look passed through Cam's eyes that made Joe shiver.

"Joe, sweetheart. There you are."

Once more, Joe jumped at the unexpectedness of a voice—this time his aunt's—hailing him from the main entrance of the barn. Cold sweat trickled down his back. He was still shaking, dammit. But Cam's hold on his shoulder did calm him, and he blinked his eyes closed for a split second to soak in the tranquility before stepping out of Cam's reach.

"I missed you at the table this morning," Aunt Marie said.

Both men turned to watch her pick her way through the straw and paper cups littering the barn floor. Seán and the younger man helping him clean up the mess took a moment to tip their hats and comment on the nice weather as she passed. She offered them kind smiles and didn't seem to notice that they continued to watch her until they saw Cam's dark glare on them.

They went hastily back to their task, but Cam scowled. "Should fire both of them," he growled under his breath.

"She's not an unattractive woman, Cam. Give them a break."

Cam shook his head. "Doesn't matter. She's their employer, and they need to respect that."

Joe just shook his head and turned his attention back to his aunt. Men on this farm had been watching her since he could remember. She wasn't a stunning woman, but she was a passionate and capable boss. No-nonsense. Her strength became her, and people, not just men, were attracted to her confidence. It didn't hurt that she had the body of a woman twenty years her junior, or that the gray in her straight black hair complimented her fine skin and bright eyes. No. She wasn't stunning with model good looks, but she was impossible to ignore.

As she approached them now, she carried an old wire shopping basket in one hand. Joe recognized it as the same one in which she had carried countless meals out to his uncle Albert. It still had the red plastic handle protectors emblazoned with the Kmart logo. He vividly remembered the snowy night she had taken him shopping for socks and underwear and pajamas at the old department store. It had been his first night in her home, and he'd been lying in bed in his soot-covered jeans and T-shirt. She'd mother-henned him until he'd bathed, even washing his hair for him, since he'd been too stunned to manage anything but stare blankly at the pink plastic walls of the shower enclosure.

She'd then borrowed too big clothes from Cam for him, and together, they had gone in the old farm truck to the department store. She had been a whirlwind of efficiency, holding clothes up to his shoulders, finding him all the necessities, and quickly tossing them back into the basket as she paid. No time for plastic bags or delay as he stood beside her at the cash register and began to shake and whimper and pleaded to see his mother.

Twelve years old, and he'd begged like a tiny child to see his parents. Parents he already knew were gone. Gone, gone, gone.

"Should have known I'd find you out here with all your four-footed friends," Marie said brusquely as she glanced around at the horses calmly munching breakfast in their stalls.

"She's a Clydesdale, Auntie," Joe said, blinking himself out of that memory and smiling fondly at his aunt's expression.

"Just a big furry baby, if you ask me," she replied, stepping into the generous stall with them. She patted the horse's nose, and the huge animal bent to nuzzle her fingers and huff softly. "Yes. You are," Marie said. "No use denying it. And you." She turned to Joe. "Skipped your breakfast."

"I'm not hungry, Auntie," Joe began, but she thrust the basket at him.

"I've brought a nice thermos of warm oatmeal. Your favorite, with apples and cinnamon and butter. And some peanut butter toast. Now sit and eat before the toast gets cold. You know you don't like cold toast."

"Auntie—"

"Cameron, be sure he finishes it all. There's some hot digestive tea in the blue mug for your stomach, and Joe, you drink the green tea in the red mug. It'll help you eat."

"Auntie," they said in unison.

"Don't you 'Auntie' me," she said, eyeing them both in turn. "You need looking after." She had her fists on her hips now, and a stern look on her face. "And Joe, drink every drop of that juice in the water bottle, as well. You're too thin, and I won't have it."

"Yes, ma'am." He plucked the bottle out of the basket and drained half of it while she watched.

"There's a good boy. Now the horse is not going anywhere. Sit and eat." She turned her heavy glare on Cam as she passed him the basket. "See that he does."

"Yes, ma'am," Cam said. He reached for the blue coffee mug. "And thank you."

"How you survived off in that city on your own, Joey," she muttered.

"Auntie, please." He held up a hand, but she shook her head sharply.

"You should come home. You've graduated, and I won't mention after today that you didn't even let us come to celebrate with you. You've got your piece of paper."

He nodded mutely.

"Then come home where you belong." Her eyes flicked to Cam, so briefly he thought maybe he imagined it. "Where you are loved, boy." She gripped Joe's free hand in strong, tight fingers. "Come home."

Then she turned on her heel and strode out of the barn without a backward glance.

"Don't know how I survived here all those years," Joe muttered, and beside him, Cam snorted.

"She is a force of nature."

Joe sighed and glanced at the basket. "Don't suppose horses like cooked oats."

"Don't even think I'm chancing it." Cam picked up the basket, took Joe by the elbow, and led him out of the stall and through the tack room. Behind a sturdy desk in the room's corner was a little-used back door that let out onto a small grassy hill flooded with morning sunshine. It was on the south side of the barn, out of sight of the house and paddocks. On sunny mornings, it was warm and secluded. Cam had discovered it was a perfect place to sit and drink a cup of coffee undisturbed while he went over the day's roster. On warm summer afternoons, it was shaded by the trees about ten feet away. Cool and ideal for escaping for a few moments of solitude in the heat of the day, the spot had quickly become his favorite bit of the farm when Cam had taken over the foreman's duties.

It had been an unofficial appointment when the past foreman, Cassidy, had had his first heart attack about five years ago. Now it was his job title, handed over two years ago when the old man had bypass surgery and his wife insisted he retire and move to a small house in town. Unwilling to take up residence in the foreman's lodgings, built adjacent to the barn, Cam had instead cleared out a corner of the spacious tack room to use as an office and kept his room in Aunt Marie's house.

The small space outside was his sanctuary. People knew better than to bother him if he'd retreated there. Only emergencies brought his workers knocking on that door, and Cam knew the farm was running smoothly at the moment.

"Sit," he ordered, lightly pushing Joe toward one of the wooden chairs on the knoll. He set the basket on the table beside him and took the other chair.

"Nice place you've got here." Joe glanced around, and Cam saw the moment he realized they were alone and likely to remain that way. His shoulders eased slightly, and the tight bend of his fingers relaxed.

"Actually, it is." Cam reached over and twined his own fingers around the nearest of Joe's wrists. "And Marie is right. You are too thin and not eating right." He squeezed and waited. Eventually, Joe glanced over at him. "Please. Just eat the breakfast. It would make us both feel better."

Joe nodded faintly and poked through the basket for the wax-paper-wrapped toast and thermos of porridge. The bread, of course, was the homemade wheat bread he loved, cold, yes, but still delicious because his aunt had made it herself. The oatmeal was the slow-cooked kind as well. Nothing out of a package ever left Aunt Marie's kitchen. Despite his lack of appetite, the food was good and he ate it all. It didn't hurt that Cam kept him under watchful surveillance until he was licking peanut butter and toast crumbs from his fingers.

"Happy?" Joe mumbled, embarrassed that he'd needed the supervision yet flushed from the knowledge that he'd actually enjoyed it.

Cam grunted and sat back in his chair. "Drink your tea."

"Yes, Sir." Joe said it softly as he picked up his mug. He watched Cam carefully for a reaction.

Cam's head lolled until his friend was gazing at him through slitted eyes. "You be careful with that," Cam said softly. "You never know if the wrong man is going to take the wrong meaning away from those words."

Joe quirked his lips but couldn't manage a smile. "I know." He knew a lot, but he wasn't going to explain it all to Cam.

His response earned him another grunt. For a few moments, they sat in charged silence, both sipping from their mugs and watching the light breeze play with the aspen leaves on the other side of the cozy clearing.

"Joe, there are a lot of medications out there that take away a man's appetite," Cam said at last. "Lots of reasons for taking them."

The spring breeze tripped cold fingers over Joe's exposed skin. He deliberately stared straight ahead. "That so."

"Your aunt's lost so many people already."

"Now she's my aunt." Joe clenched his jaw until the joint ached.

"This farm is my home, Joe. Marie is as close as I'll ever come to having a mother. If you're sick, we all deserve to know."

"And you think if I was, I wouldn't tell you?"

Cam drew in a breath through his nose, and Joe finally looked over at him. He, too, was staring straight ahead, both hands clenched on the arms of his chair. "I think you would keep a lot to yourself because you're a stubborn, unhappy—"

"You don't know shit about me."

Joe rose and turned away, headed back to the barn and away from the conversation. He didn't make it.

Cam was on him before he took three steps. "I know you held on to that tie for dear life last night." Cam was in his face, and Joe tried to go around him, but the bigger man was fast. "I wore a condom because you told me to, Joe, and I didn't press. I didn't ask, and I let you keep all your reasons and all your begging behind this stubborn jaw of yours." He gripped Joe's chin in his huge, unyielding mitt, and the pinch brought tears to Joe's eyes. A thin sound squeaked out of him when Cam shook him. "You still have that tie, but hear me now. You bring it back to me with that want in your eyes again, and we will have words. There is no scene, nothing of what you want until you tell me what's going on."

Joe shook himself free and took a step back. He would not feel his jaw. Not let on how much that grip had hurt. Or how much it helped. "Nothing's going on." He stepped around Cam and this time wasn't intercepted.

"I'm not sick," he conceded as he neared the door to safety.

"Have you been tested?"

Joe didn't answer, but he did pause before going inside.

"I fucked you last night, Joe. We were careful, but I have a right to know."

"Yes." Joe didn't dare turn around to see if Cam was watching him. He couldn't bear to find out if he wasn't. He couldn't stand the idea that if he was, he would see how much Cam's choice of words stung. But that was all it had been. It was all Joe had allowed, wasn't it?

"And?" Cam asked.

"Negative."

A heavy sigh sounded and Joe almost turned. "Good," Cam said, his voice softer. "Me too."

Joe swallowed a lump he hadn't been aware of and nodded. Just in case. Then he left. He couldn't be near Cam any longer without giving in to the man's strength and demands, and he knew, just *knew* as soon as he did, Cam would insist on knowing everything. Joe wasn't ready for that. Not yet.

For a week, Joe managed to dodge Cam and his questions. He stayed away from the tack room in the barn and the back staircase in the house that led directly to Cam's room. If Cam went to ride fences, Joe mucked stalls. If Cam stayed close to home, Joe took any and all excuses to make himself scarce by running errands for his aunt into town, riding herd on their small collection of horses, taking them out to better grazing, even offering to go out and help count sheep. Anything to maintain the distance between himself and Cam was an acceptable occupation. His only concession was to make an appearance at every meal, pile food on his plate in such a way as to make it look like more than it was, and eat what he could. It kept everyone off his back about his weight.

There was nothing physically wrong with him. He just had no appetite, and forcing food down his throat only made him nauseous. Cam watched him constantly, and the knot of nerves across Joe's shoulders kept him on high alert that he was ever under surveillance. It didn't help his mood any. It didn't let him relax. He was home, and here, of all places, he was meant to feel safe. The constant feel of being watched only put him on edge.

It didn't help, of course, that every time a car pulled up in front of the house, he expected the worst. Every noise outside at night jerked him out of restless sleep. If he didn't have a wall at his back, he was tense. Being far out to pasture where he knew for absolute certain he was alone was no proof against his imagination. Cam's penchant for sneaking up on him unawares left him jumpy and snappish too.

It was one such occasion, when Joe was just stepping out of the second-floor bathroom, one towel around his waist, another draped over his wet hair, that finally snapped Cam's patience. Joe let out a noise of surprise and took a step back, even made to close the door in Cam's face when he found him there, but Cam slapped a palm against the wood to prevent it. Joe sensed Cam's patience stretch and snap, practically felt the tension in the air slap him across the face. He stopped in the bathroom doorway, fingers tight around the opening of his towel. He shrugged the one over his hair down to cover his shoulders and back and gripped the doorframe as he willed his heart to slow the fuck down.

It was just that he hadn't expected Cam to be standing there, dirty gloves tucked into his back pocket, and boots still on his feet. He'd catch hell for that if Aunt Marie caught him up here in his outdoor footwear.

Joe could smell the hard work on the other man. Cam's blond ringlets corkscrewed in a single tail over his shoulder, and a few wisps that had escaped the elastic stuck to his skin. He had hay dust smudged across his T-shirt and along the side of his neck where he habitually ran a hand over the tickling strands. He smelled good. The T-shirt he had on was tight, curving around his biceps and over his chest, clinging and damp from the sweat. It was blue, navy, with a logo on it Joe didn't recognize. But it didn't have gold ribbing around the cuffs. Cam's arms were smooth, the blond hair nearly invisible and not dark and curling over the fabric. Joe blinked away the unbidden image.

Cam was bigger than the memory. Solid and safe and undeniably *here*.

"'Scuse me," Joe said quietly, hoping his voice didn't shake.

"What's wrong?" Cam asked.

"Nothing. Just going to get dressed." Joe tried to move around him, but Cam had the annoying habit of being in the way. And being wide and immovable.

"Joe, what? You look like you just saw a ghost."

"Just move please!" He hadn't meant to raise his voice. He couldn't help the wince when he realized he had. "Sorry."

"*What* is the fucking problem?" Cam almost shouted. "You tense like that every time I come near you. What the hell do you think I'm going to do, Joe? Force—" Cam's face went white. "Jesus, Joe." His eyes grew wide, and Joe pushed past him before he could say or think anything more.

"I'm going to get dressed," Joe snarled, hearing the flat, forced tone in his own voice.

"Joe?" Joe didn't stop to placate Cam, but hurried to his own bedroom and closed the door firmly behind him. He leaned on it a moment, then flicked the lock in the handle and quickly dressed. He could feel Cam still out there. He knew he was waiting for Joe to emerge and explain himself.

There wasn't much chance Cam was going to drop this bone. Joe should have just told him he was off the mark. Cam was never going to give him peace until Joe convinced him he had the wrong end of the stick. Again. Like the reason for his lack of appetite being due to meds Joe wasn't taking, this was a false trail. It was better Joe just told him to drop it, that he had it wrong.

"Look," he said, finally opening the door.

The hallway was empty. The looming presence he'd felt was nothing but his own mind weighing him down. Figured. Cam wasn't all that concerned after all.

"Good," he muttered, ignoring the small twist of pain in his gut, turning his stomach inside out. He didn't need people being worried over him. He was fine. He was perfectly capable of looking after himself. He'd done so for five years away from this farm and this family. He didn't need them to take care of him.

When he got to the ground floor, he could hear the boisterous gathering over the dinner table. Mindy was crowing with laughter over something Seán had said to her. Aunt Marie admonished someone, probably Tommy, their newest hire, who had arrived sometime when Joe was away. She didn't allow anyone to snag bits of the meal from her serving platters before everyone was gathered at the table and grace had been said. From the sound of her reprimand, this wasn't the first time she'd slapped his fingers.

On the other side of the wall, Tommy yelped to the accompaniment of a sharp crack that could only be a wooden spoon hitting knuckles. Joe winced, grabbed his truck keys, and hurried for the front door.

"Going out for supper!" he called over his shoulder, and fled.

seven

CAM WATCHED the gravel spin and slip under the rear tires of Joe's truck. Once the vehicle had skidded out of the drive and disappeared down the road, he let the curtain to his bathroom fall closed again. He occupied one of the two suites in the house on the third floor. The other was Aunt Marie and Uncle Albert's and was the opposite of his own, with the bedroom across the hall from his bathroom at the front of the house, and their much larger en suite bath across from his sleeping quarters at the back. Both rooms could be accessed from the front or back stairs, but Aunt Marie generally used the front and left Cam the privacy of the back entrance.

Below, on the second floor were Joe, Mindy, and Katie's rooms, although Katie, of course had moved out now. There were three more rooms on the ground floor, one occupied by Abby, their mechanic who wasn't keen on cohabitating with the seasonal male workers, and the other by Seán, who had worked for them so long, he was as good as family now. The third was an office Aunt Marie used to do her books. In a small bunkhouse across the backyard, the rest of the permanent crew, three men in all, and the seasonal workers slept and showered. Everyone but the seasonal workers ate in the main house twice a day, breakfast and dinner. Lunch most days was had on the job, or, for anyone working in the barns or in the yard, Marie would make sandwiches.

Cam could hear the madness of yet another cheerful meal taking place three floors below and he hurried to dress and join them. Marie would hold the meal until he got there. He'd learned that early on.

When he entered the kitchen, she glanced at him, worry in her eyes. He smiled, tried to make it something other than a mutual expression of concern, and knew he failed when she sighed.

"Hey," Cam said jovially to Mindy, who told him it was about time he'd showed, since she was starving. "Yeah, yeah." He flicked her hat off her head as he sat, and she squealed at him, but did toss it on the boot bench across the room as she settled onto the long bench behind the table.

"Everyone's here," Mindy said, glancing around at Abby, Seán, and the others. Her gaze lingered a second longer on Tommy, and he blushed. "Joe's taken off again. Lookin' for a date, probably." She reached for the pot of potatoes. "His loss. Nothin' beats Mom's bangers and mash." She scooped a generous portion of the mashed potatoes onto her plate and asked for the sausage as she passed the pot to Tommy.

Cam served his own food and ate in silence. He doubted Joe had gone in search of a date, but even the mention of the idea made his blood boil. He didn't dare meet Aunt Marie's eyes over the table. He knew she'd read his feelings in an instant, and he didn't need her trying to sympathize with him on top of their mutual worry over Joe.

She'd try and tell him it was hopeless and he should let his "crush" on her nephew die already. She'd been singing that tune for nigh on a decade. It wasn't ever going to happen. No use revisiting the pointless conversation. After dinner, when he would normally stay and supervise the younger hands' cleanup of the kitchen, he let them get on without him this time. Instead, he wandered out to the front porch.

It wasn't as though he expected Joe's truck to be back in the drive. He knew the other man hadn't returned. But he wanted to be sure when Joe did come back, he was there.

"Do you know where he went?" Aunt Marie asked as she came out to sit with Cam on the swing on the front porch.

"No." Cam took the oversized mug of fragrant tea she offered. "Something else for my stomach?"

"Just chamomile. Helps settle the nerves." She smiled faintly at him and blew over the top of her own mug. "Though it isn't doing me a lick of good lately. That boy is…."

"Yeah." Cam didn't need her to finish the thought for him. He was pretty certain they were on the same page of fret and bother over Joe.

"So he hasn't told you, either?" she asked, and Cam shook his head. "Oh, Cam, I wish...."

"Yeah," he said again.

They sat and sipped tea in silence for a long while, watching the sun lower and sink and stretch the shadows of the tall maples along the drive closer and closer to the house.

"You know, I know you love him, Cameron."

"Auntie, please," Cam warned.

She tsked him. "He needs someone to look after him properly. You know that."

"Don't I just."

"Does he love you, Cam? Does he—is he—?" Her lips pursed tight, and Cam sighed.

"You know that isn't a question I can answer, Aunt Marie. Even if I knew how he felt, it isn't my answer to give you."

Her lips got tighter.

Cam set his mug at his feet and turned slightly to face her. "I'll tell you what I do know. I have every intention of looking after him, to the best of my ability, as long as, and however he'll allow."

"Oh, Cameron." She blinked at him. "You shouldn't waste your life on a man who can't love you back. It isn't right. You deserve to be happy."

Cam smiled softly and settled his back against the unyielding boards of the swing. "Who says I'm not happy, Auntie?"

"So it is true, then." She peered at him. "He is... like you."

Cam almost grinned. "Auntie, Joe is most emphatically *not* like me. He is his own person. Who and what he is, who he loves, those are things you have to talk to him about yourself. I won't answer questions for him that I don't have the right to."

"Oh, Cam. I just want... I want...."

"Grandkids? Someone to carry on the family name and business?"

She snorted. "I raised five girls. I've one left to marry off, and every year, more and more grandkids spring up and get underfoot. I'm not worried about continuity. And you already know what Albert's will said. Mine is the same. This place goes to Joe if he wants it. You if he doesn't. That hasn't changed, my dear. And it never will. What I want is for you both to be happy. You know that, right?"

Cam focused on her again, met her eyes, and nodded. "I know, Auntie. I do. Sometimes, though, you have to understand there's nothing you can do about how a man chooses to live his life."

A high-pitched screech came from in the kitchen, and Mindy's riotous laughter followed, accompanied by much cursing and Tommy's name squealed in righteous, laughing indignation. Cam counted under his breath to three, and then Tommy's loud shout of pain and "Holy fuck, woman! Those are my future *kids*! Watch it!" Then both young people erupted in gales of laughter all over again.

Cam snorted. "Any more than you can make a lady out of a girl who doesn't get that she's not one of the guys." He shook his head in amusement. "One thing I always appreciated about growing up here, Auntie, is that I never felt I was anything other than family. Cared for. Wanted. Right now, I think that's what Joe needs the most. Care, and to feel wanted. I don't know what happened while he was away, and I can't make him tell me. I can only make sure that as long as he's here, he feels safe and wanted. It's all I have."

"And what about what you want and need?"

"Him," Cam said softly. "It's a done deal. Let it go."

She nodded and together, they watched as a set of headlights swung round the curve in the road, then the orange of a turn signal as Joe's truck pulled into the drive.

"Okay," she said, getting to her feet. "I'm going to see if I can't sort out the riot in my kitchen. Please make sure he actually did eat something, Cameron."

"I will."

She squeezed his fingers and left him alone on the porch to see if Joe would be willing to open up, or if he was going to remain as recalcitrant as always.

eight

JOE LET out a sigh and sat for long moments in the running truck, both hands on the wheel. He could see Cam sitting under the porch light. He wasn't sure what he wanted to do about it. He'd thought going into town, getting out from under the other man's constant scrutiny, would ease his tension.

Being away from the one place he felt even a moment of something approaching calm had backfired, though. He'd spent the entire time he was sitting in the diner looking over his shoulder. Any minute, he'd expected…. Well, he didn't know what, exactly. He just hadn't been comfortable in the diner that should have been familiar stomping grounds for him. He'd felt exposed. He hadn't even ordered, and eventually, the waitress and cook had made it clear if he wasn't going to eat, he'd have to leave. They were ready to close for the day. He couldn't stay there indefinitely.

He couldn't sit in the truck forever, either. Cam showed no evidence that he might get up and go inside. Joe was going to have to chance it. And he knew the moment he stepped foot on the bottom porch step, Cam would be on him about where he'd gone, what he'd been doing, and whether he'd eaten.

With a sigh, Joe killed the engine and got out of his truck. He took his time trudging up the lawn to the porch. He actually made it to the top before Cam said anything at all.

"I want to help," Cam said quietly.

That wasn't what Joe had expected.

"Whatever it is, you can tell me. You can trust me. I can help."

"You've never lived off this farm, Cam. You've never been anywhere. Never done anything. You don't know."

"So tell me."

And risk Cam shunning him if he knew the things Joe had done while he was earning a college degree that turned out not to be worth the piece of paper it was written on? No chance. Joe grunted and strode heavily to the door.

"Someone hurt you," Cam said. He still wasn't asking any questions. Since it was a statement and didn't require a reply, Joe thought about continuing on his way inside. He made the mistake of glancing at Cam, though, and the look of smoldering fury in Cam's eyes stopped him cold.

"Don't," Joe said quietly. "It isn't your concern."

"You're my concern, Joe. And Auntie's and all your cousins'. Why won't you let us help?"

Joe smiled, but he knew it was cold and lifeless. "You can't. Nothing can take this one away and make it better, Cam. Just forget it."

"Like you're forgetting?" Cam asked, sharpness in his voice. "It's eating you alive, Joe. Look in the mirror."

Joe snorted. He didn't look in mirrors anymore. He rolled his shoulders and felt the familiar zing of exposed nerve endings under the fabric of his shirt. He didn't say anything. There was nothing else to say, so he went inside and straight to his room.

He knew Cam would never leave it at that. Joe would have to sprint up the steps and run for his room to avoid the conversation. He was tempted. He was really, really tempted, no matter if it made him look like a spoiled teenager. But then, parts of his body still had the echo of Cam on his skin. The part of him that craved it wanted to listen to the command inherent in Cam's very touch and give in. It was a much more difficult temptation to ignore.

He twitched his shoulders. Parts of him still had more than an echo of five years of stupid decisions, he reminded himself. And even being home over a week didn't alleviate the feeling he was still running from those decisions. It didn't help that he'd had constant chills all day, running over his skin as though he was being watched no matter where he went. Or that his palms sweated. Or that when he wasn't shivering, he was sweating and feeling like a complete fool for letting his imagination get to him so bad.

"Fucking hell," he muttered as Cam's footsteps followed close behind his own. "What the hell do you *want*?" he snapped, whirling.

Cam stopped dead at the very top of the stairs. "You," he said through clenched teeth. "I want you. And I want you to stop fucking running." He approached, and Joe had the wild thought that he looked exactly as he might if he were approaching a spooked horse. He had his hand out, palm up, and he remained otherwise still and steady despite the tension Joe could feel rolling off him.

"I am not running," Joe told him. "I'm just not standing still long enough for you, or anyone else, to tie me down again. I'm not doing that anymore." He clenched his jaw as a slither of chills snaked through him. "I *can't* do that anymore."

Something calculating ghosted over Cam's face. It was there and gone so fast Joe wondered, but he didn't stay to find out if it had been there, or what it meant. He ignored his room and went for the stairs instead, changing his mind about staying home. He made it opposite of Cam, but his friend grabbed him before he could pass and slammed him against the wall.

"You won't run off on me again, Joe. I won't allow it."

Joe grimaced. "Fucking hell!" Pain zinged over his back, following the lines of the cuts, but zagging outward as well, so he felt as if his entire back was on fire. "Get off!" he shook loose and bolted.

"Joe!" Cam's call diminished, even as short as it was, as Joe put space between them.

Running was stupid but Joe did it anyway. Maybe because he hoped this time Cam wasn't going to come after him. He would only ask all the same questions, and Joe still wouldn't have answers he was willing to give. At least for now Joe was off the hook by simple virtue of being alone in his truck hightailing it away from the aggravating, addictive man.

His back ached, and finally, *finally*, that pain outweighed the faint traces left from Cam, his cock, and his demanding control. Joe refused to mourn the loss.

Pointing the truck, he drove without thinking. He was so tired of thinking, of anticipating, and waiting for the other shoe to drop. If it wasn't the thought that any moment, his past could come knocking on the front door of the ranch house, it was the thought that any moment, Cam could come knocking on his bedroom door.

One knock, he had no intention of answering. The other, he couldn't seem to ignore or refuse. The only option he had left was to not be there when Cam hammered on his psyche and demanded to be let in. So he jumped in his truck and drove. Randomly, in any direction but the farm, though there was really no place to go but back into town. Eventually, he pulled up outside the community's one bar, Reilly's. The place was mostly deserted, caught in that odd lull between dinner and drinking time. Thank God, because he didn't want to have to deal with a crowded bar. He just wanted to drink.

Inside, the same dim lighting that he remembered prevailed. He'd waited tables here for a summer, between high school and college. Even then this poor lighting hid most of the grunge he knew was there. He couldn't decide if it surprised him to see the same bartender from back then wiping down the long wooden surface. His name was Craig, and he was as bald and at least as tattooed as Joe remembered, probably more. Age had been kind to Craig. Five years older than Joe, he was still good-looking in the rough, biker way he'd always sported. Joe's time away showed in deeper laugh lines about Craig's mouth and more gray in the short hair at his chin, but his eyes were still bright and his smile just as wide.

"Hey, Joe. You still in town? I thought you would've gone back to the city by now." Craig placed a beer glass on the counter and pulled a bottle from the fridge behind him. He popped the cap and began to pour in one smooth motion. "Glad you decided to grace me with your presence, though. Thought maybe you were going to give this old place a miss." He peered at Joe from under his lowered lids. "Again."

Joe admired Craig's bartending fluency as he took his seat opposite his old boss. He had always been too graceful to fit his biker exterior. No. Joe pushed that thought aside and ignored the flashes of memory older than Cam, dirtier and less pure than That Day. He settled on the stool across from where Craig was pouring and offered a wide smile. "You remembered my brand," he said.

Craig grinned at him. "Of course. I remember all my favorite customers."

Joe chuckled. "Is that what I am then? A favorite?"

"Not like I kiss and tell," Craig said, "but check this out." He pulled up the sleeve of his shirt and showed his forearm.

Joe had spent a fair amount of time memorizing the intricate swirls of color and pattern adorning Craig's arms and torso. Some days, obediently learning how to serve another man, there had been precious little to do as he knelt, waiting, than to memorize the vibrant swirls of color within his field of vision. He knew them. He remembered them. It was the newer ink on his lower arm that caught Joe's attention now.

"What the hell?" He traced the lines of red and black ink with one finger. "Is this what I think it is?"

Craig's grin got even wider. "Well, now, that depends what you think it is?"

"It looks like a cherry stem tied in a knot around a *J*." The *J* could just as easily have been a stylized swirl broken off the background of a nearby tattoo of a small Day of the Dead skull and roses, but Joe didn't think it was.

Craig grinned. His perfect white teeth flashed, and heat flared in his eyes, searing Joe where his gaze landed. "Then I guess it's what you think."

"That me?" Joe asked quietly, setting one finger to the ink, then drawing away.

"You told me I got your kink cherry. Were you shittin' me? Because I don't think you were."

Joe shook his head. "I wasn't." He stared at the tiny mark of his presence permanently embedded in Craig's skin. "Can't believe you tattooed me on your arm."

"Can't believe you let me be the first one to tie you up," Craig said. "Not a gift I took lightly, Joe. Always hoped you'd come back so we could talk it out proper."

"Talk what out?" Joe asked.

Craig studied him a long time before he answered. "You gave me something that should have rightly belonged to someone a lot more important to you, Joe."

Joe snorted. As if there had been anyone like that at the time. He'd played with Craig more than a few times, here at the bar in the back room, or in the stock room, or sometimes, in the tiny apartment behind the bar where Craig lived. But it hadn't been anything more than play. Learning, on Joe's part, what it felt like to give up control. To just be, and not worry if it was good enough, or if it was what the people around him expected or needed. With Craig, he could give in. He could let go.

It hadn't been like that in the clearing with Cam. Then his surrender had been desperate and frightening, because he had no idea if Cam would understand, and no way to make him see if he didn't. He'd had no words to explain away the utter annihilation of his will when Cam took him over if Cam didn't get it on an instinctual level the way Craig had. And no way to stop himself falling, either. Craig had always given him an out. Not knowing any better, Cam had not, and Joe had been more terrified of not wanting one than of not having one.

Craig had let him know it was okay to be used and then taken care of. Joe hadn't been brave enough to face Cam and find out what he thought about it after it had happened. He hadn't even meant to give up control to Cam that day in the first place. It had happened because Cam was strong and gentle and kind. Because Cam made him feel safe. It had happened before he'd realized it was a possibility outside of Craig's control, and he hadn't been prepared. Neither of them had.

Joe picked up his beer and chugged it. "Gimme a shot," he said, thumping the mug down. "And another beer."

Craig's eyes narrowed, but he took down the bottle of C.C. from the shelf and poured a shot. He set the tiny glass on the counter in front of Joe, but didn't release it when Joe reached for it.

"What ain't you tellin' me, Joe?"

Joe curled a lip and stared at the shot. "You don't know me anymore, Craig. Gimme the drink."

Craig released it, but Joe felt his eyes on him as he slammed it back.

"You need groundin'," Craig said quietly as he poured Joe a second beer. He didn't allow him that drink, though. Not right away. "You need keepin'. What's goin' on with you?"

"Don't," Joe said, his voice rough. The whiskey caused that, and he thumped his chest with the side of his fist to clear the burning sensation away. "I gotta go." He pulled out his wallet to slap money on the counter, but Craig waived the cash away.

"No. You just tell me what's going on."

Joe pushed away from the bar, spinning his stool so he could stand, but he was too slow.

Craig clamped down on Joe's wrist. "You stay put. I gotta deal with these nice folks." He nodded and smiled at the couple approaching the bar and the cash register. "You keep your butt glued to that seat, Joe, or so help me, I will camp out on your lawn until you talk to me, boy."

Joe stared at his own clenched fist. For the life of him, he could not unclench his fingers. He had steady pressure pulling upward on Craig's hold, but the man's grip would not budge.

"Answer," Craig demanded, his voice and his eyes cold as stone.

A deep shiver ran through Joe and he nodded. "Yes, Sir. I'll stay put." He barely managed to force his lips to form the words. He desperately wanted to leave. To run. Again.

"Good boy," Craig said, a little more softly. He let his thumb drift over the bones of Joe's wrist once, then released him and smiled broadly, showing all his teeth, for the customers waiting to pay for their meal. He was quick with the couple, and once they left, Joe was alone in the bar with Craig.

"Now," Craig said, returning to Joe, "You come on back here and talk to me."

"You have a bar to run."

"I own the damn bar. I can flip the sign for an hour in the dead of the evening lull if I damn well please. You came home last weekend for a wedding, and you're still here. Why is that?"

"You own the bar? When did that happen?"

"Don't change the subject. You'd know all about it if you ever visited, which you never have, so now it still begs an answer. What the hell are you still doin' in town?"

Joe shook his head. "School's done. I'm done. Just haven't figured out what's next."

"You told your aunt this? Because she comes to the coffee shop about every day for her morning coffee, and all she wonders is if you're going to up and disappear one day, just like you did when you decided on this whole fool college crap."

"It wasn't crap. I wanted an education. Nothing wrong with that."

"Then you shoulda took the horsemanship scholarship the community college offered. Kept your ass in the saddle and made somethin' of yourself like we all knew you could. But no. You took off to God only knows where to do God only knows what away from all the people who give a shit about you. Why would you go do a fool thing like that?"

"You don't *know* me, Craig," Joe snarled. "You don't know shit. I only came here to have a drink in peace. You don't want to offer that, you can sit in your empty bar and rot." He was on his feet, almost yelling, but Craig didn't so much as blink.

"You sit your ass down, boy." He pointed at Joe's vacated stool. "*Now.*"

"Fuck you."

Craig's gaze was flinty again. "You disrespecting me? You really want to go down that road, boy?"

Joe fought the urge to sit. Fought the urge to run. Fought the nausea rising up through his gut. He fought so hard he was frozen in place, unable to do anything at all.

"What has got you so scared, Joe?" Craig's demeanor didn't soften, but his iron will seemed suddenly covered in velvet. The rigidity in him was muted, but it underlay the gentle question, and this was the Craig Joe remembered.

Still, Joe shook his head.

Craig studied him for a long time. They stood in silence, watching each other, as Joe's heart fluttered like a broken-winged bird behind his ribs.

"Come here," Craig said at last, holding an arm outstretched.

And Joe did. Because he was tired and sore and he knew this man. He'd trusted him with his burgeoning self all those years ago. Surely he could take five minutes and trust him now.

"There you go," Craig said, lifting the section bar that separated the serving space from the rest of the room.

Joe walked numbly through and stood before him as Craig lowered the section back into place.

"Now what do you need, Joe?" Craig asked. "Talk to me."

What he wanted, Joe couldn't put into words. He'd never had to. Craig had always seemed to read his mind and just give what Joe had needed. Now, the older man stood before him, watched him, and waited.

"You gotta talk to me, boy," Craig said softly, tucking fingers under the hair at the nape of Joe's neck and cupping the side of his face. "It ain't like it was between us. Then you were a kid who didn't know shit." Craig looked into Joe's eyes, and no matter how much Joe wanted to look away, he couldn't. "Now I think you know more than you want to. I can't help unless you talk."

Joe shook his head. "Doesn't matter. I'm just tired." He closed his eyes. He couldn't break Craig's hold on him, as light as it was. All he could do was escape the scrutiny.

"Is it Cameron? Did O'Grady do something to hurt you, because if he did—"

"No!" Joe stepped back and pushed Craig's hand off him. "No. He didn't. He wouldn't. He lo—" Joe clamped his mouth shut, clenched his teeth around that word, and shook his head. His breath came in heavy gulps.

Craig chuckled, much to Joe's shock. "You damn fool. At least you know it. Have you talked to him?"

Joe shook his head yet again.

"You should, Joe. He's pined away for years, and anyone who waits that long deserves to know what's in your head. If he's waited this long, my bet is, he loves you enough to let it go if you don't feel the same, but you gotta talk to him. You gotta be straight with him."

A soft snort escaped as Joe let out his breath. "I'm about as far from straight, in any sense of the word, as it's possible to be, Craig. He deserves better."

"You are so full of shit, you stink the place up," Craig said, a sneer of disgust on his lips. "This ain't about Cam at all. Something happened to you, Joe. While you were gone? Or when you came back?"

Joe ran both hands through his hair and ground out a moan of annoyance. "Before. During. After the wedding. So much. Most of it, I can't take back."

Headlights flashed through the front window of the establishment, and Joe glanced up to see if it was Cam's truck that had turned off the main drag and into the bar's parking lot. His blood froze in his veins at the sight of a cream-colored Hummer swinging into a spot near the front door.

"Goddammit!" he croaked. "He wasn't supposed to find me here." He didn't think when he crouched, he just dropped.

"The hell?" Craig stared down at him. "What are you—"

"Just—" Joe peered over the top of the bar to watch the tall, slender man getting out of the big vehicle. "If he asks for me—"

The front door of the bar opened and the man walked in. Joe dropped back onto his haunches to remain hidden. Through the gap in the bar, and the forest of table and chair legs, Joe could see the flash of shiny leather shoes and the fall of neat navy trousers as the guy crossed the bar. "Hello."

God, that voice. A slide of… he didn't even know what… melted through Joe, and he closed his eyes. "Please," he whispered, gripping a handful of Craig's jeans leg. He eased silently back, practically under the bar, and Craig moved to box him into the tight space. The position also served to block Joe's reflection from the glass of the beer cooler.

Joe stared into that cooler door at the spot where the newcomer's shoulder, clad in burgundy wool, was visible in the reflection.

Please, just get rid of him.

He clung to Craig's pant leg and leaned his forehead against the bartender's knee. *Just please, make him go away.*

"Can I help you?" Craig asked politely.

Joe heard the *shush* of a cardboard coaster slide across the bar's surface.

"What's your poison?" Craig asked. Even the smile in his voice sounded fake, but then, Joe knew him very well. Someone who didn't know might think it was a friendly greeting.

"I'm hoping you might be able to help," the man said. His deep voice reverberated through the empty room. Through Joe. "I'm looking for someone. He's from around here. Said he used to work at this bar, actually, but I forget the address he gave me." A soft chuckle Joe remembered too well sent a cascade of shivers over him, and he squirmed. That wasn't the man's happy chuckle. It was the one he used when he was pretending to be amenable.

Craig's foot moved to rest alongside Joe's own. The contact was deliberate and reassuring.

"He wrote it down on a slip of paper," the newcomer went on, "and I'm afraid I must have left it back home." God, he sounded so real. So sincere and plausible. "Name's Joe Conner. You know him?"

"Course I know him."

Joe clamped the inside of his cheek between his teeth to keep from making a noise and tightened his fingers.

Craig shifted his weight to his far leg, just enough to raise the toe of his near one. He tapped three times on the side of Joe's boot. Three times. It was an old signal. Tap three times if you're okay. If you trust me to go on. Once if you need to stop. Joe remembered. He squeezed his eyes shut and pressed his forehead to Craig's leg. He tapped three times with the fist holding his jeans. He had to trust him. He had to be *able* to trust him, or nothing he thought about himself could be real or true.

"Small town, mister," Craig continued. "Everyone knows everyone else around here." There was a slight pause before he said, "And I don't know you."

A short hum of agreement sounded from the other side of the bar. "I'm a friend of Joe's from school."

"Got a name?"

"Mark."

Joe very carefully rubbed his forehead against Craig's knee in a negative motion. *Not Mark. André Floros, and "friend from school." A dangerous stretch.* God, please let Craig understand. The man was lying. He was *lying*.

"Well, Mark," Craig said, his tone very neutral. "If you know him from school, you probably know more about him these days than I do. He left town five years ago. Came home for his uncle's funeral, and his cousin's wedding. He worked here for a summer, which isn't much, really. Haven't seen much of him since he left, tell the truth."

None of that was anything but strict truth. Craig had a thing about lying. He didn't do it. He didn't like it. He didn't tolerate it.

"Just want to see him," André said. "He took off so suddenly, and I thought he'd be back by now. I was worried."

Craig shrugged. "And I appreciate that. But I don't know you, and I'm not going to tell you anything you don't already know. If you'd like a drink, fine. If not...."

"No." André's voice had dropped into a range that made Joe's blood cold and his hands shake. "Thanks for your time."

Joe waited, listening to the clop of André's heels fade, the bells over the door sound, and the wheeze of air through the old workings of the door's mechanism. Faintly, he heard the rumble of the Hummer coming to life and the spray of gravel as André peeled out of the lot faster than was strictly necessary.

Beneath the bar, Joe sagged back onto his heels and released Craig's pant leg. "Thank you," he whispered, sure it was too quiet to hear.

"Don't thank me yet, boy," Craig said in the coldest voice Joe could remember ever hearing from him. Craig stepped back and looked down on him. His blue eyes were like ice, his face stone cold and blank. He reached down and gripped Joe by the back of the head, by his hair, and hauled him forward until he landed on his knees. "You'll tell me what the *fuck* is going on, and you'll tell me now."

Behind his words, Joe heard the clang of the door's bell again and pinched his eyes shut. André had come back. And here he was, on his knees in front of another man. Didn't matter what he was doing there, André would see only one thing. He understood only one thing. Joe was property. And property could be shared. Property had earning potential. *Joe* had earning potential that André wasn't about to squander.

"I sure as shit would like to know the same goddamn thing!" The bar drop bounced against the brass framework next to it as it was flung upward. It was Cam's voice reverberating through the room, not André's. Cam's bulk crashing behind the bar to loom over Joe, fists clenched and Cam's face full of thunder. Only the fury was directed at Craig, not Joe. Cam's legs pressed against Joe's side and back, offering a strange sort of reassurance and protection.

Craig released Joe and stepped back, so suddenly, Joe almost toppled on his face. Both men reached out to steady him.

"Get to your feet," Cam ordered. "And you, keep your fucking hands off him. He's mine."

Joe shot up and pushed Cam out of his way. "I don't belong to you," he snarled. "I don't *belong* to anyone. Leave me the fuck alone!"

"No chance."

"Uh-uh."

Cam and Craig spoke at the same time, and Joe stared from one to the other of them.

"I can take care of myself." He expected them both to negate him again, but neither of them spoke. "I—" A wave of chills and nausea swept over him, and he reached for purchase on the wood of the bar. Sweat on his palms made his grip slick, and his hand skidded. His legs wobbled. "Need to sit," he mumbled, and then Cam was pressed to his back and Craig grabbed his arm.

The pressure against his back was screaming agony, and he might have cried out, but it was hard to tell in the chaos. The ceiling was falling in, the floor rocking, the bar snaking away in a slithering motion across the room. Cam's voice was harsh and ragged in his ear. Craig's urgent and clinical. The bell over the door jangled and finally, things settled into a dark mist and he floated off into the shadows where it was cool and quiet.

nine

CAM PACED. Aunt Marie had begged him to sit more than once, but he never managed to stay still more than a minute or two before he had to be moving again. He thought better when he was on his feet, doing something. Not that there was anything to do but wait. He sucked at waiting.

"Why is it taking so long?" he asked for about the tenth time.

His phone vibrated in his pocket, and he jumped, then pulled in a breath and yanked the phone out. "What?" he asked into it once he'd slid the green bar across.

"Anything?" It was Craig.

"Still waiting."

"Shit. Call me when you find out what's going on. Please."

"Why?" Cam couldn't help the cold tone. The anger. The utter, furious, vibrating rage that the guy had been all over *his* Joe.

There was a pause, then Craig's voice, calm and tenaciously patient. "Because he's my friend. I want to know he's okay. I want to know what's going on."

"Just keep away from him," Cam replied, and hit End, shoving the phone away in his pocket.

"Who was that, honey?" Aunt Marie asked from her seat in the plastic orange chair against the wall.

"No one."

"Cameron." Her no-nonsense voice brought Cam about to face her. She sat quietly, contained. Her long hair was piled into a messy knot on top of her head, held in place by a crisscross of elastic bands. Her hands were folded loosely on top of the leather purse in her lap. She wore jeans and the same, short, oilskin coat she'd had forever. She was every inch the calm, centered woman who had raised him, and Cam felt every inch the boy he'd been every time she'd chastised him over the years.

"Craig Anderson," Cam said finally. "The guy from the bar."

"I know who he is."

"He wanted to know if Joe's okay."

"He's always been a good friend," she said. "Did you tell him you'd keep him informed?" She watched Cam calmly from her seat until Cam felt heat slide up from under his collar and sheath his face in shame.

"Sorry, Auntie." He pulled his phone out and dialed the last number on it. Craig's voice chimed down the line, eager and concerned.

"Well?"

"No. Nothing yet. Just. I'll call you. When we know." Cam glanced up at Aunt Marie, who still watched him. "Sorry," he mumbled, and hung up again before Craig could say anything more. He shoved the phone safely into his pocket and slumped into the chair next to Marie's. He couldn't face her. Not really.

She didn't condemn him, though, simply patted his leg and nodded faintly. "You're a good boy, Cameron. Try not to worry so."

He said nothing. After an agonized minute watching the long black second hand sweep around the face of the waiting room clock, he was back on his feet.

It wasn't that he disliked Craig. He'd never had anything against the man. But he'd walked in on… what? On Joe kneeling at the guy's feet. On him with his fingers tangled in Joe's hair. Fury seethed through him again. No. That was wrong. Joe belonged to *him*. To *Cam*.

"Fuck." He swept his hand through his own blond locks and cursed when fingers caught in the tangles still trapped in the elastic. He ripped the offending thing out and whipped it across the room.

"Cameron," Aunt Marie said softly.

He resisted the urge to apologize again, but he did go pick the elastic up and spent a few minutes smoothing out his hair and retying it into a neat queue. What the hell was taking so goddamn long?

"Cameron," Marie said, and Cam turned to look at her. She patted the seat next to her. "Come and sit do—oh. Doctor." She turned her attention from Cam to someone beyond him, and he turned to the woman standing in the doorway.

"Mrs. Conner?" she asked.

Aunt Marie nodded and stood. "Yes. Marie Conner. I'm Joe's aunt. You're Beth, aren't you? Beth Tanner? Your mom taught Joe and Cameron. Sixth grade, I think."

Beth blushed slightly. "Yes," she replied. "Dr. Beth Tanner." She met Marie's steady gaze. "But you can call me Beth. I've come from seeing to Joe."

"Is he all right?"

"Well—" The doctor glanced from one to the other of them. "Yes. And no."

"Well, I—" Marie blinked, set her lips, and squared her shoulders. "What does that mean, exactly?"

"Mrs. Conner, there is nothing life-threateningly wrong with your nephew." She glanced at Cam, but Marie reached and took Cam's hand, indicating there was nothing the doctor said that could not be said in his presence. Cam was suddenly, wearily grateful to her for that.

"He is, however," Dr. Beth went on, "suffering from a number of conditions that just do not happen to a man overnight, Mrs. Conner."

"I'm afraid I don't understand."

"Well, most notably, he's malnourished. Has he been eating well?"

Marie glanced at Cam and he sighed.

"No," Cam said. "He's been off his feed lately."

"Cameron!" Marie elbowed him. "He's not a horse."

"The results, unfortunately, are the same, I'm afraid," Dr. Beth said, smoothing over Cam's gaffe. "We've done some blood work, and the results will tell us more, but I only have to look at him, his skin color, his hair and nails, to know he isn't getting the nutrients he needs. And he's dehydrated. The two often go together. Has he been depressed? Or is he on any medications for conditions we should know about?" She was looking at Cam now, and it made Cam angry all over again.

"No," Cam said, jaw tight. "He's not on any medications. I asked. He's fine."

"He is certainly not fine, Cameron," Marie said, a burning fierceness in her eyes and that tightness in her voice that made men cringe.

"Well, no, Auntie, but—"

"This brings up the next issue," the doctor said. "Do either of you know how he got hurt?"

"Hurt?" Cam looked to Marie, who was staring wide-eyed, at him.

"No," they both said.

"Hurt how?" Cam asked. "What are you talking about?"

The doctor's lips pursed for a moment, then she opened the metal cover on the clipboard she was carrying. "Understand, we took pictures, because injuries like this, well, they are unusual, and definitely not self-inflicted."

"Self...." Her face had gone pale and she reached, gripping Cam's shoulder for support. This was not the self-sufficient Aunt Marie he knew. He wrapped an arm around her waist as the doctor turned the clipboard around.

The pictures were of Joe's back. Bile rose in Cam's throat, and a squeak of pure agony escaped Aunt Marie's lips.

Who...." She reached toward the image and then snatched her hand away.

"Now, we've scheduled X-rays and an MRI, but given how old the bruising is, and the fact he's been up and walking around the past week, I doubt there is any internal damage. It's a precaution only."

"What would cause that?" Marie asked, voice tiny and, for the first time in Cam's memory, old sounding. Frail.

Joe's back was, indeed, bruised. But besides that, there were three long gashes across the expanse of discolored skin. One crossed from shoulder blade to shoulder blade. Another angled down from his right shoulder blade to just below his left ribs, and the third marked the skin over his hips, just at the base of his spine.

"It's difficult to say," the doctor replied. "They look almost like whip marks."

"No." Cam took a step away from Marie. "I've seen whip marks. On horses and those.... No. More like a crop. Something that doesn't bend so easily. God, they'd have to hit him hard to break the skin. Why is it so red?"

"Infection." The doctor snapped the clipboard closed. "We have him on an IV and an antibiotic drip. The wounds around his shoulders had to be lanced, and we'll monitor his blood and white cell count." She sighed. "In a way, it's lucky he didn't eat today. Lucky he fainted, or this infection might have been much worse before anyone realized he was hurt." She turned to Marie and looked at her over the gold wire rims of her glasses. "Mrs. Conner, whoever did this to your nephew might still be a danger to him. I suggest you see if you can find out who, and why, and alert the authorities. He's safe enough here, but you don't want to take any chances."

"Yes, of course," Marie whispered. Then she straightened her shoulders and pulled herself up taller. She took Cam's hand in hers, desperate, but determined. "Of course, thank you, Doctor. Can we see him now?"

Beth smiled faintly and nodded. "Yes. He's been moved to a semiprivate room upstairs. Ask at the nurse's station there, and they'll show you where he is. I'm recommending he meet with a nutritionist and a counselor before he leaves here. If there's nothing physically wrong with him, then it's best to get to the heart of why he hasn't been eating. Whatever is going on in his life that got him beat up this badly, I can't imagine it hasn't affected his mental well-being as well. He needs help, Mrs. Conner." Her smile deepened and she patted Marie's arm. "He's lucky he has you." She gave Cam a nod. "Cam." She let out a little huff. "Take care of him."

Cam nodded. A lump formed in his throat, and he tried and failed to swallow it down. Even Beth sounded ripped up about this. She was only a few years older than he, had a younger sister Cam and Joe had gone to school with. This wasn't an anonymous city hospital where Joe's injuries were just another in a long succession daily ugliness. This was their home. Everyone knew everyone, and Joe had come here to be safe. Cam should have been paying better attention. He should have known before now that Joe was in trouble.

Furious, with his own blindness, now, he stalked after Marie toward the elevator. He was done letting Joe put him off. He was going to get answers.

ten

JOE WONDERED if feigning sleep would save him. He was lying on his side facing the partially open door and he could hear Aunt Marie's voice down the hall. She was exchanging pleasantries with the night nurse, who was, apparently, Aunt Marie's backup coordinator for the community center's weekend horsemanship classes for the kids who came out from the city. She offered to take over the classes for a few weeks, while Marie got Joe straightened out.

Joe sighed as he listened to his aunt accept. Why the hell did everyone think he needed straightening out? He was so not—

The door opened even while he was still listening to Aunt Marie down the hall.

"Hey." Cam's low, velvety voice filled the semidarkness of the room and chased the unsavory shadows from the corners.

Joe closed his eyes briefly and refused to let that soothing tone draw him in. "Hey," he answered.

Cam let out a heavy sigh and pulled a chair over. He set it beside the bed so when he sat in it, he and Joe were at eye level and Joe couldn't look anywhere but at him.

"Well." Cam ran a finger over the IV line in the back of Joe's hand. "Can't run away now."

Joe swallowed.

"Talk," Cam demanded.

Joe stared at him, into his beautiful, hurting, loving eyes and wished there was a way to tell him everything. He wished there was a way that would ensure Cam would still look at him like this once he'd spilled everything.

Cam took his hand, and for a moment, Joe held on tight. Then the sound of Aunt Marie's boots approaching the door made it through his fog, and he tried to let go. Cam shook his head. "She knows how I feel. Always has. She's not going to say anything."

Joe didn't want the relief to be so intense. He didn't want to need that connection. He couldn't rely on it. He didn't let go, though.

Marie entered and stood at Cam's back, gripping his shoulder. She didn't ask how Joe was feeling. She didn't touch him. She studied him, appraising, let her gaze flick to his connection to Cam and finally, *at last* reached over and tucked a clump of Joe's hair back off his forehead. "You'd better tell us everything, then," she said. "Cameron, let an old lady sit down."

Joe reluctantly let go of Cam so the other man could move out of the chair. Aunt Marie's grip, when she replaced Cam's with her own, was nearly as firm, though, and motherly enough to be comforting. And Cam didn't go very far. He perched on the edge of the bed and placed a hand on Joe's hip. It wasn't the sort of gesture that happened between friends or brothers. It was a lover's touch, and Joe should have twitched it off, but he couldn't. He glanced at his aunt, who made an uncharacteristic cooing sound and patted his cheek.

"Enough now, Joe. Cameron's been more than patient. I'm not so old—or old-fashioned—that I don't understand. Not so blind I don't see what goes on under my own roof, either." She gave him a baleful eye. "Not that I want you boys giving Mindy any ideas. She's only eighteen. Much too young." She clucked disapprovingly. "And that Tom fellow is too keen. Needs some settling out, that one."

Heat scaled Joe's neck and cheeks. He'd been barely more than Mindy's age when Craig had first caught his eye. The poor bartender hadn't stood a chance against Joe's driving need or insatiable curiosity. Neither, for that matter, had Cam. Joe glanced at Cam now to find that he was staring at Aunt Marie, gratitude in every line of his features.

Well fuck. He was definitely outnumbered on the whole coming-out-as-gay thing. Cam was getting his way in that as he did in everything, and

Joe had to wonder how long his aunt had known about them. About him. His attention was drawn back to her when she spoke again.

"Don't look so damn surprised, boy," she chided gently. "A mother knows these things."

Joe's entire being jerked in surprise. "You're not my—" Wasn't she? In a way? His own mother had disappeared into the flames after the rest of his family. She'd left him alive and followed them into death. He'd had to make do with Aunt Marie and Uncle Albert and their teeming mass of girls. And Cam. Joe swallowed and nodded. "Yeah. I guess," he said finally.

"Oh, Joey, you're a sweet boy, but daft." She caressed his face and smoothed his kinked hair off his cheek again. "Sometimes I think you forget who you are. You're my boy as much as those girls were ever my own kids." She smiled fondly. "You both are." She tossed a glance at Cam. "You both are." She gripped Cam's hand in hers and straightened. "Now enough. You have problems, Joseph Andrew Conner. Out with it."

Like this would be as easy as admitting he'd swiped a Superman comic and pack of gum from the general store when he was twelve. Or that the smokes Uncle Albert had found in an old tin in the tack room when he was sixteen were actually his. Of course he hadn't mentioned that he didn't smoke them. He only smuggled them to school to barter with. Bullies there would agree to leave off harassing a then skinny and defenseless Cam if Joe promised a steady supply of cigarettes. He also made no mention of how he'd acquired the cigarettes. In a town as small as theirs, he hadn't been the only one who kept his gayness under wraps. The general store's teenage clerk wasn't above smuggling smokes to Joe in exchange for a few secret kisses and gropes in the stockroom. It hadn't been as if Joe didn't enjoy the attention, either. It fed something in him to know the older boy wanted him like that. And it gave him the means to protect Cam. No one had to know about any of it, then or now.

The irony of that last memory was not lost on Joe as he searched his aunt's face, then Cam's and tried to find a way to explain. "I should never have gone to college," was the first thing that came to mind, and the first thing to fall from his lips when he opened his mouth. He had to wonder if the drugs the doctor had given him were making him stupid.

Cam snorted. "At last, we agree on something."

"But I did," Joe shot at him. "I did, and I had bills to pay. Tuition. Rent." He slid his gaze back to his aunt. "I looked at the books, Auntie. After Uncle Albert died. I knew—"

"Those books will be your concern when I say they are," Aunt Marie said harshly. Her eyes had gone shiny and her lips pursed tight.

"So you had to get a job," Cam said.

Joe couldn't meet either of their gazes anymore. "Something like, yeah."

"I'm not going to like this," Marie predicted. "Well, go on, then. What did you do?"

What didn't I do? Joe pulled in a deep breath and for a moment, he could feel the tension of Cam's tie around his wrist, the ache in his knuckles as he'd hung on to it for dear life. He could feel again the tightness in his chest at the thought that he needed to be tethered like that to stay sane. He settled when he remembered that the tie was still under his pillow at home. Safe. Comforting.

I answered a Craigslist ad.

And why wasn't that as good a way to begin as any other? So he said it out loud. Cam and Marie glanced at each other, then back to him.

"And?" Cam prompted finally.

And....

It had seemed so benign at the time. Jonathan Pollard. Sixty-something millionaire and philanthropist. Old, dying gay guy who only wanted a bit of companionship.

"He was nice," Joe said quietly, explaining further as the memories ran through his mind like an old film reel. He didn't tell them every detail, but painted images of the past five years in broad strokes while the minutiae dug into his soul and lodged, thorns in the most tender parts of him. "Only wanted someone to take out to dinner when he felt like it, and to keep him company when he couldn't go out. Not like it was anything. I mean, it was easy. He took me to nice places, tried to pay me when I went to his when he couldn't go out. I mean, that's a dream job. School was difficult enough. I tried a part-time waiter thing, but I was going to flunk out that way. Not enough time to study. Not enough sleep to be halfway decent at the job. It paid shit and the tips sucked because I was crap at it. This way, with Jonathan, I got fed and had time for school. He didn't care if I was doing homework. Just that I was there and he wasn't alone."

He risked looking up. Aunt Marie's lips were pulled into a tight line. Frown lines traced down from the corners of her mouth. Joe looked to Cam. His brow was furrowed in thought.

"Doesn't sound so bad," Cam said finally.

Maybe Joe imagined the lack of warmth in his tone. He looked back to Aunt Marie, hoping he could just leave it there.

"Was," Marie said curtly, waiting. "You keep saying he *was*."

Joe sighed. "He died. Maybe three months after Uncle Albert." He kept his gaze on the weave of the blanket over the bed. He couldn't look at his aunt when he talked about his uncle. Not when he mentioned him in the same breath as all the things he'd done while he was away.

Silence crept through the room. Marie's hand was motionless and cool in his, and Cam remained on the edge of the bed, but he was no longer touching Joe. If they thought keeping company with a lonely old man for money was bad, what would they think of the rest?

"You took advantage, Joe," Marie said quietly.

Joe shook his head. "No, Auntie. I swear. He took me out to eat. I did homework in his living room. I never took a cent from him, even when he offered. He paid my tuition, but I didn't ask for it. I didn't even know about it until I went to the registrar to find out about loans and they told me it was taken care of. I gave him shit and he asked me to move in with him."

Cam shifted, drawing a little farther away from Joe under guise of shifting to a more comfortable position. Joe's heart threaded through a barbed wire tunnel of hurt.

"I did," Joe said, pushing ice into his voice. If he could freeze out the emotion, he could ignore the way Cam's silent movement away tightened that razor wire around his already bleeding heart. "Eventually. He kept paying my rent no matter what I said to him. I couldn't see making him waste his money if I was at his place most of the time, anyway. I got to know him. To like him. He was a good guy. He introduced me to his friends." Joe shrugged and some of the icy resolve melted. "He thought they were his friends. Some of them were. Some."

He closed his eyes.

"This is André, Joe. I knew his father and his uncle." Jonathan *smiled sadly. "Gone now, but André is a good boy. He keeps an old man company sometimes. You should get to know him."*

André.

Joe did get to know André. He was handsome and cultured, in his forties, and very attentive to Jonathan, and to Joe. He was classy. Joe liked him, at least at first. As Jonathan's health declined, however, the shades of André began to show. The first real thing Joe learned about him was that he'd known Jonathan for a very long time, and twenty years ago, "keeping an old man company" had involved a lot more than doing homework at his dining table, or going out to dinner.

Joe had suspected as much would have been true now, had Jonathan the wherewithal to do anything about it, but the man was old and unwell. He was content with companionship. André wasn't shy about letting Joe know he expected more.

"Jonathan was so concerned about knowing he wasn't leaving me alone," Joe said. "He pushed us together. Constantly, so I let André…."

He knew Jonathan's door wasn't closed. The old man would be able to see them, and Joe should mention it. He should go close the door. Better yet, he should just go. He wasn't really interested in André. Not that way. But then he thought about Craig, about the way he liked the control, and that secret part of him that liked to be kept throbbed in response to André's grip in his hair. He had to break this off now, or he would never be able to. He wouldn't want to.

"Fuck me, you've got a pretty mouth," André growled, pulling Joe out of the brutal kiss by that handful of hair. His eyes gleamed with dark need. "Wanna give the old man a little thrill? He does love a show."

"What?" Joe blinked at him. "Show?"

André grinned. "What do you think I did for him twenty years ago? Statistics and math problems? He likes to watch, Joe. He especially likes to watch pretty young men put their assets in the air. We're going to do it anyway, eventually. You have a problem with giving old John a peek at your bare ass?"

Joe shook his head. "We're not—"

André shook him by the hair. "Eventually, we are."

"Says you." Joe tried to ignore the panic-coated need rising in his gut. Fucking hell, but the man's strength and power felt good.

That dark gleam got darker still. "Yeah, Joe. Says me. Don't think I don't see how much that turns you on." He bent and kissed Joe, plunging his tongue deep, yanking Joe into him by a grip on his belt.

André reached down and clamped thick fingers around Joe's package, pointing out the proof of Joe's want. He squeezed, and Joe grimaced and caught his breath inside the kiss. He held it, getting light-headed and going up on his toes in an attempt to escape the bruising force at his groin.

André finally relented, easing his grip, but not releasing it. He pulled back from the kiss. "You wanna get off on this?" he asked. His voice was dark and deep.

Joe fell into it, headlong. He nodded.

"Get on your knees, put those pretty lips around my cock, and suck." He smiled, and that too was dark and full of lust for Joe. *"Then we'll see."*

Joe dropped, just as he was told, and waited like a baby bird for André to feed him his thick, hot dick. God, he was so easy. But the feel of a cock in his mouth was... it had been a long time. Not since Craig had taught him to take it deep. Not since Craig had shown him all the pleasure to be had in letting another man seize what he wanted.

Fuck, and André took. Hard, fast, and deep, just like Joe wanted, with no apparent thought, at the moment, for anything but his own pleasure.

That was okay. Joe could accommodate that. Craig had shown him the possibilities in giving, even until it hurt, and the rewards that would come when he'd done a good job. He'd get his chance. He could wait.

Then, there was very little time or space for him to think. André drove deep, and his cock often cut off Joe's air. As André fucked and Joe fought for breath, everything narrowed down to the heavy cock sliding between his lips, the inflexible hands in his hair, and guttural noises André made. Joe whimpered and clutched at André's thighs, but when he gripped André's trousers, seeking some connection to the world outside the act, André yanked free of his mouth and slapped him.

"Didn't say you could touch, dog," André growled, and shoved back into Joe's mouth before he could even think to protest.

Insults had never been a part of Craig's repertoire. They'd talked about the idea of humiliation some, but it wasn't something Joe craved, and along with the lying, it wasn't a thing Craig had any stomach for. Joe dropped his jaw as André's hips jerked and brought Joe's mind back to the now.

"Oh yeah," André crooned. "Fucking hell, you've got a good mouth." He tilted Joe's head up. "Look at me."

Joe lifted his gaze to see André glaring down at him.

"You're even prettier this way, all stoppered up with a thick cock. Suck it good now."

Joe hollowed his cheeks, and when his eyelids fluttered at the taste of salty precome on his tongue, André shook him.

"Look at me."

Joe forced his attention back to André's murky eyes and the glimmer of power in them. "You'll make a good boy, Joe." He jerked his hips viciously, and Joe gagged, tried to pull away, only to have his head held tighter as André's cock bored deep. "Fuck, yeah," André breathed.

For a few heartbeats, his hips rocked and that cock was Joe's entire world. Even the pain of his scalp faded to nothing as André used his mouth and took his pleasure. Joe sucked when he was told and held still when he was forced to. It was a different sort of pleasure than he'd experienced before. If it was pleasure. He wasn't sure. He only knew it was euphoric in the way it took him out of himself and let him not think, even if it was only for as long as it took André to get off.

And get off he did, in spectacular fashion, yanking free of Joe's mouth and spreading come over Joe's cheek as he pumped the release from his body.

When he'd shuddered the last bit out, he gazed down at Joe and patted his cheek. He didn't say *anything. Joe waited, his own cock aching inside his jeans as come dried on his face.*

"Still hard?" André asked after what seemed like forever. He smiled, but it wasn't a friendly sort of expression. "Well, then, whip it out, let's see."

Joe swallowed. "Sir?" he ventured, very quietly.

André laughed as if he'd just heard the most wonderfully ridiculous thing in the world, then shrugged. "Okay. Sure. Take it out and let's see you come for me, Joe. That'll be interesting."

Joe hesitated, but he ached. He needed this. He pulled his cock free of his jeans and jerked at it, vigorous and unevenly. He saw no reason to hold back, and there, on his knees in the hallway outside Jonathan's room, he gave up the only thing he really had to call his own, and came on command. Like the dog André slowly turned him into over the next three years.

He drew in a deep breath. "Let's just say, he had me by the balls." Of course, just because he remembered that day as the slow, minute motion of humiliation it was didn't mean he recounted it. Again, he gave them the broad strokes. It was enough to close Aunt Marie's eyes in sadness. Enough to propel Cam up off the edge of the bed.

Joe looked up at him. "I know. Not the best decision I ever made in my life, but—"

Cam held up one hand and plunged the other into his pocket. He drew out his cell and held it up. "Phone's ringing," he said, voice thick and curt. He pulled his thumb across the surface of the device, turned, and fled the room. His faint "Hello?" was lost behind the closing door.

Beside Joe, Marie pulled in a long, steadying breath. When he looked to her, she was looking back. "You'd better tell me the rest before he comes back."

"What rest?" Joe asked. He tried to look her in the eye. He really did. But he couldn't. "I let him turn me into a whore." He shook his head. "No. I was—am—"

"Joseph Andrew, if that word crosses your lips again, I will wash your mouth out with soap. See if I don't."

"Gonna take the truth away from me, Auntie? The only thing I have left?" God. He sounded so bitter. He felt… like the worst, used dregs of… he didn't even know what.

Then she reached for him. The soft skin of her fingertips brushed over his cheek. He only felt the wetness when she dragged her fingers through it.

"Joey," she whispered. Her tongue clicked softly behind her teeth, and that small sound brought the scent of smoke to his nostrils. Just the memory of it. Of the orange flicker and the smell—the stench—of his life disappearing.

He waited, sitting on Aunt Marie and Uncle Albert's kitchen table. He watched the front door, waiting. Any minute, his father would walk through with the car seat, his mother haranguing and juggling all the baby gear they took everywhere they went.

"Joey, honey, let's get you tucked up into bed." He glanced to his aunt, sure in the way only kids who believed ever were that the minute he took his eyes off that door, it would burst open and his father's affable voice would fill the house. He'd be laughing, chiding Joe's mother in that way he had. "Woman, leave off the meddling and let the lad carry his own kit."

Joe smiled. Only his father had that way of drawing out his words into an accent like that. It was his job, after all, to be anyone they paid him to be onstage or in front of a camera, and right now, he was doing some English thing. He always talked like that, lately. Practicing. Joe loved to watch him recite lines. Half the time, he had no idea what any of it meant. It was like listening to half a conversation.

Only recently, his father had let him run lines too, speaking the opposite parts to those his father practiced, and Joe found he was good at it. He read fast, and remembered well. He could act, like his father, and he loved the grand make-believe of it all.

The door did open, quietly, and Uncle Albert slipped in. He looked at Joe for a long minute, then held out both arms. "Come here, boy."

Joe jumped down from the table's edge and ran for him, careening into him and burying his face against the scratchy wool of Albert's sweater. He willed the arms circling him to be another's. When he looked up, Uncle Albert's craggy, tired features would be transformed to his father's shaved cheeks and square jaw.

He clung and he buried his face and he didn't look. Not for a very long time.

When his aunt made a small, inquiring sound, though, he couldn't stop himself. He peered up at his uncle, saw the way he closed his eyelids over grief and shook his head.

Joe pulled away, tucked his arms close to himself.

"Come on, Joey," Aunt Marie said. "Bed, now."

He took her hand and followed her, up the stairs to the landing before he looked back. "They'll be here in the morning, I guess," he said to Uncle Albert, and then turned his back on the man and let his aunt bring him to his room, tuck the comforter up to his chin, and turn out the light.

"Joey, don't be daft." She tucked a clod of hair behind his ear. "The truth is, you screwed up. We all do sometimes. Your mom and dad, your uncle and I, we all taught you better than to hide behind the mistakes, Joey. Now. Was it one of your... those men who hurt you? Did he hurt you any other way?"

"No!" Joe would have sat up, but she was a practical woman and he was tired and sore. She held him down easily. "No, Auntie, nothing like that. It wasn't a client. Most of them were decent enough. They wanted certain things from me, were willing to pay for it, and I...." He swallowed. "I supplied what they wanted. But there were rules, and people like that, people like I... entertained... were willing to abide by the rules because usually, they're important. They don't want the world to know they do what they do, and people like me, we have safeguards. Precautions to keep the more reckless ones from doing something stupid."

"Then...," she prompted, "who?"

The door to his room flew open then and Cam was back. "He was *here*?" He practically shouted. "Here? He came after you?"

"Who?" Aunt Marie asked.

"André," Cam snarled. "Come looking for his lost puppy." He held up his phone. "That was Craig. He wanted to know you were okay. He told me some guy named Mark stopped by the bar, but Craig figured he was lying. About being your friend. Probably about his name. Did you know he was here?"

"No. I mean yes, I knew," Joe said, closing his eyes, trying to grapple his thoughts back into line. They skittered away under the weight of Cam's anger, and the cutting echo of André's favorite insult echoed through Cam's voice. "Just. I only just saw him a few minutes before you showed up at the bar. I didn't know before tonight."

"But he did come looking for you. Craig said he acted like he owned you." Cam's eyes narrowed into slits. "Does he?" In the question, another question hid, disguised from Aunt Marie, but easy to read in the hard clench of Cam's fist. The Dom in Cam glared out at Joe and demanded a reply.

Does he own you?

"It's not like that," Joe said, forcing the words out through his closing throat. "I left. He didn't want me to. Said I still owed him. He tried to make me stay. When I said no, he...."

"He did this," Marie said, indicating Joe's back with a wave.

Joe nodded. "I honestly didn't think he'd follow me. I figured he'd just... give up. I don't know."

"Do you?" Cam asked.

"Do I what?" Joe looked to him and saw the frosty anger all over his face.

"Owe him," Cam said. Every line of him was rigid and cold, and Joe shivered. "Do you owe him money or something?"

"No. Good God, no. I'm not an idiot. I always gave him his cut. I never held back. I let him keep all the shit those guys gave me. I didn't need their trinkets, and André liked the perks. I only ever kept enough to pay my bills. He arranged my schedule. I gave him his share for that."

"You paid him to pimp you out." Cam's words cut.

Joe said nothing, because what the hell else was there to say?

"Cameron," Marie stood and placed herself between Joe's bed and Cam. He couldn't even see his friend as she took a few steps toward him. "It's getting late. You should go back." A tight silence wrapped invisible, strangling cords around them all. "Boss is always the first one up," she said quietly, rubbing up and down his arm and reminding him of the lesson both Uncle Albert and Cassidy had been fond of drilling into them as teenagers reluctant to drag themselves out of bed for morning chores.

Cam sniffed, a sharp intake of breath through his nose. "I'll stay with him."

"No, honey, I think you need to go back to the house. If this André turns up, I want you there. Joe and I are perfectly fine here. I'll bring him home when they check him out tomorrow. You have a farm to run, and I want you there."

Cam didn't say anything else, and Joe couldn't see his face, only his back as he turned and left the room. When the door was closed again, Joe finally let out his breath.

"That's that, then, I guess," he said. The weight of Cam's anger crushed him, and he dug deeper under the covers, wishing he could turn his back but knowing it would hurt too much to roll over. "I'm sorry to have made such a mess of everything. I'll make sure I take it all with me when I go."

"Joseph," she admonished him gently as she retook her seat, this time with an extra pillow behind her head and a blanket over her knees.

"You saw him, Auntie, he hates me now."

She smiled at that and shook her head. "Your Cameron doesn't have a hateful bone in his body. He's hurt. Yes. As am I. Disappointed. What did you expect?"

"Nothing but what I got, I suppose."

"Shush, Joseph. You go to sleep now."

"Auntie—"

"I said shush. You're tired, and no good decision was ever made by a tired mind. Sleep, now."

As if he could. Instead, he lay and watched her face as she closed her own eyes and sat quietly. He couldn't really tell if she was sleeping. Knowing her, she did that with as much grace and elegance and strength as she did everything.

"Joseph," she said warningly, a slight, firm whisper over the air.

"Yes, Auntie." He closed his eyes, and somehow, sleep did come. Eventually.

eleven

CAM HAD run hundreds of scenarios through his head since Joe had come home. A bad breakup had been his first instinct, maybe even a violent one. He'd also considered poor grades, stress, even flunking out. A year's worth of wasted tuition would account for the guilt and depression. Cam knew the farm's financial status as well as anyone. They weren't in dire straits, but they didn't have extra, and Katie's wedding hadn't been free.

Frustrated, he took the heavy snips to the twist of wire he was using to fix a fence. The tool was old, dulled, and chipped, and it took him a few tries before he realized the wire had slipped into a notch of the blades that had only cut through a small portion of its thickness.

"For fuck sakes!" He flung the offending things across the small paddock. A foal whinnied and shimmied closer to its mother. Seán glanced over at him and Cam sighed. He was tempted to go on a rant about proper care of the tools they all needed to do their jobs, but the man's soft nod of understanding closed Cam's mouth.

"Aye, lad. We've got a list compiled," the man said. "Tools that need replacing. Think Abby's got it to go over the mechanical whosits."

"Mechanical whosits," Cam muttered as he fetched back the snips and examined the oft-sharpened blades. "That what I put on the order form?"

Seán chuckled. "Now an' I ain't the mechanic, am I? That'd be Abby's area. She'll give you the goods when she's through with it."

Cam smiled at Seán's thick Irish brogue. Uncle Albert had been Irish, albeit second or third generation. He held to the old Irish loyalties, but he didn't have the lilt of green and moss in his voice. Seán did, and it always eased Cam's mood. It brought out a feeling from somewhere deep. Not a memory. Just a mood, an emotion too far back in his mind for images. Maybe his father had sounded like that. He couldn't remember.

"You all right, lad?" Seán asked after a few moments.

"Yeah. Fine." Cam sighed and was more careful about how he placed the snips over the wire this time. He found a still sharp section of blade and squeezed. The wire gave neatly, and he bent the sharp edges in to keep clothes and horse hide from harm.

"And Joey?" Seán asked. "They find what ails him?"

Cam looked up sharply. "What do you know about it?"

Seán, easily forty years Cam's senior, didn't even flinch at the ire or disrespect inherent in the curt words. "'Now don't get thick. You know me wee one drives the ambulance. She doesn't usually be tellin' tales outta school, but this is Joey, isn't it? When she brings one of our own into the hospital in a terrible state, she's not gonna keep it hush. Did ye think she would?"

Cam sighed. He hadn't thought anything at all. Hadn't even bothered to note that Seán's daughter, Jessica, had been the ambulance driver. His heart and mind had all been on Joe. Images of his pale features, and of Craig clutching his hair, took turns burning themselves into the headspace behind Cam's eyes. Now the fire of fury over Joe's confessions only served to fuel the heat of those branding irons of memory. All his being had been taken up with Joe. God. For how long now had all of him been taken up with Joe? And where had Joe been in it all? Denying him and….

"Fuck!" The snips caught a pinch of skin and he threw them again.

"Lad." Seán fetched the tool and brought it over to him. "Lad, this ain't the place for you today, surely?" he said gently. "Your head's a thousand miles away."

"Everything is a thousand miles away," Cam said, just for one minute letting the balloon of anger and regret well up and clog his throat, push the tears to the very surface of his eye. Just for a moment. A heartbeat. One space in time where someone, anyone, could see he wasn't head of any household or manager of any farm. Just a boy left behind. Again.

"Your da," Seán said, and Cam's head shot up.

His da?

"Uncle Albert—"

"No. Your da." Seán set the snips on top of the fence post, took Cam by the elbow, led him the few steps to the truck's tailgate and set him on the edge.

"What do you know about him?" Cam asked. He'd long, long ago stopped wondering. He'd bled every scrap of information out of Aunt Marie and Uncle Albert that they'd had, and that was not a whole hell of a lot.

"He weren't a bad man."

"Just a lazy one." He worked jobs none else would bother with.

"No. Not that, either. He worked hard. He worked jobs none else would bother with. He made a place here. We all thought he'd stay, but he didn't."

"Why?"

Seán shrugged. "Never said aught to any of us. But the place he made, he made it for you. He carved out a spot in this family for you. Whatever pulled him away, he knew when he arrived he weren't takin' you with when he left. He worked to give you a home. Every penny he made, he gave back to Marie and Albert the day he left. Dunno what they did with it, but they accepted his decision, I reckon, and gave you the home he couldn't. Didn't question why he couldn't. Just did what he couldn't outright ask of 'em."

"Yeah," Cam said "I suppose that's one way to look at it."

"Only sane way to look at such a thing as a man leavin' his young 'un to strangers."

"This isn't the dark ages, Seán. He abandoned me. He left me here and went"—Cam waved out over the fields—"wherever. Couldn't be bothered. I wasn't worth his effort."

Seán settled his rump on the tailgate next to Cam. "Lad, sometimes there's no way t'know what a man's thinkin'. Why he does what he does."

Cam snorted. "And that makes it okay to just accept it?"

"Okay?" Seán shrugged. "Somethin' you'll hafta decide for yourself. I worked side by side with the man for nigh on a year. He weren't a talkative fella. He did go on about you, though. Any who'd listen, and oft those who wished they didn't hafta got an earful o' your antics. If that man didn't love ya, lad, then I haven't a drop o' good Irish blood in me veins."

Cam couldn't stop the bark of laughter, and the grin Seán gave him was like sunshine through the fog and wet of the morning.

"Love, lad. It comes to ya all ways. Some?" He shrugged. "Some ways we just don't know. Your da loved his wee lad enough to know when he had to give him up, maybe." Seán fixed him with a stern gaze. "You love our Joey enough to be right good an' thick at him for Lord only knows what. The lad makes some daft choices, and that's truth."

Cam shook his head sharply. "It isn't like that."

"Are ye goin' to make me deny me Irish blood twice in one day, lad? Don't take me fer a daft old man. Not in this." He laid a hand on Cam's thigh. "You grew up under me roof, lad, as much as with Marie and Albert. As I say, I don't understand all the ins and outs o' love, but I know when I see it. You love him, an' he loves you."

"No." Cam got up, snipping the word off as he had the bit ends of the wire, and leaving behind just as sharp a point on it. "He doesn't. Of that, I can assure you."

"If you weren't a grown man, Cameron Miles O'Grady, I'd box your fool ears." Seán hadn't moved from where he sat on the tailgate.

"What would you know of it?" Cam asked. "You just said you don't understand love."

"Made me promise ne'er to tell you this, he did."

Cam stopped the angry shuffling of tools he'd been doing, trying to make room for the old snips in the wooden tool kit sitting in the back of the truck. The tools had been Albert's, and many had belonged to Albert's father. A few were new additions Cam had made, but most were a generation or more old, the snips included.

"Tell me what?" Cam asked.

"You were a stripling lad, you were," Seán said as if gone off on a tangent. "All beanpole arms and legs. Not a strip o' meat on your long shank bones."

Cam tightened his lips, neither denying nor agreeing. He had been a skinny-ass weakling most of his teenage years. It had taken him time and hours upon hours of steady, grueling work to grow into his long limbs. He'd gotten enough grief at school over his straw-blond hair, pale blue eyes, and gaunt body, so different from Marie and Albert's kids. Even Joe had always been stocky, short, almost beefy next to Cam's thinness. Cam had stood out. He'd worn his differences like a shield, even his gayness, as out and flaunted as he could manage, to hold off the hurt of other kids' words.

He'd built up pride in how he was different, made those differences his strengths, but it hadn't always been easy, and he'd found himself on the wrong end of a fist more than once.

"You'd come home with a split lip or a black eye, and Joe was fit to be tied. Wild-cat mad when you'd be hurt like that."

Cam smiled faintly. "I remember."

"Never knew how he don't get into fights o'er it meself. Then one day, I find a stash of smokes in the tack room."

Cam nodded more deeply. "I remember. Uncle Albert tanned him good over that. Told him if he ever smoked again, he'd get worse."

Seán chucked, and even that sound had the song of Irish running through it. "He never smoked a day in his life, that lad. He traded 'em. To them bullies as'd harass you. Don't know how he got 'em, but he bartered with 'em t' keep you safe. He were always a right devious lad, that one."

"He's not devious," Cam said. A sigh escaped when he thought back on the ruckus those cigarettes had caused. Uncle Albert had been furious. It was the only time Cam could remember the man ever raising his hand to any of the kids. It was the only time Cam could remember ever seeing Joe cry. He'd slept on his stomach that night, in the bed next to Cam's because his backside was too sore even for the light caress of a sheet or underwear. He'd sniffled quietly because he didn't want Cam to know he was crying.

But Cam could feel the hurt coming off him through the dark, and that one time, Joe hadn't denied him when Cam had snuggled onto the bed next to him and held him close. They'd whispered in the dark about what had happened, and when Cam had gone off on Uncle Albert for being a tyrant, Joe had told him no. He wasn't angry, even. He'd accepted his punishment and said it didn't matter what had happened to him, it was all okay. All worth it.

Cam had never been able to really understand that. He'd thought maybe Joe meant it was worth it to have been set on the right path, to know Uncle Albert cared what happened to him. He wasn't sure. He hadn't understood, but he'd agreed, because Joe had asked him to, that he would let it go and not be mad at their uncle for the incident.

Now it made sense.

"He never told me," Cam said.

"Of course he didn't tell ya, lad. Your pride is so dear to you. The one thing he'll never take from you is that. He cares too deeply for you to hurt you like that. But to see another take up against you?" Seán shook his head and offered Cam a small grin. "He'll not stand fer such a thing so long as he breathes. Mark me."

And so there was something else pitting Joe against his confessed mistakes. He'd never allow his bad decisions to embarrass Cam. The idiot. Cam could care less about pride when Joe hurt as much as he was hurting now.

For a long time, Cam studied the old man, his sun-touched, leathery skin and sharp blue eyes. "You don't miss much, do you, Seán?"

"I may well be old, lad, but I ain't dead nor blind."

"You know Joe thinks he's in the closet around here."

"What he chooses to reveal is his choice, after all," Seán said. And a moment later, "Not that it matters one way or 't other to any who live and work here. But his reasons are his alone, and neither you nor I have rights to question them."

"No." Cam felt that giant bubble of emotion try to choke him again. "I suppose not."

"But he'd walk over flames for you, so don't ever tell me he don't love ya."

"Sometimes I wonder."

"Well, you'd be wrong."

"So what do I do about it?"

"Love him back, you bloody fool git. Love him back."

"And if he won't let me?"

Seán turned bright, knowing eyes on him. "The lad needs protecting. Sometimes from his own daft ideas. You man enough to do that, Cameron? You man enough to take charge of a wild thing and bring him to heel? Because I think you are. Meh." He gave a small, one-shouldered shrug as he pushed himself to his feet from the tailgate. "Mayhap you get bit a few times, but that ent always a bad thing. It's the ones with fire, ones what need a bit o' shacklin' what ends up bein' the ones a man like you needs, lad. Ask me, you and our Joey, you're made fer each other. Time you let him know enough is enough, yeah?"

As he walked out of the paddock without waiting for a reply, carefully latching the gate behind him, Cam had to wonder if the old man knew more than his slightly mixed metaphor hinted at.

Enough is enough. As far as Cam was concerned, *enough* was far and away entirely too much. The things Joe had admitted to were… too much? Certainly, the thought of it made Cam writhe with fury. There was no way to undo the last five years. He'd been so busy resenting Joe for leaving, he hadn't noticed just how thoroughly he'd gone. How far. Maybe too far to get him back.

"No." Cam tossed the last of his tools into the box and closed the tailgate. No place was too far. Nothing was too much, because Joe was his, always had been, and dammit, he would get him back. Every piece of him.

"Seán!" He called across the yard to the old man, and Seán turned.

"I'm headed into town for a bit. Something I have to do."

Seán waved. "'Bout time."

Cam didn't have to worry about the farm for today. Joe was family, and if everyone knew he was in the hospital, then Cam's and Marie's absence was not only accepted, it was expected. They should be at his side. Well, Cam would be. Soon. Or, rather, Joe would be at his, where he belonged, but there were just a few pieces of his man he had to claim first, beginning with any ounce of Joe Craig thought he might still lay claim to.

twelve

CAM REALIZED as he pulled up in front of Reilly's that his plan had been an idiotic one. Seán's estimation of Joe's inability to make good decisions should have been extended to himself. The bar, of course, would be closed. It was barely half past eight in the morning. If Craig was even up, he certainly wasn't pouring drinks at this hour. Still, Cam pulled into the parking lot and put the truck into Park so he could take a moment to think.

"Now what, moron?" he wondered out loud.

As he sat there, the small door at the far end of the building opened, and one of the hairdressers from the shop across the street came out, carrying a cardboard tray stuffed to capacity with tall paper cups.

Of course. Craig had renovated two years ago and opened a small corner of the restaurant portion of his establishment to supply coffee to the very early risers. Once, there had been a café attached to the bakery next to the general store. Cam remembered it, and Mrs. Doherty, a sweet, pudgy little woman from when he was a child. She'd been free with cookies and other small tidbits for her youngest costumers, and Cam had loved trips into town that inevitably passed through her homey-smelling little store. When she'd finally retired from the place, the bakery had shut down and the diner had eventually closed.

A couple of years ago, Craig had taken over the lunch business at the pub, and a young, energetic man in his thirties had reinvigorated the bakery, but it was more a catering facility than an eat-in establishment now, supplying Craig with a fair amount of his baked inventory.

Cam shut off his truck and headed for Reilly's Coffee Corner. The bell over the door gave a soft tinkling of music that could have been a dusting of fey voices through the fog if Cam was in the mood to think of such fancies. When he walked in, the baker was just straightening from where he had been leaning over the counter toward Craig.

He smiled broadly at Cam and nodded a hello. His lips were shiny, red, and his gaze soft.

"I'll see you then, Pete?" Craig asked, licking his tongue over his own plump lips.

Pete nodded and turned his attention back to Craig. "Your loaves will be out of my ovens in another twenty minutes. I'll have the crusts for the hot pies ready then too, so make sure your stew is… stewed." He blushed a bit and grinned. "See you soon."

Craig gave him a wink, and the man's cheeks flushed a little more.

He nodded again to Cam as he left.

Cam swiveled back to Craig, ready to let fly at him about how he'd manhandled Joe, only Craig was still watching the door. Or, more precisely, he was watching Pete's ass through the glass as the door swung shut behind him.

Cam tightened his fingers into fists. "Fucking hell!"

Craig blinked at him. "Oh? That bad?"

"You." Cam pointed an accusing finger, but immediately lowered it again and curled it back into its fist.

"Coffee, then?" Craig asked.

Cam glared through narrowed eyes. "You're fucking the baker," he said as he plunked down on one of the red, vinyl-covered stools at the counter.

Craig set a large ceramic mug and a spoon in front of Cam. He poured coffee as he poured behind the bar, efficiently, and importantly. As though what he did mattered.

"Hmmm," he said. "Not sure why who I fuck is any of your business, actually."

"Joe," Cam said flatly, picking up his mug almost before Craig had done pouring. He sipped the scalding brew and drew the back of his knuckles across his mouth.

"What about Joe?" To someone who wasn't paying attention, Craig's outward demeanor hadn't changed. He remained casual and relaxed. But he looked at Cam from a head-lowered position. For all the world, the man looked like a wolf sizing up his next meal, even while the meal was still breathing.

Cam studied Craig just as malevolently. The man had had *his* Joe, on his knees, fingers tangled in his hair, just the day before and here he acted as though it meant nothing. And for Cam to explain how very much it meant to a man like Joe would be to out them both to things Joe surely didn't want the world to know.

"All right." Craig set his bar rag aside and pulled up a stool across the counter from Cam. "Here's the thing. You and I"—he waved a finger between them—"have a certain taste in men."

Cam opened his mouth, but Craig held up a stalling hand.

"Let's not dance around the issue. We've seen each other at munches. You've seen me at clubs, and the fact I know this means I've seen you there. Just because we don't acknowledge the fact to the world at large doesn't make it less true. I'm a Dom, and I'm a very good one. Come on, Cam. I've run seminars, and you've attended. I've been at this longer than you, and I know protocol. I'm a decent kind of guy. I had a thing with Joe, yes. Before he went away to college. I trained him. But it wasn't love. It was—"

"Before?" Cam gripped the edge of the counter. "Before."

Craig nodded. "You didn't know."

Left behind in that too.

Cam closed his eyes and tried desperately to prick the bubble of emotion cutting off his air, his thought, everything but the hurt of one more thing he hadn't known.

"Look," Craig said. "I don't know what the deal is with you two, but I swear, nothing has happened since he left. Not between us."

"Yesterday," Cam managed to choke out.

"Yesterday, he was disintegrating. I was trying to get his attention. Lord knows someone had to, before he caved in on himself."

"Better you than me," Cam ground out, swinging his knees out from under the counter and standing.

"Sit the fuck down," Craig said softly, an edge to his voice.

"Fuck you." Cam was halfway to the door when Craig spoke again.

"I'm not the one he needs."

"And I'm not the one he wants. He's had an entire life I knew nothing about."

"Because he didn't want to tell you?" Craig asked. "Or because you didn't want to know?"

"He never talked to me."

"But did you ever ask?"

Cam glared at the door pull. His knuckles were white where he'd wrapped fingers around it. His arm shook.

"Joe will take direction because it's in him to do so. Has been ever since he came here. Everything he had was stripped away in that fire. Everything he knew about himself, gone. Marie's a good woman. She bandaged him up, swaddled all that rawness in wrappings best she could, but the hurt, Cam. It's still there. The healing's been spotty, at best. He's tried, over and over, to put on a new skin, but that isn't how it's done. Especially not for a guy like him."

Cam eased his grip on the door and let his arm fall.

"He needs a safe place to grow into who he is. What he wants. I tried to be that safe place for him. I taught him, but I'm not what he wants. He needs more than rules, and more, I can't give him. I'm not built that way."

"More?" Cam asked, the word croaking out past the balloon of feelings.

"The next person who ties him down, Cam, has got to hold on while he thrashes. He'll hate it. He's scared of it, but God, Cam, he needs it."

Cam said nothing.

"If you can't be the one to hang on and watch him tear away all the old pus and scabs, then for God's sake, don't be the one to rope him in the first place."

"He belongs to *me*." Cam thumped his chest with a fist. "Me."

Craig chuckled. "Yeah, okay, He-Man."

"Yesterday," Cam said, finally turning around again. "What was it?"

Craig sighed and motioned to Cam's abandoned coffee and stool. "It would have been me telling him all this, but we never got that far. That guy. What did you say his name was?"

"André."

"André. He came in and Joe freaked the hell out. Hid from him. Who is he?"

Cam shook his head. "Not mine to tell except that he's the one who'll never get within spitting distance of my Joe again or I'll kill the fucker."

Craig studied him for a long silent time before he finally nodded. "Note taken," he said at last. "You're not alone in feeling that way if he's had anything to do with how Joe is now."

"He had everything to do with it."

"Then you and I are on the same page all round, Cam. I get that he's yours, long as he feels the same. Don't for a minute think I won't protect him from you if I have to."

Cam looked up and Craig held his gaze.

"If he asks, Cam, I'll protect him. Even from you."

Cam nodded. He still wanted to rip Craig's head off, but that was the heat of anger, not the cold realization that lurked beneath it. And not the clawing knowledge that if Craig was someone Joe trusted, then Cam owed it to both of them to preserve that, for Joe's sake.

"Okay, then." Craig picked up his bar cloth and ran it absently over the breakfast counter. "After André left, there was about a minute and a half of me trying to calm him down and figure out what the hell was going on before you got there. And then you know the rest."

Cam nodded. He knew the rest. He hoped to hell he did, anyway, because if there were more secrets Joe was hiding in his damaged heart, Cam wasn't sure he'd be able to deal himself, let alone help Joe figure any of it out.

They remained quiet for a long time while Cam fought the floating mass of anger and frustration down far enough to have anything like intelligent conversation. When he thought he might be able to keep it together, he glanced up.

"You said you trained him."

Craig nodded, guarded.

"When?"

"The summer before he left for college."

"How… how'd that happen?"

"Gradually, Cam. It wasn't a big revelation for him. It was something I began to notice the more he came on to me. The more we fooled around, I started to see what he really wanted, but he had no idea how to ask. He had no idea he *could* ask, or that anyone would get what he was asking for."

"So you showed him."

"Someone had to."

Cam nodded.

"Look, it wasn't like I was trying to…." Craig threw up a hand. "He was a young, inexperienced, very submissive man. He wanted connection he wasn't getting anywhere, and I was worried he'd end up with the wrong guy because he didn't know what was right. You know how this works. You were new at this once too."

Cam nodded without looking up. He had been. He hadn't gone into it blind, though. He'd had the Internet for one thing, and he wasn't submissive. It wasn't the same.

"You fuck him?" Cam asked. It was Neanderthal. It was a pissing match he couldn't win after the fact. He knew that. But he had to know.

Craig didn't seem perturbed or upset by the question. Maybe he understood. "It was less about sex than it was about understanding what he wanted. Needed."

"Doesn't answer the question."

"Because the question isn't about sex, either."

Cam looked up at him then. "Yeah, it actually is. Did you fuck him?"

"It's about whether what he had with me was more important than what he had with you."

Cam continued to stare him down.

"He left me too, Cam. No good-bye. No contact. He left me too." Craig's nostrils flared, and Cam saw that the cloth was fisted under white knuckles. "I moved on, because there's no teaching someone who doesn't want to learn any more. You still love him because love is different. I was his mentor. That isn't what you'll be if you take him."

"If."

"If you don't mean to be his just as much as you want him to be yours, then don't do it at all. He won't survive it."

"I'm not going to kill him, for Chrissake."

"No. But whatever it is he's been turning into over the past five years, it'll harden. It'll be the new skin he wears, and it'll be impossible to chip it away because he won't want to hurt like that again. No one would. But if you do it now, if you peel that away, it'll still hurt. He'll bleed all over you, be exposed, and frankly, I'm not tough enough to hold on to him when he's begging to be let go. You have to be."

"He's been begging me to let him go since forever."

"And yet, you still think of him as yours, so clearly, he isn't getting what he thinks he wants."

Cam looked into Craig's eyes, and that emotional bubble rose and swelled to bursting. The cascade wasn't anger or frustration when it washed over him. It was fear, sticky and cloying. "And what if it isn't just what he thinks he wants, but what he actually wants?"

"Then he wouldn't have crawled under the bar yesterday and hid. He wouldn't still be here. He'd have gone back to André, but he's here, and this is the last chance you're likely to get."

"So." Cam picked up his mostly cold, almost empty coffee and swigged the last bit. He set the cup down and once more met Craig's gaze. "I guess it's true, then."

"What's that?"

"Bartenders really do have all the answers to life."

Craig shrugged. "I'm mostly an annoying prick."

Cam nodded. "I was going to rip your head off. You know that."

Craig grinned. "I have had that effect on a lot of people, actually. It's why I'm tending bar in backwardville and not bike jockeying with my old crowd. They said I caused too much trouble. I'll tell you what, though. Some of them are all right. They'd back me if I needed it. Nothing illegal, mind you. But they can be a pretty intimidating lot. Joe's friend might not be so quick to throw his weight around if he thought it might bounce off a few of my old buddies and back in his pretty, over-made-up face."

Cam felt a mean grin twist his lips. It did satisfy the still burning anger in his gut to imagine that scenario. When he rose from his stool this time, he realized that anger, as hot and consuming as it was, could be controlled. And it was no longer directed at Craig, at least. He might not be ready to be the guy's best friend, but he could appreciate the man for the role he'd played in Joe's early foray into the lifestyle, at least. Not everyone would have been so kind.

"I'll see you around, then," he said finally.

"Sure."

Cam got to the door before Craig spoke again.

"And Cam, thanks."

That surprised Cam and he looked back, questioning. "For not ripping your head off?"

Craig shrugged. "Only proves you're a lot stronger than I am. I'd have gutted you if the places had been reversed. It's why Joe's better off with you than me."

Cam nodded. "Fair enough." He opened the door, almost stepped out, but turned back a final time. "And thanks."

Craig grinned and waved him out.

ALTHOUGH HIS natural inclination was to move as little as possible, and certainly not to get out of bed, Joe knew his aunt Marie had other ideas. Still, he remained where he was until she'd returned from the nurse's station and was flinging open the curtains. Her dramatics were only slightly thwarted by the dismal fog blanketing the outside world. The light she let in was still brighter than the hospital room had been. Joe winced and tightened his eyes against the demand daylight made to be noticed.

"Really, Auntie?"

"I was just asking the nurses, and they expect to have time to check your bandages before breakfast. I want to see the procedure and talk to them so that when we get you home, I know what to do and what to look for."

Joe groaned and buried his face into the flattish hospital pillow.

"Sit up." She clapped a few times and then smacked him on the hip as she passed. "None of that."

"I'm not ready."

"Well, get ready, because it's time you came home."

"I can't leave until they say so, Auntie."

"Not what I mean, Joseph."

He moaned and rubbed like a cat and finally turned his face out of the pillow to look at her through one eye. "Last night I was Joey again for a little while."

Aunt Marie gave a faint, twisty smile and pecked his cheek. "You're always Joey in my heart, but today, you'll be Joseph because...."

He waited as she bustled about the room tidying things that didn't need tidying.

"Because you're too angry with me to be gentle," he said softly when she had stopped, both hands smoothing repeatedly over his jeans she'd folded over the back of a chair.

"I'm angry, Joey, yes."

"I'm sorry, Auntie. I really am."

She sighed and dipped her chin toward her chest. "I know, baby."

"And I'm done with all that. I'm not going back."

She nodded. "You certainly are not."

"Like you said, it's time to come home."

Again, she nodded, and they were spared having to find something else to say when the door opened. Joe didn't know he was hoping it was Cam returning until he saw that it wasn't him. Everything in him deflated.

"You're up." The nurse smiled. "That's good. I'd like to take a look under the bandages, and Marie would like a walk-through of how to care for the lacerations and what to look for. You up for that?"

Joe nodded and hauled himself upright. He swung his legs over the edge of the bed, and the nurse walked around behind him. Aunt Marie joined her, and for the next while, Joe listened absently as the nurse described the red, puffy mess on his back.

She talked about inflammation and soreness, lines snaking out from the wounds like bluish spiderwebs, and generally made it sound like alien body-snatch invasion if his cuts should get infected again. He shuddered and as he did, the nurse yanked off the pad and tape on the highest cut. He was pretty sure a few hairs went with it, and he flinched. For an instant it felt like....

Oh fuck, don't. He closed his eyes.

"Joe?" Marie placed a warm hand on his shoulder.

"I'm fine." He shimmied his shoulder out from under her well-meaning contact.

"Don't what, honey?" she asked.

"Nothing. I—" *hadn't meant to say that out loud.*

"Well, it looks like everything is healing well, now. The antibiotics seem to be working, and the redness and swelling are pretty much gone." The nurse poked at a cut and Joe growled.

"That hurts!"

"Yes. But see, the discharge is minimal, and it's clear. That's fine. It's what you want. If it isn't, there's a problem, so watch for that. Change the bandages every day, and Joe, remember to take the pills with meals. And sponge bath for a few more days. Let the wounds scab over before you soak them through." She was slathering something on them none too gently, and Joe ground his teeth. "Once they look like they've closed up, let the air at them, but be careful," she admonished. "We don't want to see you back in here."

"Yeah," Joe mumbled. "Sure."

"And eat, boy. Everything your mother puts in front of you." The nurse gave his shoulder a small, vehement pat.

"Oh," Aunt Marie said gently. "I'm not—"

Joe reached back and gripped Marie's hand, squeezing her fingers tight to shut her up.

"Yes, ma'am," he said quietly. "I will."

The nurse pulled a deep breath in through her nose and continued her ministrations in silence, but with far more gentleness than she had begun with.

Before he was allowed to leave the hospital, Joe was "advised" to make a follow-up appointment with his family doctor, which he did without comment, a nutritionist, which he did under duress, and a counselor, which he flat-out refused.

"I don't need to talk about my fucking feelings, Auntie," he snarled, and immediately regretted it. He didn't swear at her. It wasn't done. "Fuck, I'm sorry. Shit, I—shit." *Fuck.*

Marie took him by the elbow and led him through the doors and out into the hospital's main lobby. Was she *smiling*?

"Shit, Auntie, I—"

"Dude, best shut your mouth before you make it ten times worse." This came from the orderly wheeling the chair along next to him. He'd refused that too, but hospital policy dictated the chair arrive at the front door when he did, so the affable young man walked beside them and pushed the empty chair along. Joe remembered the guy from high school, though he couldn't remember his name.

"Yeah, right," he agreed, and fell into silence.

The ride home was silent too. He'd said everything he had to say, bared everything there was to bare, and his aunt didn't seem inclined to talk about any of it. She drove and he sat, watching the town fall away and the pastures and cornfields rise up.

A few times, Joe pulled in a breath to speak, thought better of it, and closed his mouth.

They were less than five minutes from the turnoff that lead up a long lane to the house when Marie finally broke the quiet.

"Cameron had the farm to see to. I sent him home last night."

"I was there."

"He had work to do. I'm sure you'll see him at lunch. I doubt he went far from the property today."

Her prediction proved false, though. While Joe sat and choked down the thin broth and toast with Seán and Abby, the only workers not out riding fences or inspecting sheep or crops, Cam remained absent. Joe didn't ask where he was. It was best this way, anyway. Cam wouldn't want him now that he knew who Joe really was. What he was.

"Help me do up the dishes, Joseph," Marie said as they finished eating. Abby gave him a small smile as she left, and Seán patted his shoulder.

"Good to see you back home, Joe," he said. "We missed you. Hope you stick around now. This is where you belong, lad."

Joe nodded but didn't say anything. He rounded up the dirty dishes and carried them to the sink, then washed them in silence.

After lunch, when Cam still hadn't shown his face, Joe dragged his ass up the stairs to his room. He didn't bother to undress or close the curtains. He fell across his bed and allowed sleep to fold him under where no pain, physical or otherwise, could get to him.

He only woke when the room was chilly because the sun had gone down and Aunt Marie brought him a tray with more soup and toast. He ate some of the offered meal in bed before setting the tray aside. He went to the bathroom and washed what he could reach of his body with a facecloth. Once he didn't stink, he poured himself back into bed. Between the pain medication and the emotional exhaustion, he didn't have to hope for sleep. It came with a vengeance and swamped him under even as Marie returned and tutted over his unfinished meal.

THREE, MAYBE four more days passed like that, though after that first night, he was never allowed to get away with not eating every bite brought to his room. No one tried to talk him into eating at the table with the hands, and Cam remained conspicuously absent.

Joe did crawl out of bed long enough to watch out the window. It was warm enough to leave it open a sliver, and the distant sound of Cam's deep voice calling to the horses was enough to send a shiver of yearning through Joe. Goose flesh would wander from the roots of his hair to his toes. He wanted that voice, those soft commands, that expectation of being obeyed, directed at him.

And then he'd think how he'd longed for it from André, and his aching body reminded him how that had turned out, and he'd return to his bed with a sigh. At least it was safe there. Secure and isolated. No one could be disappointed if he never left his room, never promised anything.

Never tried.

A soft knock brought his attention from the lone figure standing in the pasture below to his door. Well. He knew it wasn't Cameron. Again.

"Who is it?"

"Joey?" Mindy's tentative voice trickled through the wood.

"Yeah, Min. Come in." He expected her to be laden with his evening soup and sandwich—he'd progressed to cheese on toast and real bits of chicken in the broth, at least—but she was carrying only her hat and an apologetic expression.

"What?" He tried not to sigh. He really did. He failed.

Her face pinched tighter. The apology vanished to be replaced by something sharper. "What are you doing, Joe?"

"Nothing." He glanced back out the window, but Cam was gone. The paddock was empty, gate locked. Even the light in the barn was dimmed to the low wattage they left on overnight that wouldn't bother the horses kept stabled for whatever reason.

"Yeah. No shit," she muttered. A few quick steps brought her to the window, and she glanced out. "You ever going to work up the balls to leave your room?"

"You care?"

She rolled her eyes at him. "Don't be an ass. Of course I care. You're the only brother I got."

"Cousin," he reminded her.

"Ass," she replied. "That's semantics, and I don't give a shit."

"What do you want, Mindy?"

She turned from the view to study him. Her face was somewhat in shadow with the light hitting her from behind, but her eyes were still dark, shaded with uncertainty. "I want you back," she said. Her thin arms crossed over her stomach, and she scowled. "I hate this. What's wrong with you?"

"It's really none of your business."

"Fuck you."

"Aunt Marie is going to wash your mouth out—"

"I'm eighteen. Like to see her try."

"Then I will."

She glared at him, but the look held a gleam of triumph. "Is that what it'll take? Then fuck you, Joseph Andrew Conner. Fuck you, fuck you, fuck you."

"Mindy."

She stomped her foot, the effect ruined by the carpet and the fact she had only her socks on, but her face was thunder. "I hate you like this. Come back and stop being the creepy guy who lives down the hall. I want to go riding with you, and you need to be all big brother and kick Tommy's ass for me."

"Did he do something?" Joe couldn't stop the churn of his gut, the raw anger, the clench of fingers into fists.

She laughed. "No, asshole! Fuck." She scurried to him and threw her arms around him. "But you'd punch his lights out if he did, right?" She clung, and Joe ground his teeth at the pressure on the too tight skin of his back. "Right, Joe?"

"Yes, Mindy." He pried her off him and held her at arm's length. "Baby girl, of course you know I'll murder anyone who hurts you."

"Or sneak ciggies from the general store and bribe the bullies?"

"Fuck, how do you even know about that? You were what? Eight?"

She tilted her head slightly, and her signature impish expression bloomed. "Nine, and I know everything."

That sobered him. "No, Baby girl. You really don't." Suddenly weary, he shuffled to his bed and slumped down.

"Yeah, Joey. I do."

"Listen, you're just a kid, and you don't know." He smiled, a wan, bland attempt at some expression he didn't really remember how to make. "That's why you need me to kick asses and take names."

"Actually, I don't, but I love you for saying it." She plopped down beside him. "You know I live here, right?"

Joe groaned.

"And you know none of us would ever tell your secrets."

"But."

"But this is about all of us, Joey. We're family. You were in the hospital. That guy, whoever it was, he put you there. What that creep did to you, he did to all of us, because we lost you."

Joe shook his head, wanting to deny that she had any idea what she was talking about, but it didn't faze her in the slightest.

"We'll bring you back from this. Because we love you, and we made a new family for you. I know it's not the same as your own, but nothing can be. Nothing can be the same, except you can always come home. Always, Joey."

"You don't know anything," he said weakly, but he wrapped an arm around her shoulders and pulled her tight to his side. She snuggled there for a long time, not saying anything else. He didn't need her to say anything else, really, but it was nice to have the warmth of another human being who didn't want anything at all from him other than just him.

"Baby girl," he said after a while.

She *hmmmmed* at him.

"You're eighteen. And you're not a virgin."

She snorted.

"So you know enough to know that what I did, it isn't a solution, right? It was a really, really terrible idea."

"I know."

"Not just the whor—"

"That's not you, Joey," she said quietly. "Please don't call yourself that."

He sighed and kissed her hair. "I was a prostitute, Mindy. There isn't any other way to put it."

"So what's your point?" She sounded irritable, but burrowed closer into his side.

"Maybe I'm not the best person to be giving you advice about sex, but—"

"Oh dear God, please don't," she whispered, and that small, horrified plea finally made him smile for real. Almost, it even made him laugh. She grinned at him, though. "Oh, fuck it. What?"

"The usual, baby girl. Don't do what I did. Don't let some guy talk you into it because you want to keep him, or because he says it'll be good. Just...."

She curled her feet up onto the bed under her and pushed her shoulder into his side. "I actually am a virgin, you know," she said, not looking at him.

"Huh."

"Had you fooled?"

Joe swallowed a lump of emotion he couldn't identify. "I think you've got everyone fooled, including Tommy. Don't fuck around, Min."

But she was already shaking her head. "He knows, actually. He's cool with it."

Joe studied her for a long minute. "You like him?"

She nodded and pulled in a deep breath. "Scary."

"Yeah." He hugged her close again. "It's terrifying."

"Well." She giggled. "Not that scary." But then she was pulling away and gazing up at him. "Is it? What don't I know?"

"Nothing. Don't listen to me. I'm an idiot."

She wiggled up so she could kiss his cheek. "Only if you let him stay mad at you and don't try to fix it. Just make up already, because this all sucks and I want my guys back."

"Him?" He raised an eyebrow, making her giggle.

"Cam, idiot."

Joe shook his head. "It was never a secret, was it?"

"Wow, Joey. You really are an idiot."

"Brat."

"Jerkwad." She pecked his cheek again. "Come down and have breakfast with us tomorrow. Please? I miss you."

"Did Aunt—"

"Don't. I'm a person who lives here too, and you're my big brother, and you've gone off and left me here, and now you're back, and I am so allowed to have my own fucking opinion about that. Do not put everything I think and do at Mama's doorstep. I came up here because I wanted to see you and it seems the only way anyone can. Including Cam, by the way, and if half of what I think is going on in your head is, and he's half the kind of guy he'd better fucking be to deserve you, he's never going to come in here until you come out."

Joe blinked at her. "What?"

"If you're traumatized or some shit, what kind of boyfriend would come barging into your bedroom? One who you should be kicking to the curb. So he's staying away because that's the vibe you're giving off. You want him, you have to go to him. You get that, right?"

"I thought you were an eighteen-year-old virgin."

"Doesn't make me stupid."

Joe snorted. "No. I guess it really doesn't."

"So you'll come to breakfast?"

"Do I have a choice?"

"Yeah. Of course you do. No one is going to take those away from you. You do know that?"

Joe furrowed his brow. "What do you mean?"

Mindy rolled her eyes. "You ever heard of this thing called the Internet? It's this big, freaky place where even teenage virgins can get their hands on all kinds of kinky shit." She leaned past him and gently, slowly, pulled a yellow tie from under Joe's pillow. "Now, I'm sure you sleep with Cam's tie under your pillow because it smells like him, or some shit." She grinned as she wrapped it around her hands. "Or, you want him to do something else with it. That's cool. It's between you two."

"Yes." Joe snatched the tie from her. "It is." He shoved it back under his pillow.

"Okay." She got up, leaned over him, and kissed his forehead. "I'll continue to pretend I don't notice him boss you around or you get that look of utter peace on your face when he does. It's cool."

"Good God. Mindy—"

"There is no closet deep enough, Joey." She grinned wickedly. "There are no doors on the net." She sauntered to his door.

"Stop surfing gay porn!" he called after her.

"Come down to breakfast," she countered.

What could he say to that? No? Hardly.

AUNT MARIE'S favorite country music station played softly in the background of the blaring quiet. He watched out the window as Abby worked on a tractor in the yard. Her tiny, lithe body seemed misplaced here when she wasn't dressed in those ridiculously huge overalls. She had them rolled at ankle and sleeve and belted around her slim waist, and she climbed nimbly over the fenders of the huge machine to get at the parts needing her attention.

Joe remembered when she'd applied for the job, the summer before he'd left. She'd appeared on their doorstep, the perfect image of a white, middle-class city girl with her tight jeans, tight tank top, and knee-high combat boots. She talked with a lilt of something East Coast, long descended from the Irish who had settled there, and she'd held up the flier Cam had pinned up at the pub.

Marie had been bemused, Joe flat-out thought the girl was off her rocker to even bother, but Cam had heard her out because he was Cam, and that's what he did.

Turned out, Abby was from some small town in Nova Scotia, but had moved to Halifax when she was fourteen. She didn't mention during the interview that she had "moved" alone and had managed to survive by attaching herself to a young man who worked in a garage and taught her how to fix cars. Not that fixing cars was of any use on a farm, she knew, but she could learn, and she would if they just gave her a chance.

Cam was the type to give people chances. So was Aunt Marie, and Uncle Albert couldn't do the physical labor the farm needed, so he had all the time in the world to teach her about farm equipment. Her employment began as more of an internship, room and board for her, a potential new mechanic for them if she proved up to it, which she had.

She'd later confessed to the teenage-runaway thing, and that when the garage had gone bust, she'd had few choices. She could sell her mechanic skills, difficult, because no one would hire a barely sixteen-year-old girl, or sell herself. Easy, given the way she looked. But she'd decided there had to be a third choice, so she'd hitched a ride west and eventually found the farm. She was seventeen when they'd hired her full-time, barely a year after that first knock on the door.

"Ironic, isn't it?" Joe said softly.

"What's that, honey?" Marie asked. She was ladling the leftover stew into a smaller container for the fridge and didn't look up.

"Abby. She's...." He shrugged and dropped his attention back to the sink and his task.

"She's what, darling?" Marie came to the window and looked out.

"She had no choices. She had no... well, nothing. And she still managed to make the right decisions. She came from nowhere and has everything and I—"

Marie clucked her tongue but said nothing.

"How the hell did I get from here to there?" Joe asked. "She was already there, and look at her now. Here, doing what she loves, making her life something else."

Marie set the ladle carefully into the soapy water and patted Joe's arm. "Just proves the road between here and there runs both ways, Joey. Turn your steps around and walk back the way you came, that's all."

"That's all." He let out a sour chuckle. "Just like that. For fuck sakes, Auntie… shit!"

"Joe?"

But Joe had abandoned the sink and the dirty dishes and flew out the door as a cream-colored Hummer wheeled grandly into the yard.

Abby jumped down from the tractor fender as the Hummer pulled to a stop. She greeted André with a sunny smile as he stepped out of his vehicle. Puffs of dust lifted around his shiny shoes, and he made a slight sniff of distaste. The expression changed as he looked Abby over, head to foot, in her snug pink tank, overalls bunched around her waist, and grease smeared from fingertips to elbows in random streaks.

"Well, hello," André said, offering her a wide smile of his own.

Joe stormed across the yard, made sick to his stomach by the expression. How had he ever thought that was anything but smarmy? Maybe it looked different under city lights than it did under the brightening glow of sun finally burning through fog. Maybe because André fit so effortlessly into the cityscape this expression didn't look so grotesquely out of place there.

He certainly did not fit in standing beside his oversized rental in his slick city gear ogling Abby like the fucked-up shark he was.

"Get the fuck off my land!" Joe shouted at him.

Abby turned big eyes to him and took a step back. "Joe?"

"Go see if Seán needs any help in the barn, Abs," Joe snapped, reverting to the teasing nickname they'd given her. He didn't spare a look to her, though.

"It can wait, lad," came Seán's voice from the barn door. The old man wandered out, a large wrench in his hand, to stand behind Marie, who must have followed him out, and Abby. They all stood at Joe's back.

André eyed the huge spanner, but his gaze quickly glided back to Joe. "Good to see you, Joey," he said smoothly. It could have been mistaken for kind, even. Only Joe knew better. Now.

Joe crossed his arms and said nothing.

André smiled, unperturbed. "I only came to see how you were doing. I know you were a little under the weather. I expected you back sooner, though." His words were concerned, his voice soft. Steel underlay it all, though. He was slick enough none of that was obvious if you didn't know.

Joe's back itched with the sweat suddenly snaking down between the bandages. *Under the weather my ass.*

"Had a bit of back trouble," Joe said through clenched teeth.

André smiled, careful, just on the friendly side of neutral. "So I understand." He shrugged as if Joe complained about a dodgy knee. "Part of the job sometimes, I guess."

Joe's breath came in soft little pants. He couldn't pull enough air into his lungs, but he remained still.

"Every man has the right to refuse dangerous work, lad," Seán growled from behind him in his thickest, dirtiest Irish brogue. "'Tis the law."

André's smile broadened. Thinned.

"Seán," Joe warned. "Leave it."

"Well," André said, dismissing Seán, "if you're feeling better, and seems you are, since you're back on your feet"—he smiled, and there was no mistaking the mockery—"we should talk a bit of business. I've had to do quite a bit of rescheduling. We have clients who need attention. It's getting difficult to put them off. They've made investments. We really need to deliver the goods, yes?"

Joe shut out Aunt Marie's small gasp. He couldn't think of what was going through her head right now and get through this intact. "No," he said. "I told you when I left you'd have to find someone else to take over my workload. Permanently. I'm not coming back."

"Joey." André's smile softened, but not enough. "Let's take a little drive, shall we? And talk business. Privately."

No fucking way.

Joe stood his ground, arms still crossed, knees locked against the wave of revulsion threatening to buckle him. Because Aunt Marie knew, she *knew* exactly what André was implying, it was beyond humiliating to be doing this here, like this. But the prospect of going anywhere alone with André made him want to vomit. To run. To hide, just as he had at the bar. Only knowing Marie was there, watching him, listening to him, judging his intent with every word out of his mouth gave him the will to stay. He didn't have the strength to speak, though.

"Nonsense!" Marie's amiable laugh carried over the wave of heavy silence. Joe heard the dangerous edge to it. He recognized that fatal calm, polite, nearly invisible sneer from the times she'd confronted Cam's bigoted teachers, Uncle Albert's snotty bank loan officer, and any other snide fool who thought he was too smart or tough to be taken down by her seeming frailty and sweet charm.

"Come inside. We haven't met any of Joe's coworkers, so he can introduce us. I was just about to heat up some stew for lunch. Abby, Seán?"

Joe glanced from her to the others. Seán's gaze made a calculated circuit from Marie to Joe to André and back to Joe before he nodded smartly. Abby opened her mouth, but Seán was first to speak.

"Grand! Abs, this the spanner you be needin', lass?"

Praise the brilliant old man for catching on to Marie's ploy. Joe had no idea what she intended, but she wasn't about to face André down without backup, and she wasn't going to leave Joe to deal with him alone, either. He loved this farm, these people, so very much.

Abby took the wrench, a little hesitantly. "Um. Yeah. I think?"

"Good, then. Go put it with the rest. I'll give you a hand after lunch. We can twist a few nuts, you and I, yes?"

Abby glanced to Joe. He had no idea what to say to Seán's viciously emphasized last sentence, but Abby suddenly grinned. "Grand, as you say, Seán." She mimicked Seán's accent—terribly— and followed them inside. She never did go put the overlarge wrench with the pile of tools near the tractor, but kept it firmly in her small little fist. Deceptively smooth muscles bunched in her forearm as she clenched her fingers and shot Joe a fierce look.

Absolutely. Loved. Them all.

Inside, they settled back around the table. Abby set the spanner between her placemat and Seán's, and Marie began to ladled stew into bowls from the pot she'd only just put it in. Joe ran the mostly hot stew through the microwave, a bowl at a time, and handed the servings around the table. André made himself at home, the bastard, removing his suit jacket to hang it over the back of his chair before he sat at their dining table.

Marie prattled on about the farm, the sheep, cows, ducks, and corn as they worked to serve everyone. André nodded, largely silent, watching Joe like a cat, crouched and waiting among the weeds. It was all Joe could do to keep his hands from shaking.

The inane small talk continued as André grew visibly more and more agitated. His veneer of politeness wore thin, and Joe was grateful the man couldn't help but show his true nature beneath. It also made Joe nervous, though. Before the day he'd returned home, he wouldn't have thought André capable of hurting anyone. He knew better now, and trying the man's patience didn't sit well with him.

If the others saw André's thinning tolerance, they said nothing, just ate their second lunch and talked about the farm as though this was nothing but a friendly introduction to someone from Joe's city life. It all made Joe twitchy.

"Auntie, I think once we're done eating, André and I will go to the office and discuss what we need to discuss," Joe said at last.

"Excellent idea." André shoved his bowl back. "Excellent stew, Marie, but I really am on a deadline. Joe?" He stood and actually held out a hand to him, as if Joe would ever lay a hand on the man again.

Joe shivered and stood.

"Nonsense." Marie stood as well and collected Joe's barely touch food and André's half-empty bowl. "Joe has no secrets from us, do you, Joe?" She smiled at him, her eyes sharp and bright behind the kind expression.

Joe shook his head. "Of course not." *Not now, anyway.*

André smiled, and it was a mean, sinister expression. Joe doubted even those in the room who didn't know him would be able to see anything friendly remaining. "Fine." He returned to his chair and straightened his tie down the front of his shirt.

Joe had a flash of memory, come to him from the dark of his brain and the sweet depth of Cam's bed, involving a different tie. He let the memory surface. He clung to it as he had the tie that night, and stared André down.

"I made appointments for you this week, Joe," André began. "Ones you didn't keep. The men who pay to see you pay good money. I can't run this business without that money. Every missed appointment is an expense I can't afford to swallow." He made eye contact with Joe, and everything friendly or compassionate was gone from the cold look. "You missed six appointments."

Behind him, Marie made a small noise, but Joe didn't turn. Yes, that sounded about right. A client a day. Thank you, Uncle Albert, for instilling that fantastic work ethic. Made him a good earner.

"You'll have to reimburse me for those missed appointments." André's voice, affable despite the chill in his stare, broke through to Joe.

"They don't cost you anything if they don't happen," Joe said.

"Oh, but they do. In reputation, lost business, sometimes in fees for space or to hire someone to take your place if the client can't reschedule." He pinned Joe with a look. "By my calculations, you owe me close to twenty grand."

The number took a moment to sink in, and Joe gaped. Behind him, Marie made another noise that sounded more angry than distressed this time.

"I don't have—"

"Oh, I know." André smiled at him. "But you can earn it back over time. I had to let your place, obviously, so you'll have to stay with me when we get home, but that's better anyway. I can keep a close eye on you. Your back, of course," he added when Seán growled. "And if you don't have rent to pay, you can pay me back that much quicker."

Joe was shaking his head. "I'm not—"

"You owe me money, Joe. How do you intend on paying it back? You think anything else you know how to do is ever going to raise that kind of surplus?" He smiled again, and Joe was getting heartily sick of the expression. "Sheep aren't worth what you are, Joe. Be reasonable."

Joe snorted. "Because twenty grand is reasonable for a missed week of work."

"In your field?" André snarled and sat forward. All pretense of nice vanished. "It's me being generous, and you know it. Now stop being a baby and get your things. I have my own schedule to keep. The longer I have to slum here, the bigger your bill gets."

"All right, that's quite enough." Marie got to her feet and began clearing the table. "Mr....?" She lifted one eyebrow at André.

"Floros," Joe supplied when André glared back at her and said nothing.

"Well, Mr. Floros, Joe has made his intentions perfectly clear. His home is here, and he is not going back to the city. Now or ever."

"Ma'am, with all due respect—"

"Respect?" She narrowed her eyes at him. "You have no respect for me, my home, or my nephew, Mr. Floros. Let's not beat that horse to death as well. Joe no longer works for you. Consider this his official resignation and be happy he hasn't brought you up on charges of assault or any of the many other criminal acts involved in coercing a minor into the sex trade. You may leave my table, this house, and this land at once, and the matter will be considered closed. Do I make myself clear?"

André stared at Marie for a moment before his face turned stony and cold. "I wish it were that simple, Mrs. Conner. As far as coercion, for instance, I can assure you, Joe made all his own decisions. If he took money for sex, I'm sure that was none of my doing."

Joe slumped. He really would have rather not talked about his prostitution in front of their employees, but when he snuck a glance at Seán and Abby, they weren't looking at him in disgust. Seán was watching André through icy, narrowed eyes, and Abby had her small hand firmly around the spanner. Her face was a mask of chilly anger. Whatever the exact moral or legal details of his past were, they seemed to be on his side. That fact, and Marie's mama-bear fierceness, kept him from complete disintegration under the scouring of the shame.

Marie pulled herself up tall, shoulders squared, chin high. She looked down her nose at André as she spoke. "It certainly hasn't stopped you claiming far more than your fair share of the spoils, Mr. Floros. Rest assured, you'll get nothing more from Joe or any of us. You may leave."

André rose stiffly and retrieved his suit jacket from the back of his chair. "Thank you for lunch. It was delicious."

Marie snorted.

André turned to Joe. "This isn't the end of this, Joe. Some of your clients don't like loose ends, and I can't afford to pay them all off. You owe me. Fail to pay up, and I might not be able to pay enough to keep them from tying things up on their own. Am *I* clear?"

Joe kept his mouth shut, jaw clenched tight over the anger and humiliation. He didn't dare look away from André, though. He'd shown the man his weakness once, and paid for it in pain and bruises and permanent scarring, inside and out. He wasn't going to make that mistake again.

"You think you can get away—"

"None of the men I serviced are going to lift a finger against me as long as you keep them happy, and we both know it," Joe said. "They don't want trouble. They want…." He shook his head, unable to say it in front of Marie again, or where Seán and Abby, supportive as they were being, could hear. "They'll pay plenty for it. You've got what they want. You don't need me."

"I own you."

"No one owns me."

"You can't survive on your own, boy."

"He's not on his own," Seán pointed out, moving to where he could rest a heavy hand on Joe's shoulder.

"Is that what this is?" André sneered. "You really think this little squadron of family enforcers you've got going on here is going to stand by you when they know the truth?" He bared his teeth and glared right at Marie. "Your little boy is a whore, in fact. He puts out and takes money to let other men fuck his ass. That's what filth you're defending."

The wrench made a loud scraping sound as Abby pulled it off the table and hefted it.

"Time to go, prick," she snarled, advancing on him. "You don't get to call our boy names. You don't get to call judgment."

André turned his sneer on her. "Oh really?"

"Really. Out."

"Don't believe me, then," he said, turning back to Marie. "But the truth is, he sold himself to those men, and all I did was watch."

"And exploit what you should have protected," Abby said. "Get the fuck off our property. Marie will call the cops, but I doubt they'd get here in time to help you."

"Abby," Marie said calmly.

"You really think I'm lying." André sounded bemused.

"I already told them everything," Joe said. "You aren't shocking anyone. Just showing what a complete fool I was to trust you in the first place. It won't happen again. Leave, or we will call the police. Who do you think the local sheriff is going to side with? A city pimp or the farm widow he's been sweet on since high school? Seriously. Leave."

André made a frustrated snarling sound. "This isn't over!"

"It's so over," Joe said, suddenly tired beyond imagining. "Go away."

There was nothing André could say that was going to intimidate them. Joe couldn't understand why they all stuck up for him so fiercely, but he was willing to accept it. More, it seemed, than André was willing to accept defeat. He kept hurling insults at them as he swept out of the house.

They all sat in silence as they listened for his Hummer, and then heard the clatter of gravel as he peeled away down the long drive.

The sound hadn't even faded away before Joe became aware of another vehicle motor, and he looked up to see Cam's truck roll into the yard. Cam jumped out and ran for the house, fury on his face.

Perfect. Joe set his head on his arm on the table and closed his eyes.

"What the hell?" he snarled as he entered. "What was that piece of shit doing here?"

Marie sighed, and Joe sat back up and watched her reset her determined stance as she faced Cam. "Have you eaten, Cameron?" she asked. Always practical. As though food could solve all the world's ills.

Cam stared at her for a moment, then glanced around the table, taking in Seán and Abby, both of whom were watching him carefully.

"What's going on?" Cam asked, turning at last to Joe. "Why was he here?"

"Trying to extort money," Marie said in disgust. "Well, he won't get any from us." She sighed as she served Cam a bowl of stew. "Not that we have any to give." She shook herself. "But not the point. Joe has been through enough. He doesn't owe that monster another thing."

"Auntie," Joe said tiredly. "Not arguing that's he's the bad guy, but he was right about me."

Everyone jumped with surprise at the sound of a loud clank as Abby slammed the wrenched against the tabletop and stood. "Bullshit!"

"Abigail," Marie began, but Abby held up a hand, palm out and turned to look at Joe.

"I know how these things work, Joe. I lived it, remember? And they are insidious. They find your weakness and make you think they're helping you, when all the time, they're prying under your shell and finding the softest part of you to sink their hooks in. I saw it. I watched it happen. I *felt* it. I know how it is, and if he managed to get under your defenses, no matter what part of you thinks this was your fault, it wasn't."

Joe shook his head. "But you didn't live it, did you?" Joe asked quietly. "You walked away. You said no. You were at least smart enough not to fall for it. I did."

She was shaking her head, though. "I wasn't alone, Joe. I had Mickey. He taught me a hell of a lot more than how to fix a car. He protected me. Who protected you?"

Joe shook his head. "I shouldn't have let them…."

"You made some bad decisions," Seán said gruffly as he, too, stood. "We all get that, lad. But you are here, now, and you have family. You have help. Let us help."

Joe swallowed his protests. They went down with a lot of sharp corners, scratching up his throat and making his eyes water, but he nodded.

"Good." Seán picked up the wrench and motioned Abby toward the front door. "Off wi' you now, lass. We have work to do." She preceded him out, but he stopped at the door and turned back. "I expect that arse weed'll be back, and you have what help I can give." He hefted the spanner and grinned, but then turned his attention to Marie. "He may be right about the trouble from… others, though, Marie, and if it's money he says'll keep the lad safe, then you have that too. I' mayn't be much, but I have a bit."

"Seán, no," Joe began, but Marie cut him off with a look.

"It's a generous offer, Seán, and I thank you. It won't come to that, but we appreciate the sentiment."

Seán grinned and winked at Joe, then left.

"Auntie, I won't have him giving me a cent because I was a damn fool."

"Nor will I, Joe, but the offer, that is the thing you need to accept. Do you see?" she asked fiercely. "Do you? This is your home. Your family. Don't ever run from us again, do you understand me?"

Joe nodded.

"Good." She got up from the table. "Now I have things to do. Clean this mess up." She waved toward the dirty dishes and sighed, then left the room.

Joe slumped in his chair. He couldn't move. Definitely couldn't look at Cam. Silence filled the kitchen, once more overlaying the soft drone of the country music station and the occasional clink of Cam's spoon in his bowl as he stirred his stew.

"Did you eat?" Cam said at last.

Joe nodded.

"And the others?" He nudged the mostly full bowl in front of the chair Abby had vacated.

"They ate. Lunch was over when André got here. Aunt Marie put on a nice show for him is all."

"So they all know?" Cam asked.

Joe shrugged. "Seán and Abby. It just sort of… happened. I was useless." He shoved himself away from the table and grabbed up a few dishes. "Always have been."

He forced himself not to hesitate as he moved, not to wait for Cam to tell him he was being hard on himself. He forced down the disappointment when Cam merely took a spoonful of stew and ate. He blinked and didn't let the crushing hurt show when Cam said nothing at all.

thirteen

CAM BIT his tongue. *Hard.* Then he scooped up a spoonful of stew to give his mouth something to do instead of spew platitudes. He needed his brain engaged in anything he said to Joe right now. It was too easy to let his heart overtake everything. The last thing Joe needed was empty lip service. And Cam couldn't quite bring himself to blindly tell Joe he wasn't giving himself enough credit. Certainly, like everyone else, Cam wanted to believe Joe had been hoodwinked into this disaster, but realistically, he knew better.

Joe had made decisions. Poor ones. Maybe he hadn't been thinking. Or he'd been thinking with his heart—or worse, his dick—instead of his head. Cam didn't know because he hadn't been there. But before he sank much further into the morass of feelings he had for him, Cam had to figure out exactly how Joe had gotten into that lifestyle as far as he had.

"When you're done the dishes," he said at last, "we need to talk."

Joe stilled, back to Cam, hands immobile in the soapy water.

"About?"

"Really?" Cam asked, watching Joe carefully.

Joe's head and shoulders drooped. Through his thin T-shirt, Cam could see the outlines of the bandages. He could also see the defeat in Joe's stance, and the way his jeans hung on his too narrow hips. The bones of his elbows pressed against skin with too little muscle to hide the angles.

"What's to talk about?" Joe asked. "I already told you everything."

Cam lowered his voice so he was sure it wouldn't carry through the house. The last thing he needed was Aunt Marie interfering in their relationship. Bad enough she had to deal with Joe's handler sitting at her kitchen table and bringing his filth into their home. He was not going to put her in a position to arbitrate between them.

"You let me fuck you, Joe, without—"

"We used a condom, Cam," Joe whispered fiercely, turning to face him. "I would never take a chance—"

"You let me tie you up!" Cam struggled to keep his voice low, his temper in check.

"So?" Joe curled a lip. "You think you're the first one to go all Dom on my ass? You aren't. Not even close. Never forget, I *let* you do what you did. Most people have had to pay for that privilege."

Cam pulled in a sharp, burning breath and clenched his teeth. Logically, he knew what Joe said was the letter of the truth, that he was leaving out a lot of the reality of what he'd been through. Intellectually, he knew Joe was lashing out, trying to protect what little dignity he had left. Knowing it didn't make it hurt any less. And if it hurt him just hearing it, how much more damage was it doing to Joe, living with those truths inside him all this time? How much did it hurt him only letting out the barest facts and keeping the rest, the true pain, bottled up inside?

Cam set his spoon down and rose. He should, he knew, keep his distance. There were a dozen shrinks within a reasonable drive who could help Joe deal with all his shit. They would all try to talk him through the feelings of inadequacy and all the crap that he heaped on himself for letting André and Jonathan cozen him into something he hadn't wanted to do. But was there one close enough to home who would really understand that some aspects of Joe's experience were as much a part of him as being male, being gay, and being human? He didn't think so.

"It can't happen again," Cam said, ignoring the way the certainty of that tore at him.

Joe turned to stare at him, wide-eyed, forlorn. "What?"

"I can't do that to you again, Joe."

"But—" Joe stared up at him. "It's different. You're—I can—"

Cam cupped his cheek, and Joe immediately fell silent. His eyes remained riveted to Cam's, and all his need shone out.

"Nothing about what happened between us has been—"

"Don't." Joe was shaking now, tearing up. His face reddened, and the vein down the center of his forehead began to pop and pulse. "Do not tell me anything between you and me has anything to do with that." He pointed out the window, out to the world in general. The wave of his hand swept Cam's off his face, and Cam took a step back, out of reach.

"Look at you," Cam said gently. "Just look at yourself. You are so turned around you have no idea what it is you even want."

"I know what I want," Joe growled. "Do not treat me like a little kid who did a bad thing. I fucked up, but I am a grown man and I can deal with it."

Cam shook his head. "Last week, you did everything you could to push me away, Joe, and I couldn't figure out why, what I'd done, what was wrong. You didn't trust me enough to tell me anything, yet you let me put you in the most vulnerable position...." He wanted very badly to hold Joe again, but he didn't trust himself to keep it safe and sterile. "And I was selfish enough to let you. You say Jonathan cared about you, but did he ever say one word about what André did?"

Joe's brow crumpled in confusion. "What do you mean?"

"Did he say anything about André 'giving the old man a show' as he put it?"

Joe shook his head. "Of course not. It was my choice."

Cam nodded. "Yes, it was. But a man who understands anything about being risk aware should have realized André was using your love for the old man against you and put a stop to it the first time it happened. Did he even try?"

"He didn't say anything," Joe said softly.

"And since he's dead, you'll never know why he didn't. Maybe he just really thought André was an old friend and that you and he were a couple and happy together. But maybe he was being selfish. Maybe it was the show he wanted, and he let himself believe you weren't being manipulated so he could have what he wanted. Maybe he accepted it was what you wanted, because that was easier than seeing that there was something else going on. Who knows?"

Joe remained silent.

"I could easily let myself believe the same thing, Joe. That this is what you want, and I should just accept it, because it coincides nicely with what I want."

"It *is* what I want."

"But what I see is a man who needs to be told he isn't a failure or an idiot or a fool." He slowly lifted an arm, cupped Joe's face in his palm, and wished desperately he could kiss him. God, how he wanted to tell him exactly what Joe wanted to hear. It was, after all, exactly what Cam believed about him. "But telling you all those things is not going to erase what's in your heart. Until you can say it to yourself, and believe it, nothing I say or do is going to make a difference."

"And so you're just going to walk away," Joe said, yanking free and backing against the counter. "Because I'm not worth it."

Cam retained eye contact with him. Angry, apparently, was better than hurting, because this quarrelsome side of Joe demanded contact and confrontation, and if Cam could keep him engaged, he could maybe figure out a way to get through to him.

"If I didn't think you were worth anything, Joe, I would do what everyone else has done. Tie you down and fuck you. Only your payment would be in how it feeds your need to be accepted back into my life instead of a fat bank account. I want you back in my life, but not like that. I have too much respect for myself to let you use me like that. And I won't use you and give you so little in return, either. You deserve more."

Joe stared and said nothing. His eyes glimmered, and his face was a pasty, sickly pale. He was tired. Strained.

"Finish the dishes," Cam said softly. "Then go upstairs and take a nap."

"Why should I?" Joe asked, soft, but raggedly defiant still.

"You need to get your strength back. You need rest and quiet for a few more days."

"You don't know what's best for me," Joe said.

Fuck it if he wasn't right. Cam didn't know everything Joe might need, because he didn't know everything that had been done to him. He didn't know everything Joe had done to himself. But he knew this, at least. The man was tired and wrung out, probably in way more pain than he wanted to admit, and it was more than just because of the infection. He was done. Physically, at least, Cam could see to it that he got strong again. With any sort of luck at all, the rest would come as they fumbled along.

"So you going to stand there and tell me you aren't ready to fall over?"

Joe looked away for a moment, conceding that point with silent belligerence.

"Then do as I say," Cam suggested gently.

"Because you told me to?"

"Yes, Joe." Cam slipped his hand around the back of his neck, pulled him close enough to kiss his forehead, then stepped back. "Precisely because I told you to." When he looked back into Joe's eyes, he could see the two of them, as they'd been That Day, so young and stupid, and yet so completely, instinctually right, as well.

"That isn't a reason."

"For you it is. It always has been."

Joe continued to stare at him, though, searching. "I did everything André told me to do, and look where it got me."

"Then instead of asking what your reason is for doing what we say, ask yourself what our reasons are for telling you to do it."

Joe's nostrils flared. "André wanted the same thing, always. Money."

"I only want one thing too," Cam admitted.

"Me." Again, his nostrils flared, and he leaned away from Cam.

Cam took a deep breath, but he nodded. If he was going to do this, on any level, it had to start from the truth. "Yes. So I need you to be healthy. Strong. That's the only way I'll have you."

"And what if I don't want you?" Joe asked, still poised, the need to flee obvious and visceral.

"That's your choice. Don't do what I say because I say it, do it because being healthy and back in shape are good things for you anyway."

Joe's breath came out in a heavy, short huff. "Bastard," he muttered, turning back to the sink.

"So I've been told," Cam agreed and fetched his own dishes from the table so Joe would not be able to see the small twitch of triumph on his face.

When he faced the table and the doorway out to the hall, it was to find Marie standing watching them. Cam caught her eye. Her lips were thin and her expression stern, but she nodded once before she turned her back and disappeared in the direction of the office. Cam didn't wonder how much of their conversation she'd overheard. Her expression of disapproval told him enough.

It hurt that she didn't like what he and Joe were, but there was no more he could do about that than about being gay, or loving the man. He was not going to hide anything about how he chose to love, and if Joe thought they could hide it, or if he wanted to hide it, they were in for a very rocky road that might not lead anywhere at all.

"One thing at a time, Cameron," he muttered. "All you did was get the guy to take a fucking nap."

"What?" Joe asked.

"Nothing." Cam set his dishes on the counter next to the sink. "I have to get back to work, but I'll be in to check on you."

"I'm not three."

"Then stop acting like it."

"Fuck off."

Cam gave Joe a lopsided smile. "As you wish." He spread his arms wide and bowed slightly, backing toward the door. Joe's mouth dropped open, but Cam turned and left before he had a chance to say anything. It was a decent note to go out on this time.

fourteen

"FUCKING NAP," Joe muttered. "I fucking don't need to take a fuck"—
he yawned, cracking his jaw with the enormity of it—"nap." He let out a
sigh. "Man's a bastard. Always thinks he's right. Burns my ass."

But he finished the dishes without any more childish tantrums and
he did go upstairs to his bed. It was quiet, at least, and private. The
afternoon sun sprawling in through the windows was warm and bright
now that the fog had gone completely. It shone with soft polish off the
hardwood floors and left a welcoming spread of brightness over the
multicolored quilt.

It wouldn't hurt to lie down. He stretched on his belly across the
bed, letting the sun play across his back and ass, warming him through
T-shirt and jeans. After a few minutes of catching his breath through
the pain of his lanced wounds, he managed to relax and let the burn and
throb go. He didn't remember falling asleep.

Chills woke him. The sun had moved far enough across the room
it no longer sent a cozy glow over him, and the loss left him cold. The
shivers pulled at his sore back and healing skin. He thought about
pulling a blanket on over himself and going back to sleep, but he could
hear his aunt moving around in the kitchen below. That meant supper
would soon be ready, and he didn't think either she or Cam would
allow him to skip a meal, no matter how little appetite he had.

Grumbling, he pulled himself up from where he lay and shambled
to the bathroom. When he returned to his room, he found Cam sitting
on the edge of his bed.

"I've made a decision," Cam said.

Joe grunted at him and peeled off his shirt. He kept his back facing away from Cam at first. Not because he needed to hide the injuries anymore. Just because... well. Because.

"Before we can go anywhere, I need to know, Joe," Cam said softly.

"Know what?" Joe didn't make eye contact as he decided to turn his back to root through his dresser for a clean shirt. Letting Cam see the marks was better than letting him see the way Joe's body broke out in goose flesh at just his presence.

"Everything."

Joe found a T-shirt and pulled it free of the tangle. He closed the drawer and stood facing the dresser and the mirror on top. He could see Cam in the reflection, and the man was watching him carefully. His big brown eyes studied Joe. Not his back, and the telltale marks all over it, but Joe's face. He watched Joe as intently as Joe watched him

"What do you mean, everything?" Joe asked.

"Come sit." Cam patted the bed beside him.

Joe leaned on the dresser, resting his ass on the pale wood and watching Cam from there. Sitting next to him would put him within reach. He wasn't sure about that. He shoved his arms into the shirtsleeves, but remained with it stretched in front of his belly as he waited.

Cam nodded as if Joe's action confirmed something. "Every time I tell you to do something, you question, second-guess, or outright refuse."

Joe shrugged. "Learned the hard way, I guess."

Again, Cam nodded. "I wish I could convince you that I'm never going to tell you to do something that's going to hurt you. Not ever on purpose, anyway. But there is no way to make you see I mean what I say if you won't take a single thing I have to give at face value."

"I can't."

"Yeah, you can. If you let yourself. Believe me, I get why you don't want to, but at some point, you're going to have to."

"Only if I want—" Joe snapped his mouth shut. *If he wanted Cam. Only if he wanted Cam.*

Cam nodded one more time as he stood.

"Wait!" Joe yanked the shirt over his head and stood straight, grimacing as the fabric scraped over his back.

"For what?" Cam sounded tired. "I waited five years only to find out you went on ahead without me. What is there left to wait for?"

"You didn't sit at home and do nothing," Joe countered. "A guy doesn't learn to top like you did without practice."

Cam nodded. "Okay. Yes. I've been around."

"So why don't I get to know everything you've done?" Joe asked. "It only goes one way, and you want me to trust you? You're as much an unknown to me now as André ever was."

"Fair enough." Cam went to the door. "Supper will be ready in twenty minutes. Aunt Marie expects you there."

"No shit."

Cam said nothing. He didn't even address the griping. He left the room, and Joe listened to his footsteps travel down the hall and up the steps toward his own room.

Dinner was mostly silent and tense. When Marie rose to begin clearing it away, Cam placed a hand on hers and told her to leave it. He'd bring her tea out on the veranda. Once she was gone and the kitchen had cleared, Joe glared at him from his place at the table. "This where you tell me to clean up?" he asked.

Cam nodded. "You don't get a free ride, Joe. There are things needing to get done, and if you aren't fit to ride the fences or any of the other shit needs doing, you might as well give Aunt Marie a break for a little while."

Joe remained silent. Cam was right, of course. Still, he didn't get up until Cam had boiled the kettle and brought tea out to Marie. Everyone else had long since left to do evening chores.

He didn't see Cam again that evening, though he did hear him come in the back way and go up to his room as Joe finished up the dishes. There was a lot of movement upstairs as both Cam and Marie got ready for bed and the other people who lived there moved about the house. Joe lingered in the kitchen until it all quieted, then snuck up to his own room and hurried inside, closing the door behind him.

He was exhausted again, and couldn't really figure out why. All he'd done was eat, wash dishes, and brood. Still, his body felt heavy and his mind sagged. His heart was comatose. He could use a good sleep, so he stripped down to his boxers and headed for his bed.

There was an envelope on his pillow, and he picked it up, turned it over, and saw his name scrawled in Cam's messy handwriting.

"What now?" He sat and ripped open the seal to pull out the folded papers within. It was a list of sorts. There were no names, no dates other than a vague sense of a timeline, but it was, essentially, exactly what Joe had demanded. Cam had given him a surprisingly detailed outline of what he'd been doing over the five years since Joe had left.

It included the fact he'd taken some correspondence courses that were heading him toward a college degree, his sadness over old Cassidy's having to retire, and his uncertainty about taking that job on himself. It talked about his learning curve, the office in the tack room, and his struggle to fill the old manager's boots.

It also talked in frank detail about Cam's love life. If it could really be called that. It explained how their encounter had affected Cam. It talked about his struggle to understand the dominance that had manifested that afternoon in the clearing, and his search for some way to explain to himself how he could be that aggressive when he didn't ever feel that way at other times. The last half of the note was all about his voyage of discovery through munches and seminars and eventually clubs and play partners.

There was no mention of any of the partners ever being more than that, though. If Cam played around, he did it without investing his heart, it seemed. Sure, he had a few men he played with regularly, but the tone of the encounters sounded tactile and physically satisfying. Nothing more.

If Joe had ever thought Cam was an inexperienced hayseed, that idea went up in smoke as he read. Cam didn't stint on the detail when it came to the sex he'd had. He wanted full disclosure from Joe, and he gave it in return. The details sent Joe up in smoke too and left him heated and fumbling for a grip on everything he'd believed about Cam. He shook as he flipped to the last page, which was a copy of blood test results. All negative and recently dated.

When he'd finished, he carefully folded the papers back inside the envelope. What was he supposed to do now? He lay back, but his head reeled and he had no inclination to sleep after that.

Eventually, he got up and snuck down the hall to the back steps and up to Cam's room. He had to knock twice before he heard a muffled response on the other side. He slipped inside and waited near the door for his eyes to adjust.

"Joe?"

"Yeah."

"What are you doing up here?" Cam's bedsheets rustled, and Joe twitched, wondering if he was naked under them.

"Read your... note."

"Oh." In the darkness, Cam's arm was a long shadow as he reached for the bedside light. He switched it on, and Joe blinked into the glare.

"Yeah." He held up the envelope. "That was a lot."

"Yeah." Cam sat up, pulling the sheets around himself as he did. "It was, Joe. Five years' worth. It's a lot."

"I had no idea." He hefted the note again. "You're taking classes?"

"Slowly. When I have time and money all at once. It's taking a while."

Joe nodded. "Wish I'd have thought of that," he joked.

"Would have suggested it if you'd asked. Or called. Or emailed. Or, you know, gave a shit."

Joe sucked in a breath. "You think I didn't give a shit? You think I did all that because I didn't care? I did it because I couldn't ask Marie and Albert for money they didn't have."

"Neither could I, Joe, but when I asked about college, they had ideas. They had solutions that had nothing to do with selling—"

"I wasn't you!" Joe said harshly. "I wasn't here to ask them."

"Because you chose to leave and not come back. That wasn't because you wanted to go to school. It was because you wanted to get away from me. From us. From what we were becoming. You couldn't handle it, yet you ended up giving it all away to strangers for money. What you couldn't bring yourself to give to me, you sold off, piece by piece."

"How were you any different?" Joe stalked across the room and slapped the fat envelope against Cam's chest. "How were you any different, going to clubs and strangers to get your fix?"

Cam stared up at him, jaw clenched. "I knew what I was getting into, at least. I did it with forethought and knowing how to stay safe. I slept with men who wanted to sleep with *me*, not with guys who didn't care who they paid. We never pretended it was love, sure, but at least it was always mutual."

"Well, bully for you, Cameron O'Grady. You always do the right thing. Everyone should be so perfect." He turned to leave, but an implacable grip clamped around his wrist and he froze.

"No."

Joe strained against his hold, but Cam didn't let go.

"I don't. I screw up too. I let you go. I didn't come for you."

"You didn't know."

"I should have. When you didn't call, I should have known. When you didn't email or answer texts, I should have known. When you didn't come home for holidays, I should have known. I should have figured it out and come for you. I'm sorry."

"You couldn't know," Joe said again, tightly. "You don't know everything."

"No, but I know you. Or I did then, and I knew it was wrong that you never came home even to visit. I should have found out why. I should have tried, but I was so angry. I was confused. I thought maybe it was because of me. Because of… what we did. How we did it. I thought I was the reason you stayed away, and I thought I should have left so you could come back, and I never did because I didn't know how to. I didn't… don't… know how to be anywhere but here. It's all I've ever known, and going out there?" He shook his head. "I can't. I'm not brave enough. I thought, for the longest time, that I was the reason you stayed away, and instead of doing something about it, I left you out there alone so I didn't have to be. So no. I don't know everything, and I don't do everything right. I screw up too. That's why I want this—us—to start right."

"What us?" Joe asked, his teeth clenched so the words were thin and jagged once they made it through.

"The us we build, Joe. Whatever it ends up looking like. I know what I want. I'm willing to help you figure out if it's what you want too, but I'm not going to jump in like I did then and just take. That was wrong."

Joe stared down at him, at the pain and uncertainty in Cam's huge brown eyes turned up to him. "I gave," he said softly, giving in to Cam's hold on him. "I gave, Cam. I did. Don't think you took something I didn't want you to have. Never think that."

Cam nodded. His grip relaxed and they stayed that way, Cam's fingers circling his wrist, him letting the hold remain. Eventually, though, someone had to say something.

"So what now?" Joe stared at him, searching, hoping, but he had no idea what for. He wanted to run from this thing he saw in Cam; the implacable will. It was frightening, how huge it was. Nothing he'd experienced, no matter how uncomfortable, had scared him like this did. It was as if, out in the world, he'd given parts of himself to those men, and replaced them with fabricated bits made from the money they gave in return. Here, in this room, whatever he gave Cam, he would have to replace with something else. There would be no invented, made-up persona to hide behind while he did this. Whatever pieces he gave would leave holes, and he had no idea how to fill them again.

"I should go." He twisted free and fled for the door.

Cam let him go.

CAM HADN'T been so sure leaving that letter for Joe would be wise. Part of him was sure Joe would fling all his meaningless affairs back in his face. He'd been right. Joe had held those encounters against him. But he hadn't hung on to the argument very tightly or very long, and Cam had to take that as a good sign. Didn't he?

Either way, he was not getting back to sleep anytime soon, so he got up and paced to the window. The casement was closed against the still chilly spring night, but he opened it and went out onto the tiny balcony. It was large enough only for a café chair and table arranged on the half-moon-shaped space sticking out from the gable, but it faced the backyard and looked over the treetops to the pond in the near distance.

He loved the private nature of it, even as it was exposed to the world. No one could see him up here, but it felt as if he could see the whole world stretched out before him.

He'd spent hours and hours out here over the years watching the water ripple in moonlight and sunlight, pimple in the rain and disappear into the fog. He couldn't see their clearing from here. The leaves obscured it from above. But he could remember.

Joe's sunny smile lit up the sun-dappled place like nothing else could. He looked so alive and vibrant, and Cam wanted—needed—to touch that light. He reached out, and Joe laughed and shoved him playfully off.

"What the hell, O'Grady?" he laughed again. "Getting horny on me?"

"Always horny," Cam replied.

"I know. Horndog."

Cam grinned and slowed. "What's your hurry?"

"We're on a mission, remember?"

"Yeah, yeah. But she said she doesn't need them until tomorrow, so why rush?"

"This is you, Cam of the great work ethic?" Joe laughed, but he did slow. "You playing hooky?"

"Maybe." Cam ambled to a stop and waited to see if Joe would disappear through the trees on the other side. He didn't. He slowed and stopped, his back toward Cam at the far end of the clearing. He bent and set his pail down near the side of the gravel path and turned around.

"What?" Joe looked at him, a quizzical grin on his face.

"Nothing."

"Bullshit." He returned to give Cam a playful shove. "What're you looking at?"

"You." Cam reached up and snatched Joe's hand out of the air as it came for him again. His fingers closed around Joe's more slender wrist, and Joe froze, eyes wide.

"What?" Joe practically whispered.

"Just you," Cam said. "Come here." He tugged, and Joe stumbled the few steps toward him and landed with both palms on Cam's chest.

"What?" Joe's breath and lips formed the word, but not much sound.

Cam felt the soft warmth of it on his lips and he reached to capture it. He saw Joe's eyes go wide as he closed the space and brushed his lips over Joe's

"What are—"

"Kiss me," Cam demanded. He tightened his grip on Joe's wrist and pulled him closer.

Joe shook his head very slightly, but his eyelids had drooped and his gaze seemed stuck on Cam's mouth.

"Yes. Kiss me."

"I'm—" Joe closed his eyes, frozen, inches from Cam.

"I won't if you don't want to," Cam told him, and he meant it. He wouldn't do anything Joe didn't want. He wished, very much, that Joe wanted what he wanted, though. Since Joe wasn't pulling away, wasn't decking him, maybe he would get his wish.

Joe's eyes flitted open, and he leaned back far enough to come into focus. "Gonna make me?" he breathed.

Cam stared "N-no."

"Please?" Joe blinked and licked his lips, once more riveting his attention on Cam's mouth. "Make me." He pulled slightly, but Cam was slow to let go and Joe moaned softly. "God, hurry up before... please hurry up and do it!"

So Cam did, taking Joe's mouth for his own until Joe was squirming and groaning and pounding softly on his chest with his free fist.

Cam pulled himself away from the rest of the memory. It was too dangerous. He'd spent years trying to recapture that sense of surrender Joe had instinctively given that day. Lots of guys had been good. Spectacular, even, but none had been Joe.

"I am so fucked," Cam muttered.

A chill breeze blew over him, reminding him he had no shirt and only a loose pair of boxers. He went back inside and closed the casement behind him. He could still see that same yearning in Joe he'd felt back then. He knew it was there, shuttered away where the tricks couldn't get at it. But Cam wasn't another trick. He was Joe's truth and he was going to make Joe see that. Somehow.

"It starts with that list," he decided, going to the desk he'd used all through high school and pulling out a pile of loose-leaf paper and some pens. "I can't do anything without knowing, Joe, so you're going to have to do this, whether you like it or not."

Even if he and Joe never materialized, Cam knew Joe had to do this. He had to look at everything that had happened and figure out what had been choice and what had been manipulation. He had to know what was desire and what was coercion. For his own good, he had to know where he drew his lines, and if that was all Cam could do for him, it would have to be enough.

He arranged the papers and pens on the desktop along with a coaster and a pillow on the wooden chair. This was going to be Joe's world until Cam had his list. They might never be together again, never even kiss again, but that didn't make Cam's responsibility any less. He'd claimed Joe the minute he'd got back, and until someone Joe wanted more came along, or he could trust Joe to take proper care of himself, he would honor that. Even if Joe fought him on it, there were some things Cam had to see in him before he could let him go. He laid a palm on the pages and sighed. Was this any of his business? He wasn't a shrink.

"But I'm the guy who knows him best. Or did know him best. He needs to do this." He slumped, all his weight on his hands. "God, what am I doing?"

"Cam?"

Joe's voice at his door startled him and he turned.

"Needs to do what?" Joe asked. "What do I need to do?"

Cam sank onto the edge of the desk. "God, Joe, I don't know. I just... I...."

The look of loss in Joe's eyes made Cam's gut twist. It was too much to let that look be what defined them, so Cam straightened. "I know I want you," he said calmly, because that much was true, so it was easy. "I know I can't blunder in and just take what I want. Not now."

"So I have to do the list."

"You have to."

Joe motioned to the desk. "Is that what that is?"

Cam nodded.

"Now?"

"In the morning. After breakfast."

Joe nodded. "I'm not stupid, you know," he said softly. "And neither are you. I trusted you five years ago, and I wasn't wrong then."

"Then why did you run?"

Joe shrugged. "Not because of that. Not because of you. Because of me. Because I couldn't be everything everyone needed me to be. Or what I thought everyone needed. I was wrong, but I didn't get that back then. I get it now." He came into the room and held a hand out, which Cam took. "I want this. You. Us. I don't know how to do it right. I don't know if I can do all the things you need me to."

"So try. It's the only way to figure it out."

Joe nodded again and moved a little closer. "Okay."

"Joe."

He was so close now that their legs brushed and Cam could feel Joe's breath on his lips. Joe's eyes fluttered closed. "Kiss me."

"Joe."

"Please."

Cam cupped his face and place one firm, short kiss on his lips. "Trust me, baby. This is not how to begin."

Joe's eyes remained closed, but Cam could see the disappointment in his features even still.

"Trust me," Cam said again.

Joe backed out of his grip and turned, left the room without speaking. Again.

It was a long time before Cam found his way back to his bed.

fifteen

JOE WILLED himself to sleep when he got back to his room. At least, that was what it felt like. He didn't want to think or feel anything else. It had been a bear of a day, and he just wanted oblivion. He wanted it in Cam's arms, under Cam, because that was where it came easiest, but that wasn't to be. So he turned out the lights, hid under his covers, and blanked his mind.

It worked. Morning came and he knew he'd slept. Poorly, maybe, since he had a head full of half-remembered crap that had to have been dreams, and the light of the early sun was too bright, but at least whatever had been going through his skull, he hadn't had to consciously deal with it.

Stiff, still tired, achingly sore, he wandered down to the kitchen and helped to get breakfast on the table, then cleaned up afterward. He was debating what came next, thinking maybe he'd go out to the barn when Cam stopped him even as he reached for his boots.

"Where do you think you're going?" Cam asked, placing a hand on his forearm.

Joe froze, then glanced around the room, but they were alone. The men, and Abby, had all filed out ahead of him, and Marie once more had disappeared into her office. He could hear the shower running upstairs, which meant Mindy probably hadn't left for school yet. "Thought I'd see if there was work to do in the barn," he mumbled, knowing it was an attempt to cop out of the decision they'd made the night before. Knowing Cam wasn't likely to let him do so.

"I have something for you to do upstairs. Or did you forget?" Cam peered at Joe with a stern light in his eyes.

Joe watched him. His heart seemed to slow as he lost himself in Cam's gaze. He could have stayed there, but Cam said his name and he blinked.

"Yeah." He shook his head. "I mean no. I hadn't forgotten."

"Well, then?" Cam pointed toward the stairs.

"I—" He what? Was he going to say no? After last night, Cam's letter, and what they had talked about, was he really going to refuse? He wasn't. How could he? Cam had laid it out for him. Didn't he owe it to the other man to at least try?

"Okay." He dropped his gaze and gave a small nod.

Cam moved out of the way to let him up the stairs, and Joe trudged up. He didn't look back to see if Cam followed. He wasn't even sure if he wanted him to. In Cam's room, he stood and eyed the desk and tried not to acknowledge the queasiness in his belly.

He must have stood there for over five minutes because when Cam appeared, he had a cup of heated coffee, had donned his barn jacket, and had his gloves tucked into his back pocket. "Work better if you actually sit down," Cam said softly.

Joe nodded. "Yeah."

Cam strode over and set the coffee on the coaster beside the paper. He pulled out the chair and motioned to it. "Sooner you start," he said.

Again, Joe nodded.

"Pen doesn't bite."

Joe eyed Cam at that. "You sure?"

Cam offered him a smile. "I am, actually. I thought it might when I started, but look at me." He held up both hands. "All ten fingers accounted for. I survived."

"Yeah." He pulled in a deep breath and approached the chair, but stopped in front of Cam. Slowly, he lifted his gaze to about the third button of Cam's shirt.

"Joe." Cam placed the side of one finger under his chin and lifted. "You can do this."

He was glad Cam thought so. He wasn't so sure.

"I have to get to work. The guys will be waiting."

"Yeah." Joe tried to lift his chin away, but Cam was quick and had a grip on him in less time than it took Joe to make the move. He didn't say anything when Cam leaned in, and Joe let his eyes drift closed. Let himself hope for this one small thing.

Cam's lips brushed his, and Joe let out a breath, a small, indistinct bubble of acceptance as he felt Cam move away.

"Okay," Cam said softly. "I'll see you soon."

Joe nodded, but remained where he stood, eyes closed, until he heard Cam's tread on the stairs and eventually, the front door bang shut.

Only then did he force himself to pull in another real breath and make his eyes open. He blinked into the shaft of morning sunlight streaking across the room into his face, and focused on the papers. He could do this. He had to.

So he sat down and picked up a pen and hovered over the paper with it.

"And write what?" The lines slanted across the page, blue brighter in his mind than in reality, and getting brighter the more he stared.

Good God, where to start? Cam had said he needed to know what had been done to Joe. No. He was wrong about that. It was what Joe had done, and that was a different thing altogether.

So he wrote.

I fucked men for money.

It was hardly the pages of soul-baring honesty Cam had given him.

"Doesn't mean it isn't honest," he whispered, and began writing again.

Men fucked me for money.

Because that was more accurate. He'd never fucked anyone in his life. Didn't particularly care to, but then he'd never been offered the option, either.

Men fucked me for money because that's what I wanted. Because Cam wanted truth.

He stared at that sentence. Reread it. And read it again.

"Fuck."

He swept up the sheet, crumpled it, and threw it against the wall.

Men fucked me for money because I let them.

"Good God." He pulled in a pained breath, and his fist clenched on the desk beside the sheets. That sucked a little bit more than admitting he liked bottoming. He scrunched up that piece of paper, and it joined the first in a ball on the floor.

I have been kissed, sucked, tied up and screwed, displayed, shared, spat on, humiliated....

His chest hurt, and he had to stop to breathe and will his hand to quit shaking.

I chose to submit to them. I took the money.

And handed most of it over to André.

He crumpled the paper tight and heaved it at the wall. It hit, bounced, landed, and rolled with a series of soft crinkling rustles, so ineffectual a reflection of the ache and the anger he'd used to hurl it.

"Fuck. Me."

He lowered his head to the desk and choked on a few breaths. He didn't realize how much tension he held himself under until the pen he held snapped where the two sections joined. He dropped it with a clatter.

"Shit."

Picking another out of the jar, he stared down at the next unoffending sheet of paper.

André:

Kissed me. That was true.

Touched me. Also true.

Fucked me. He ran a finger over those words. Good God. Why? Why had he let him? *In front of Jonathan. (mouth).* The first time.

He was shaking again. He glanced at the coffee next to the pages and considered. He didn't think he needed anything putting him more on edge, but Cam had brought him the cup, and when he sipped it, he realized that his... his what? That Cam had fixed it with cream and sugar exactly how he liked it. He tried to think if André had ever made him a cup of coffee.

He had done so for André every day. And for Jonathan.

Jonathan:

He stared at that name for a long time before writing: *nothing*.

Then he reread the whole thing, scratched out "nothing" and wrote *DID nothing*.

And then: *Died*.

And all he'd had left was André.

Maybe there was truth written on that page, but it didn't matter. He crumpled it and threw it. He swept the entire pile off the desk and growled, then threw the pen. It impacted the wall, leaving a thin streak of blue where it struck.

He was still heaving, trying to control his breathing when the door opened.

"Marie almost has lunch ready," Cam said, then stopped as he looked around.

"What?" Joe stared at him. How had that much time passed? He glanced at his coffee cup, still mostly full, but now cold. He looked out the window to see the sun had fled around the building, leaving Cam's room in cool shade until it made it over the zenith and began to fall toward evening.

Cam didn't mention the fallen pages. "Go eat, Joe."

"I'm not hungry." Joe refused to get up. Refused to do as he was told. He held ferociously to his autonomy and turned back to stuff his knees under the desk.

"Joe."

"Fuck off!"

"Joe!" Cam's hold on his shoulder was implacable. "Come and eat."

"Leave me the fuck alone!" He surged up and away from Cam. He didn't need him or anyone else telling him what to do, what was best. He needed to be left alone.

"Not going to happen," Cam said, his voice calm and gentle. "Pick up the papers and come down to eat."

Joe turned a stony glare on him. "Fuck. You." He left the room, took the stairs down as fast as he could without tripping, and was out the back door before Cam could stop him. He didn't think where he was going, he just went, down the path and through their clearing without slowing or thinking. He hurried, as fast as bare feet allowed, to the rocky edge of the pond and glared out over the sparkling water as he crossed toward it.

A stone, less round than the others, dug into the meat of his sole, and he grabbed it up and flung it into the water. It went far and landed with a plop. Scooping up a handful of stones, he shouted obscenities out over the expanse, then began throwing them, with no pretense of trying to make them skip. He just hurled them, one after another, and when that was gone, he scooped up another and another until he was flinging whole bunches out into the water at once. As though he could clear the beach of every stone, every bit of memory, every tiny thing that could hurt him.

He was heaving and out of breath in a short time. Too short. He wasn't right in his own skin. Too thin, too tired. Too hurt. His back throbbed and stung where sweat trickled into his remaining cuts, and he winced as he rolled his shoulders to ease the discomfort.

Cam hadn't come after him. Cam hadn't followed and forced him back to the house and his lists. Why hadn't Cam come for him?

"Fuck that." He didn't *need* Cam to come after him and fix him. He slumped down onto the small space he'd cleared of stones and sat, watching water spiders glide over the surface. They didn't seem to care what was beneath them. Fish, frogs, maybe the occasional snake, they would come along and snatch those spiders out of their lives because they weren't paying attention. They weren't quick enough to get away. They stayed there, right up on top, thinking nothing could touch them just because they didn't see it coming.

The same thing he'd thought. He'd gone out in the world armed with Craig's lessons, thinking he had everything figured out. It had been easy to let Craig have his way with him, but then, Craig had never snuck up on him or taken anything Joe hadn't been aware he could give. Craig had laid it all out for him, and he'd walked into the bonds and the toys knowing what was to come.

Out in the world, with bigger fish like Jonathan, he hadn't had that luxury. He'd seen the surface of the world and skated over it, thinking he knew enough to keep himself safe. And with Jonathan, at least for most of their association, he'd been fine. It had never occurred to Joe he was giving more than he had to Craig. But then, Craig had never really scratched below Joe's surface, either.

And it hadn't been Craig's fault, he reminded himself. Craig had been teaching him, slowly, maybe, but teaching him. The man could not have known that the moment Joe realized what was underneath the submission, he'd bolt. And since it hadn't happened with Craig, but with Cam, Craig couldn't have prepared him for it, or helped him understand it. He hadn't been there, and Joe had run. From both of them.

Joe would never know if Jonathan had any idea what Joe had offered him, or what he'd taken. He'd been a dying old man in need of company, and they'd never talked about what shape their relationship took. They'd just let it form organically, and for the most part, it had worked. Until André.

Joe closed his eyes and rested his forehead on his knees.

André.

The muscles of his back twitched.

"What do you mean you're leaving?" André glanced around the room, and Joe noted the way his eyes narrowed. The deep blue grew dark under his lids, and Joe swallowed.

"My cousin is getting married," he said, glad he managed to keep his voice calm. "I told you this. I'm going home for the wedding."

"You told me when?"

"Last week."

"You said you wanted a weekend off and I said I'd think about it," André replied. "I need you this weekend. I made an appointment with—"

"The wedding is this weekend, André. I can hardly ask her to postpone it for my convenience."

He knew who André had made the appointment with, and he frankly didn't want to think about that. The man he was scheduled to see was one of his least favorite clients. He was rough, and Joe wasn't a fan of rough. He'd told André as much, but André had waved off his concern, telling Joe that the guy was willing to pay more for Joe than for any of the guys who preferred his style of... use.

Joe shivered. The guy would pay more to see him in real pain, fighting true fear than he would to play with a guy who preferred his games.

"I told you I don't want to work with him anymore," Joe said quietly.

"And I told you, we would work on your issues. Make you more comfortable with what he needs."

"What about what I need?" Joe asked, feeling oddly brave as he stuffed jeans into a suitcase.

"You need training, baby, that's all. I'll help you with that." André moved in and caressed Joe's cheek. "You know I'll help. You've got to trust me."

"What kind of training?" Joe asked, searching André's face, his eyes, for any hint of softening. All he needed was a hint that the man understood how he felt about this one small thing. All he wanted was the assurance that whatever happened, André could respect this limit, and if it absolutely had to be moved, take the time to move it at a pace Joe was comfortable with.

"You're just not used to taking a crop. We'll work on it." He said the words. Maybe he thought those were the words Joe wanted to hear, but the tone was hard. His eyes were empty.

Joe shook his head. "I don't want to work on it. I don't like impact play."

Joe lifted his head and stared out over the pond. He didn't like impact play. He never had. He'd talked about it with Craig, but they had never tried it. Joe hadn't been ready, he'd thought at the time, but now he knew he never would be. It wasn't what he wanted or liked.

And that was why André's actions that night before he'd left were worse than any other time he'd given in to the man's demands, had sex when he wasn't interested, or let the man use him when he wasn't in the mood. Worse than when he'd agreed to let André sell him off, piece by piece. It had been his choice to submit and that those acts were part of the submission. Wrong of André? Maybe. But to Joe, at the time, acceptable.

He'd not known why being tied and at the mercy of the man's crop, then, had been so devastating. André hadn't touched him sexually. Had barely touched him at all.

The cuts on his back itched and Joe squirmed. That made them ache all over again. The pain he tried most of the time to block out overwhelmed him, and he hunched, as if he could escape it.

Every stroke had cut, deeper than flesh, into Joe's trust. Every impact had been a violation Joe couldn't forgive. Everything else André may or may not have done to him over the years was beside the point. There were probably reams of studies on it all, and diagnoses about conditions he might have that would allow him to let another man use him in those ways. There were probably even opinions inside the world of the lifestyle he'd chosen that would say André had been a predator right from the beginning. Maybe they were right.

Joe could reconcile everything he'd done as choices he'd made, good or bad. But the night before he came home, André had stepped over the line. He'd opened Joe's eyes to the truth about what they were, and Joe had broken. Fled.

Everything he'd accumulated in five years, he'd left behind. His clothes, belongings, his diploma, still in the tube sitting on the hall table. Everything. Because what he had left of himself wasn't enough to let him stay even the length of time it took to collect things he could replace.

Trust wasn't something he could replace. Yet trust was the only thing Cam asked of him. And how could he give someone—even someone he cared about—something he didn't have?

With a sigh, he rose, took a moment to gently drag a few stones into the bare place he'd created on the beach. It wasn't perfect, but maybe nature would cover the mark eventually. Turning, he hobbled back toward the house. The kitchen was quiet when he got there. Seemed there wasn't anyone around for lunch today. Marie was washing up a few stray knives, and there were sandwiches on the counter.

"Cameron brought a plate up to your room," she said. "Are you all right?"

Joe grunted and went to the stairs, but he stopped and looked back at her. She was watching him, stern, kind. Frightened.

"No," he said softly, smiling at her. "But getting there."

She nodded and went back to her cleaning. Funny how a few honest words set her mind at ease enough that the relief showed so clearly in her eyes.

Joe started up but went to Cam's room rather than his own.

Cam was sitting at the desk writing something. The pages Joe had crumpled and tossed away were spread out, wrinkled and refusing to lie flat on the desk at Cam's elbow.

"Hey," Joe said quietly. He entered the room and wrapped his arms around himself.

Cam acknowledged him without looking up from what he was doing. When Joe looked over his shoulder, all he saw was a string of numbers down the margin of the page. Cam wrote *100.* And set the pen down. He rearranged the pages so the one with number one was on top. Above the numbers something was written, but Cam was getting up and Joe had to move back, out of his way, and didn't get a chance to see what it was.

Cam pulled in a deep breath and let it out as he studied Joe. "Okay?" he asked.

Joe thought about the question a moment, wondered if the same truth he'd given his aunt would hold sway here, then shrugged.

"No idea."

Cam nodded. "Fine." He motioned to the desk. "I brought food. You'll eat every bite."

Joe looked back to Cam, a digging *Yes, Sire* on his lips, but he swallowed the snark and nodded. "Okay."

"You're pills are there too. Make sure you take them. Then before you get on with your list, there's something else you have to do." Cam picked up the top sheet of paper and held it up where Joe could see it.

"I will not verbally abuse my Dom," Joe read.

Cam set the paper back down and their eyes met. "No swearing. No yelling. No throwing things or telling me where to get off. I demand respect. I would if I was your Dom, your best friend, or your brother. If I was just the farm foreman, you would owe me that much. So that's what you'll do this afternoon. Write that out until it sinks in."

"Lines." Joe glanced at the paper. "Seriously?"

Cam folded his arms over his chest, but said nothing.

"That's ridiculous."

"You can't trust someone you don't respect. You don't throw insults and swear at a man you respect. You find a way to talk to him around the bullshit, Joe. Or you walk away."

Joe swallowed at the thought of Cam walking. But the task was a child's punishment. And who was Cam to punish him anyway? He pointed at the desk. "That assumes you hold a position I haven't agreed to."

"It doesn't say 'I won't swear at Cam.' It doesn't say 'Cam is my Dom and I will show him respect.' It says 'I will not swear at my Dom.' Whoever takes that dominant place in your life. Maybe it will be you." Cam then cupped his cheek. "Maybe the one in charge of your life, ultimately, will always be you after this. Maybe you won't trust anyone else with it. All the more reason to respect the person in charge."

Again, Joe swallowed his response and stared into Cam's eyes. He didn't know what to say to that. He didn't know what it meant. He didn't know if that was Cam backing off, but his gut churned at the thought.

"Okay," he said at last. "Okay."

"Okay." Cam leaned close and kissed him, as he had that morning, too light and quick, but still, contact. "I have to get back to work. Will you be okay?"

"Yeah." Joe glanced at the desk and sighed. "Yeah. I'll be fine."

Cam left, and Joe stood for a while staring down at the papers and thinking about what Cam expected. He still thought it was foolish, but it was a small thing. Something he could do to fill the time and keep his mind from wandering. So he sat, picked up half the sandwich, and started writing.

I will not verbally abuse my Dom. He wrote it about a dozen times as he ate, trying to keep his mind focused on the simple formation of lines into letters, letters into words, words into a sentence. But the sentence refused to be silent in his mind, and it formed thoughts he wasn't able to quiet. They took him out of the task mentally, and he constantly had to haul his attention back. Around the twentieth repetition, he focused on his words, and heat flashed up into his face as he read it.

I will not verbally abuse my Cam.

Well. What the fuck? He scratched out the mistake and corrected it, then proceeded to write *my Dom* on every line down the page, and on the next, leaving room for the rest of the sentence before it.

Half way down the second page, he stopped. Deliberately, on the next line, he wrote *my Cam* and sat back to stare at those two words. He set the pen down and ran a finger over them.

Cam was his. That was a truth of his world. The fact was, he refused to let himself trust that he could belong to Cam, and that was a different truth. He set his chin down on his hand and stared at the words close up. They didn't change. He traced them, and they remained the same. He closed his eyes, and there they were, on the backs of his lids, as indelible as if they'd been written in the same ink that scribed them on the page.

His truth. Cam's truth. *The* Truth. He watched them float in the darkness and marveled that they didn't go away, didn't diminish.

They followed him into sleep.

sixteen

CAM DIDN'T ask where Joe had gone during lunch, or what he'd been doing. He desperately wanted to, but afforded the other man his privacy. He wasn't sure himself where they stood, and so he kept their interaction to the relative safety of what had already been established between them. He could dictate the path they took. He had an unsettling feeling Joe would follow where he led, but he didn't think that would be healthy for either of them. Joe needed to make some of these decisions for himself, and Cam had to be patient enough to let him. Not that it was easy. What his head knew, his heart was all for ignoring.

Firmly, he told himself to remain calm and ignore the burning curiosity as he mounted the steps to get Joe for supper. When he had come in from the barn, he had been a little surprised not to find Joe in the kitchen helping Marie, since Joe had never been a slacker, but then, if he were in Joe's position, maybe he'd want to keep to himself as well.

The door to his room was only open a crack, and Cam gently pushed it the rest of the way, so as not to startle Joe. Not that Joe could have missed his tread on the stairs. He'd been sure to hit all the squeaky spots, just to announce his presence before he got there. He wasn't sure such caution was necessary. Joe didn't seem traumatized in that way, as Abby had when she'd first arrived, but still. It didn't hurt to err on the side of caution. Abby's first few months with them had taught them all about triggers, how to deal with panic attacks, and better yet, how to avoid them.

He needn't have bothered. As soon as he saw Joe, slumped over the desk and snoring softly, he had his answer as to why he hadn't been helping Marie.

"That can't be comfortable," Cam murmured, crossing the room to the desk. "Joe?" He laid a hand on Joe's shoulder, careful to avoid the lumps of bandages under his T-shirt. "Joe. It's suppertime."

Joe stirred softly.

"Joe?"

His head came up and he looked at Cam, a groggy expression on his face. The expression cleared quickly, and Joe moved in a frantic, spastic motion to cover the page he'd been writing.

Cam glanced at the back of Joe's hand, caught off guard by the fragility of his long fingers and thin wrist. They lacked the strength he was used to seeing, and he couldn't quell the impulse to run a fingertip over his skin, from knuckles to wrist. "You awake?" he asked.

Joe just looked at him from that semicrumpled position.

"Joe." Cam crouched and curved his fingers around Joe's wrist, wrapped it up in his firm grip, prepared to lift him from the chair.

Joe's breath caught, and Cam loosened his hold, ready to let go.

"No!" Joe said, voice raspy and soft. "Don't." He swallowed, as though something huge blocked his throat. "Let go. Don't let go."

Cam lifted the hand higher and peered under it. He read the words there and looked back to Joe. "What does that mean?"

Joe stared at him. He was still bleary from sleep, but his gaze didn't waver. He shook. His whole arm, in fact maybe even his entire body trembled, but he continued to look Cam in the eyes. "I trust you," Joe said. "It means I trust you."

"To do what?"

Joe swallowed again "I don't know." He sat up straight, never looking away from Cam. It was probably the most sustained eye contact he'd managed since he'd returned home. "You're mine, though," he said softly, and Cam wasn't sure if he was asking or informing.

Cam nodded. "Always have been."

Now Joe returned his nod. "I should have seen."

"We were kids, Joe. How could we know anything back then?"

Joe smiled, but the soft curve of his lips fled almost as soon as it manifested. "I did. I had an idea, anyway. From Craig. But you." He shook his head. "That was so much more, and I didn't know how to feel about it. I didn't know how to tell Aunt Marie and Uncle Albert. I didn't know how to be... yours. I still don't know."

"You were a kid," Cam said, lowering Joe's hand to rest on Joe's thigh and removing his touch carefully.

"Now I'm not." Joe let out a long breath. "Not by a long shot." He blinked, and finally, he did look away. "You wouldn't be getting—"

Cam laid two fingers over Joe's mouth. "Don't." He said it more harshly than he'd intended, and Joe flinched. "Joe, do not tell me what I may or may not be getting. I can decide that for myself. You are in no position to make a fair assessment right now, anyway."

"I'm the one who knows all the things I did."

"You're also the one who has decided you're not worth taking proper care of, and that's bullshit. No one else here thinks as poorly of you as you seem to."

"You don't know everything I've done!" Joe said harshly, and he was back to not being able to look Cam in the eye.

"And you don't seem to want to tell me." He indicated the crumpled pages with their incomplete lists still sitting on the desk.

"Because—"

"Because you're afraid I'll start thinking as poorly of you as you do."

Joe clamped his lips shut but said nothing. He wouldn't even raise his face enough for Cam to see his expression.

Cam had to physically make him lift his head. "Instead of forever focusing on all the things you did wrong, all the decisions you made that were not the right ones, let's focus on the fact you came home. You broke free of that, and you decided to come back. Knowing what you know about yourself and what you did, Joe, that has got to be the hardest thing anyone I know has ever done. If that doesn't make you strong, if you can't *see* that it makes you strong, then you need to take a better look." He tangled fingers in the deep reddish locks at the back of his head and gave a little shake. "You need to focus on here and now.

Today. Look at tomorrow instead of yesterday. Look at what you can do instead of what you didn't do. Fix what you can and get rid of the rest."

"I'm not a broken piece of tack or farm equipment, Cam."

"No. You're infinitely more valuable than anything else in the world."

Joe blinked at him. "It isn't that simple."

Cam stared into his eyes a moment, then found himself nodding. Because it was simple. It was the plainest, most uncomplicated thing in the universe. He leaned in and kissed Joe. Deeply.

For a heartbeat, Joe was stiff and unresponsive, and Cam thought he wasn't going to allow it. He feared, just for a moment, that Joe would not let this lesson in. Then Joe's lips parted and he moaned. He kissed back, and it was tentative and yielding, but it was a response. Cam pulled slowly away to look at him again.

Joe's dark eyes were blown wide, his pupils deep abysses of need, and Cam had to hold back a groan of his own. His fingers twitched, and Joe's breath caught at the tug of his hair. "It's only as complicated as we make it, Joe, and I'm done with making things difficult."

Joe snorted, and Cam managed, barely, to give him a stern look.

"If Aunt Marie doesn't understand—"

"Marie has understood me since I was fifteen years old, Joe. She knew I was yours then, and she knows it now. If she understands now how you love, then she's going to figure out how I do." He cupped the side of Joe's face. "Do you honestly think it'll change the way she feels about either of us?"

Joe said nothing for a long time. Finally, he made a halfhearted attempt to meet Cam's gaze. The contact lasted only the barest fraction of a moment. "I guess if she doesn't hate me yet, she maybe never will."

"Joe." Cam moved from his crouch to his knees and pulled Joe to him in a tight hug. "No one hates you. We love you." He pulled Joe away from him so that he could see his face and give him a small shake to get him to look back. "*I* love you. Always have." He kissed him again, less demanding, this time, but just as firmly. "I love you. That isn't going to change, you understand?"

Joe nodded.

"Good." He rose and held out a hand for Joe. "Because that is exactly how simple it really is. Now come and eat."

The table was full when they arrived in the kitchen. Abby, Seán, Mindy, Thomas, and Marie were arrayed around it. Cam was slightly surprised to see that Marie was sitting in the same chair she'd occupied most of his life at the end of the table closest to the kitchen counter. Since Albert had passed, she usually sat in his chair, at the head of the table. That chair, presiding over the rest, was empty. Cam's seat, to the right of it, was empty as well, and he moved to stand behind it.

Joe stood in the doorway at the foot of the stairs and stared. "I—"

"Sit down, Joseph. Your plate is getting cold."

"Auntie?" He looked to her, and Cam worried at the terrified expression etched on his face.

Marie only smiled. "Joe. You're home."

He nodded.

"So"—she motioned to the chair—"sit in your place."

"That is not my place, Auntie," Joe said. "I am not—"

"Joe." She said his name sternly and glanced at his younger cousin and Thomas, who were motionless, watching the exchange.

Joe squared his shoulders. "You think Uncle Albert would really turn this farm—this family—over to me, knowing what you know about me, Auntie? He'd be ashamed—"

Marie slapped her palm down on the table, and everyone started. Her expression was fierce, and her eyes blazed.

"Mama?" Mindy asked, but Marie didn't so much as look at her.

All of their matriarch's attention was riveted on Joe. "Enough!"

Joe took a step back.

"No one can tell you how to feel, Joseph, but I sure as hell can tell you your uncle would be damn proud of you right now. You are the only one who doesn't see the amount of courage and strength it takes to come back here now and own what you've done. I don't have to be happy about your choices, but it isn't my place to judge you."

"I can't be head of this family, Auntie," Joe said. "I'm not—"

"The only thing stopping you is your own lack of faith. And the only thing Albert ever abhorred was self-pity." She settled her clenched fist into her lap, picked up her fork with her other hand, and fastidiously took a bite of her supper.

She was seething. Cam could see the rapid rise and fall of her chest and shoulders and he understood her anger. He understood her frustration. They could only give so much support. If Joe refused to believe in himself, there was nothing they could do to give him that confidence.

Joe stood for long moments at the foot of the stairs and watched them. Only Aunt Marie ate. The others watched him back. Seán was the first to look away, and then he only took up his own fork and began to eat, tossing a quick, accepting glance at Joe as he popped a bite of chicken into his mouth. Abby followed his example, and after a moment of glancing around, so did Thomas. Eventually, Mindy picked up her fork, fiddled with it, and shot Joe numerous fretful glances.

"Joe," Cam said as he took his seat. "Come and eat." He motioned, as Marie had, to the chair at the head of the table.

Joe hesitated, and Cam pulled in a long, fortifying breath.

"Joe." He hardened his voice and squared his shoulders. "Sit."

Joe's Adam's apple worked. He searched Cam's face, uncertain, hopeful, and Cam pulled himself up as straight as he could.

"Now."

Joe bit his lip and finally moved. He made his way to the chair and pulled it out, sat gingerly, and tucked in to the table.

"Good," Cam told him quietly. He longed to append the praise with some sort of endearment, but that was too much for this setting, so he settled for an encouraging nod. "Now eat."

"Yes…." Joe's lips worked, as though he, too, wanted to add something to that acquiescence, but he just nodded and dropped his gaze to the food on his plate. "Thank you."

Cam reached over and stroked the back of Joe's free hand. When Joe didn't pull away from the contact, Cam took a moment to wrap his fingers around Joe's and hold on. He only moved when he had to pick up his knife, eventually.

"Thank God," Mindy breathed, her gaze obviously caught on the connection. She reached over and patted her mother's arm. "You're right about Daddy, Mama," she said. "He never brought up anything we did once we'd caught hell from him about it. Remember that time I threw Katie's prom dress in the pond?" She shot a glance at Joe, who frowned at her. "Daddy was so pissed at me. We couldn't afford a new one for her. He tanned my hide for that," Mindy confided in Thomas, who was sitting staring at her. "Couldn't sit without a pillow for three days. But he never brought it up again, and he never let me whine about my paddled ass—"

"Mindy, language," Marie admonished.

Mindy sighed. "Oh, Mama." She smiled at Thomas. "My sore *bottom* even once. I begged donations from every one of Katie's friends, and mine, everyone I knew, and scraped together enough to buy her this cute vintage pink thing at the secondhand store. I frickin' learned to sew so I could make it frilly enough for her. Took me weeks."

"You sewed a dress?" Thomas said in disbelief.

Mindy shrugged. "Well, I sewed beads and shit—stuff on it, sure. Ask me, it looked better on her than the fancy new one she'd bought anyway. I still say that's the dress that attracted Jarrod. He snuck her out of the dance and that's the first time they—"

"Mindy!" Marie glared at her.

"Well, they did!" Mindy said. "In the barn. The hay loft—"

"Mindy, enough."

"Oh, Mama. You want us to be perfect, don't you?"

Cam shot a glance from Mindy to Marie and then to Joe, whose attention was firmly fixed on his plate. He picked at his food, prying bits of chicken off the bone, but not putting any of it in his mouth.

"I want no such thing, child. Mind your manners."

Mindy sat back and crossed her arms over her chest. "I will not. I know no one is going to tell me what Joe did because I'm all young and innocent and all that—" She snorted. "All I'm saying is that we're not perfect. We are who we are. Katie married some old fart she was sleeping with when she was my age, and I'm not frilly and sweet, and Joe's not straight."

"Mindy!" Cam almost stood, furious that she would so callously blurt out something as private as Joe's orientation.

"Cam," Joe said quietly but was cut off as Mindy continued.

"Please. It isn't a secret. Never has been."

"It still isn't yours to talk about," Cam said, concentrating on not clenching his fists or raising his voice.

Mindy turned to Joe. "You know what the saddest thing is, Joe?"

Joe lifted his head and watched her without saying anything.

"We all knew. Even Daddy. But you never trusted him enough to actually tell him. And you never bothered to think if that hurt him or not."

Joe frowned.

"It did, so you know. But he loved you, so he let you keep it to yourself and accepted it even if you were too ashamed to admit it."

"I wasn't—"

"So fucking what." She waved an arm to sweep the issue away. "Doesn't matter now, since there's no going back." She grabbed her mother's hand when Marie slammed her napkin on the table, and turned her gaze back at Marie. "All I'm sayin', Mama, is that we don't do any of it to make you hurt. We can't be who we aren't. I know you get frustrated with me, but you love me. I know that." She shrugged, let Marie go, and turned to Joe.

"So whatever you did, Joe, just move on already."

"I can't sew a bunch of beads on this and call it fixed, Mindy." He lifted his gaze from the plate as if pulling it through the air was a monumental task, and made eye contact with her again.

"So try sequins. Or, you know"—her gaze flicked to Cam and back—"handcuffs." She purposefully dropped her attention back to her meal and popped a bit of pickle into her mouth as the rest of the people around the table squirmed. "Or whatever. Just do something and stop moping. It doesn't solve anything."

"Melinda," Marie said, her voice low with warning. "You will stop talking now."

"No, Auntie." Joe shook his head.

Cam shot him a look. His heart skipped at the determined expression on Joe's face.

"Mindy's right. I have to do something." He looked around the table at the people watching and waiting for him to continue and he sighed. "Just… not sure what. But something."

"You can start with puttin' some meat back on your bones, lad," Seán said, and pointed to Joe's plate. "You ain't foolin' a damn soul pickin' at your food like that."

Joe stared at the older man for a heartbeat, and Seán just stared back.

"No one ever solved the world's problems in a day, lad. Focus on what's on your plate right now, yeah?"

Joe nodded. "Yeah." He even smiled. "Thanks, Seán."

Seán nodded and turned his attention back to his own meal, which he resumed eating with the gusto of a man who had done a lot of physical labor all day.

Cam was certainly not going to argue the man's methods as he watched Joe actually put some of the food in his mouth. Whatever worked at this point was perfect.

Much of the meal after that passed in silence. Cam supposed he wasn't the only one who had a lot to think about. Marie sat with her lips tightly pursed whenever she wasn't eating, and she seemed almost as distracted from her food tonight as Joe ever did. Finally, though the meal ended and people began to look as though they might like to make an early retreat, when Joe set his fork down and cleared his throat.

"I have to go back," he said quietly to no one in particular.

"Joe?" Marie said, very carefully. "Honey?"

He smiled at her, a faint, ghostly expression, and got up. Without explaining, he picked up his half-empty plate, stood, still stiff and wincing, and went to the compost bin with it. "I have to go back," he repeated.

"No." Cam stood, too fast, nearly toppling his chair, and he spoke too loudly. His heart jumped from chest to throat in a game attempt to get to the floor at his feet and make a run for it.

Joe's posture, straight and careful, didn't change. If not for his reflection in the window over the sink, Cam would not even have known Joe heard him.

As it was, his response was that same, faint, knowing smile, as though he'd already predicted Cam's response to his announcement.

"I left my life behind, Cam. I have to go back."

"Your life is *here*!" Now he really was speaking too loud, and Seán was on his feet and herding the younger people out with haste. "*Our* life is here," he said more quietly once they had gone.

Joe turned and leaned on the counter in front of the sink. He looked from Marie to Cam and back again, more than once, eventually settling his gaze around Cam's chest. "When I was twelve, my life vanished. Just"—he made a motion, splaying his fingers out in front of himself—"disappeared. Puff of smoke. Everything. Gone. I had to start over with nothing. My family gone. Friends, school, soccer, Boy Scouts, drama camp. Everything, Cam. Every last thing I knew went away, and I had to just do—be—some other thing."

"Oh, Joe." Marie looked devastated, and he turned his attention to her.

"It wasn't your fault, Auntie. It wasn't anyone's fault. It was a ragged wire and old insulation in a building that needed to be renovated by a landlord who didn't want to spend the money." He shrugged, rested his palms on the counter at his hips, and it looked as though he was holding himself up that way. It made him look hunched, caved in, and Cam want to go to him to lend support. "Fact is, I wouldn't have been able to do anything at all if not for you, Auntie. You and Uncle Albert. I mean I survived, and some days, that was shitty and some days"—he glanced at Cam and gave a slightly more substantial smile— "it was worth it to just try. And some days, it even felt like I was someone." His gaze dropped again, and he lifted his arms, crossed them in front of himself, then put his hands back on the counter at his sides.

"I never thought I could be who I should have been. I never thought I could be someone Uncle Albert would leave his farm and his life's work to. I thought that would be—should be—Cam, and I was okay with that. I needed to be someone, though, so I went away." He snuck a glance at Cam.

For a moment, their eyes met, and Cam saw him searching. He didn't know what to give. All he could do, really, was let him talk.

"That's wrong." Joe sighed, and Cam watched him struggle with the truth.

He wanted to tell Joe it didn't matter. That he understood, because he did. They had already talked about Joe's reasons for leaving, but he still couldn't speak. He didn't have words, either. And, it was unfair to take Joe's story from him. This was Joe's. As much as he wanted Joe's story to be his story as well, it wasn't. He had to let go.

Blinking, he looked away, down at the floor and fought back his own whimper when he heard Joe's intake of breath.

God. This hurt too much. Cam pressed a palm to his chest and rubbed vigorously. Fucking hurt.

"I didn't leave to find myself," Joe said. "I walked out of my life because I saw it getting to be too much. I saw what it could be, and it terrified me. So I ran. Good God, Cam, I left everything behind and took off to school and told everyone I was going to make something of myself. All I really wanted was to be right here. It just terrified me too much to accept it." He shuffled his feet, and Cam watched them shift, presumably to take Joe's full weight.

He didn't look up. He'd known this, in his gut, even at the time. But to hear Joe say it was like that slow-motion instant when a horse threw him. He knew he was going to hit the ground. He knew it was going to be bad. He just couldn't anticipate how he'd land or how hard. Or what might break when he did.

Joe had left *him*. He hadn't left the farm because he didn't want to be a farmer. He hadn't left to go to school. He hadn't gone off to get an education he'd bring back to do a better job here. Those were just excuses. He had left Cam. Deliberately.

"Then I fucked that up too," Joe said, his voice softer now. "I fucked it up, and whether or not André was ever in the right, I did leave him in the lurch. I made commitments and I walked out on them."

"He used you!" Cam found his voice at last, and it flared out of him, hot and furious. "He doesn't get compensation because you decided enough was enough."

Oddly, Joe smiled at him. "Yeah."

Cam stopped, confused. He realized he was halfway across the kitchen, arm raised, finger pointing in ire, and Joe was smiling at him. "Yeah? Yeah what?"

"He's an asswipe. He doesn't get to use me and then tell me I owe him. He's a douche bag." He took a big breath and curled his fingers around Cam's wrist, pulling it out of the air and gently leaving it at Cam's side. "But I walked out on my life there too. It got dicey and I ran away. I don't get to keep doing that. And I can't stop doing it until I fix it. I can't start over here until I finish what I started there. I can't be here until I go back and deal with that shit, Cam." He let out a breath.

"I left my life behind. Everything I own. My clothes, books, CDs, my diploma. Everything I built, despite André trying to undermine me the whole time, I just walked away from, and that shit, it's mine. Do you understand? The good and the bad."

"Good?" Cam fought to keep himself from losing his temper. "What good?"

"I finished college, didn't I? Everything I went through to pay my tuition and rent, I did finish, and I have a piece of paper that says so. I want it back. The watch Uncle Albert gave me before I left. My books that *I* paid for. I want my stuff back, because it's mine and dammit, I might have had a shitty job, but I earned the money to pay for that stuff."

Marie made a small sound, and Cam looked over to her. She was trying valiantly not to make noise to accompany the tears on her cheeks. Cam's heart jolted again and he went to her, wrapping her in his arms. "You can't do this, Joe. It's just stuff. Let it go."

But Joe was already shaking his head. "I have to."

"Then let me—"

"You can't." Joe stood his ground. "I let you do this for me, and"—he threw his arms out to the sides and let them fall—"I have nothing to give you that's worth anything. I might as well leave for good and let you find someone who deserves what you can give."

"No," Cam said, choked. "We're—"

"We are nothing, Cam. Not if I can't do this."

Cam wanted to protest further, but Marie was sobbing against his chest now, and Joe was walking away, and Marie didn't break down in tears. She never broke. Not when Joe's family had died. Not when Albert had passed. He couldn't leave her. He could only watch Joe walk away and do nothing.

seventeen

JOE TOOK one step, then two and found walking across the kitchen wasn't as impossible as he'd feared. Cam had his arms full of Aunt Marie, and Joe regretted that. He hadn't meant to make her cry. He didn't remember ever seeing her cry. One more notch on his idiot belt.

But it meant Cam couldn't reach out and stop him. Maybe he was playing the coward card there, but he knew, if he allowed so much as a touch, he would permit Cam to stop him. Cam would talk him out of doing this, or worse, let Cam do it for him. And that was no good. This was his life. The fuckups and the meager successes. If he wanted to claim those miniscule triumphs, he had to take the rest too. All of it. And if he didn't get it back, he'd have nothing to offer Cam. He couldn't stand the thought of returning all of Cam's years of loyalty with the bucket full of nothing but shit that he had to offer right now.

When he looked down, he was at the bottom of the stairs. He took the first one, and the second was easier, and then he was flying up them two at a time and made it to his room with the door closed. Safe.

He had already calculated that if he took the truck and left now, he'd arrive at the apartment he'd shared with André for the past year by around three in the morning. If André was there, which he probably wouldn't be, he'd be asleep. More likely, he'd be out supervising his cadre of boys. That usually took him into the wee hours of dawn, and he'd crawl home around six or seven and fall into bed for the day. With any luck, Joe could sneak in, grab his stuff, and get out again before André even got home.

He crossed the room to his closet, ignoring the fire of pain in his back. He had painkillers for that. He could take them, once he was safely in a hotel with his things, somewhere André wouldn't find him. He'd spent enough nights tied uncomfortably, fucked without mercy, and just plain used that some pain, however bad, could not stop him doing what he had to do. If he'd made it through all that just to please André, just to make a few bucks for his Dom, he could make it through the pain of a few stitches and lanced cuts to get his fucking life back.

Okay, so it was more as if he was going to steal his life back than take it, but still. His stuff was his stuff, and it mattered to him. It was the principle of it.

"Joe?" A knock accompanied Cam's voice at his door, and Joe hurried across to flip the lock.

The door handle rattled, and there was a distinct silence on the other side.

"Joe."

He tried to decide if Cam sounded angry. His voice was so flat.

"I have to do this."

"You don't have to do it by yourself."

"I'm going to pack and sleep. I'm leaving first thing in the morning," he lied. "And you have work to do here. Just trust me that this is what I have to do."

"You want me to let you go back there alone. Are you crazy?"

"I have to do this." He leaned his forehead on the door. "You aren't going to talk me out of it, so don't bother trying."

"At least let me come with you."

"No."

"Joe."

"No." Good God, was he going to stand there and just keep saying his name, wear him down? He wasn't sure how many times he could say no.

"Joe!"

"No!" Joe slammed a fist against the door, and it vibrated, bouncing his head off. He laid it back. "No," he said more quietly. "I'm not yours, Cam." He squeezed his eyes shut and grimaced around the hammering in his chest.

"Joe." Broken, this time. Angry, hurt, and broken.

"I'm not. Yours." He crumpled, sliding down and around until he had his back against the door so he could feel the pain, the true accomplishments of the past five years dig into his gut. It made him queasy, and he thought he might puke with the intensity, but it also gave him resolve.

He loved Cam for wanting to help, but this was the last thread of that old life. He had to do it himself.

Silence. If Cam left, he didn't make any sound, but there was not a whisper of protest from the other side of the door.

What he had, what he was, could never be Cam's. The man didn't see that. He'd fallen in love with an image of Joe, or maybe some construct Joe had fashioned while he'd lived here, but if Joe had ever been the person Cam thought he loved, he wasn't now.

And it was unfair. He knew that. He'd agreed that Cam was his, that he knew Cam had always been his, but as he'd tried to imagine what to write on that list Cam insisted on, he'd come to also realize the opposite could never be true.

"Fuck it." He got up and hauled his duffle from under the bed. It didn't take long to toss in a change of clothes and his toiletries. He changed into his best jeans and shirt, his newest boots, and hefted the bag. When he peeked out into the hallway, it was empty. He snuck quietly to the top of the front stairs and listened. He could hear the clatter of dishes in the kitchen, but if he was quick and quiet, he'd get out the front door before anyone realized he was leaving. So he slipped down the stairs, careful to dance around the squeaking spots and loose boards.

He made the front door, slipped out, and got in his truck in a few seconds. He had it going, backing out of the drive in another minute. When he looked up, it was to see Cam appear at the front door, anger in every line of his body. Joe turned his attention to his driving and sped away.

eighteen

"FUCKING HELL! That asshole!" Cam dropped the glass he was washing into the sink with a crash. He heard it shatter but he was already at the door, Marie close on his heels. He was too late, of course. Joe was already backing around and speeding off down the drive.

"You fucking asshole!" he shouted after the taillights.

"Cameron, honey." Marie tugged on his arm, and after a moment, managed to guide him back into the house. "Calm down."

"Calm—?" He glared at her. "He is going—" He pointed to the front door. "Without me, Auntie! He left! Again!"

"Cameron."

"He left." Cam sank onto the arm of the couch near the front door, hands limp in his lap. "Auntie, he just... left."

"Oh, sweetie. I know."

Cam was not going to break down. Not in front of her. He'd already held her through this, and he was not going to do the same. He wasn't.

"What we have to do, then, is find out where he's going, and you will just meet him there."

"Yeah, right."

"Well, I have his address, don't I?" she said, leaving him where he sat and going to her office. "It's not like he kept that a secret. Let me go find it. Then you can take the farm truck. It's newer than my car. I think my car would leave you stranded somewhere on the interstate." Her voice faded as she hurried away.

She came back a moment later with a slip of paper and a handful of money. "Take this too. You'll need to gas up a couple of times, and eat. Stop and eat, Cameron. The last thing he needs is you showing up light-headed and too tired because you didn't take care of yourself. He'll need you ready, so—"

"Auntie." He closed her fingers around the money. "I have my own money, and I know what to do."

"He loves you, you know."

Cam nodded.

"And he needs you, whether he wants to admit it or not."

Again, Cam nodded, but he was less convinced of this than she seemed to be.

Needed? Maybe Joe didn't really even want him. Maybe he wanted just the idea of what they could be. Or something. He sighed. "I'll go get ready. I have to talk to Seán, and I have to make a phone call."

Marie nodded. "I'll make you some coffee and sandwiches."

"Thanks."

She seemed so convinced going after Joe was the right thing to do. Cam wasn't so sure. Joe had been pretty definite that he didn't want Cam there. Didn't want him involved. Didn't want him. Full stop.

He forced himself upright and went to his room to gather a few clothes and make that call. He dialed Reilly's and was relieved to hear only a moderate amount of noise in the background.

"Craig?"

"Yeah." Craig's business voice crackled over the line.

"It's Cam. I need your help."

What he needed was advice. And Craig's tough-guy exterior as backup, though he wasn't sure he had the right to ask. Still. He figured it couldn't hurt to ask for the latter, even if he didn't have the guts to ask for the former.

"What did he do now?" Craig asked, and Cam noticed the background hubbub died away as he spoke. There was a sound of a closing door, and then Craig's voice was more immediate and less crackling. "Is he okay?"

"I—"

"Cam. What did he do?"

"He went back."

"That son of a—I met that asshole ex of his—"

"Wait. He told you André was his ex?"

"He didn't have to. I could tell from how he acted. Why would he go back to that Neanderthal?"

"I don't know. I mean, I don't think he did, exactly. He said he had to go back because that was his life and he needed it back. I—"

Silence hissed down the line.

"I don't know what to do."

"You go after him, because this asshole will hurt him, Cam. I mean really hurt him. Like punish him, and it will be brutal. He thinks he owns Joe, and if he gets his hands on him again—"

"It isn't like that."

"Bullshit. He might put on a civilized front, but did Joe tell you exactly how he got those marks on his back?"

"Not exactly."

"They were deliberate."

"I know. I saw them."

"If I had a sub who liked pain, who was really tough, who really wanted to be marked, I might leave lines on his back, but not like that. And Joe was never that kind of sub. Unless he's changed more than seems possible, he didn't consent to being marked at all. Never like that."

"I know."

"So where are you now?" Craig asked.

Cam looked around his room, at the papers on his desk, and wandered over to read the last line Joe had written. He traced the words. *My Cam.*

"Going after him."

"Stop by the bar and pick me up. I'll make some calls. We'll have backup by the time we get to the city."

"I—thanks."

"Just hurry the fuck up."

Cam nodded and hung up, tossed a few clothes in a bag, and took the steps back down to the kitchen two at a time. "Marie?"

She was there, by the back door with the thermos and a bag of sandwiches. "You should bring Thomas, maybe," she said. "I don't want you boys dealing with this alone."

Cam smiled at her. "I know. Not Thomas, though. He's a kid and we don't pay him danger pay." He grinned, because he had to, and bent to yank on his boots. "I called a friend. I'm picking him up in town, and we'll go from there. I just have to speak to Seán."

"I know how to run my own farm, Cameron. And for that matter, so does Seán. He taught you a good deal of what you know. Now go."

Cam squeezed her shoulder. "Thanks, Auntie."

"Keep your cell on."

"Of course." He kissed her cheek. "We'll be back before you know it."

He hoped he was right about the "we" part, but he didn't want to think about that right now. He climbed into the truck and headed as fast as speed laws allowed into town.

Craig was waiting for him outside the bar. A huge man on a motorcycle was with him, and Craig introduced him as Pip. He was fully bearded, broader than most barns, and when he stood from his bike, he towered over Cam, who was no slouch at six foot three already. He wore leather and a powder blue bandana over his bald pate. Except for his face, every inch of bare skin Cam could see, neck, throat, the back of his skull, and the backs of his hands, were painted in ink.

Cam blinked at the giant of a man. "Pip?"

"As in Pip Squeak." The man nodded. He rumbled out a bass laugh. "I can thank my brother Cage for that one. Always called me that since I was a kid. Suppose to him, it's always been true. Man's a frickin' mountain."

"And you're not," Cam muttered.

"Pardon?" Pip eyed him with a vaguely threatening expression.

Cam looked him up and down. "You telling me that compared to your brother, you're a pip-squeak?"

Pip nodded. "You'll meet him when we stop for a piss break along the way. We have to drive right past his place, so he decided not to come into town. He'll join up on the highway."

"Um." Cam glanced to Craig. "This is your backup?"

Craig grinned. "Cool, huh?"

"This is the guy who told you to settle down and stay out of trouble?"

Pip crossed his arms over his chest. "We look out for ours," he said darkly. "Even if it means saving the dumb ones from themselves."

Cam held up both hands. "That's good." He took a breath, then looked up into Pip's face. "So. Help me look after mine?"

Pip gave him a nod. "Ready?"

"Yeah."

"I'll ride with Cam," Craig said, jerking a thumb at Cam's truck. "Convoy?"

Pip nodded and swung a leg over his bike. "We'll pick up a few besides Cage along the way. Most will join us in the city."

"Most?" Cam asked as he and Craig climbed into the truck. "What does that mean?"

"The group's a few dozen strong. They'll all come."

"Um." Cam started the truck, but didn't pull out of the lot right away. "I don't want to start a war. I just want Joe back."

"And we'll get him. Trust me, these guys will not do anything dangerous. Usually, they don't have to. They just have to show up and be... big, tattooed, and intimidating." He offered Cam a devilish smile that transformed his affable features into sly, knife-edged danger. "I'm just a pansy runt next to most of them."

Cam snorted. "That so." He pulled out of the lot, then, and the roar of Pip's bike followed them down the street.

"They're good guys, Cam," Craig said after a few minutes. "They'll help because they get how easy it is to go down the wrong path. They kept me off it, and they won't let Joe go back to it, either."

"But they don't even know him."

"They don't have to. They know me, and he's—" Craig shot Cam a look. "Never mind."

"He's what?"

"He's my friend."

"You were going to say he's yours," Cam realized. His gut roiled at the idea, and he had to fight back a dangerous expression of his own. It was ridiculous to even want to voice a claim over Joe. He knew Craig had no designs on him. It was instinct. It was a lifetime of protective feelings and wishing, is what it was, and he ended up snarling at himself.

As if he sensed the uncontrollable surge of anger rising through Cam, Craig lifted a palm in peace. "Relax. I know the score. But as far as they're concerned, I claim him as something important to me, and they help me take care of it. They'd do as much for my baker"—he shot a sideways, half smirk at Cam—"or you if I asked."

"Why would you ask them to help me?"

Craig rolled his eyes at Cam's question. "Because, idiot. In the world where that"—he pointed out the back window, and Cam glanced in the rearview to see they hadn't even left town yet, and there were now two bikes behind them—"is real? I can say, 'This is mine,' and they will make sure it stays that way."

"And if they asked that of you?"

"Do you really need to ask?"

Cam kept his gaze and attention on his driving, but didn't respond for a while. "How far do you people go to do this protecting?"

"You mean did I just enlist the help of an illegal biker gang to retrieve Joe for you?"

It sounded stupid when Craig said it in that tone of voice, but Cam nodded anyway.

"Not everyone who rides a bike is a Hell's Angel, Cam. Even if some of them really look it. You'd be surprised how well the real Angels actually clean up. You could walk down the street next to one and never know it. No. They're just bikers who get that sometimes the world tries to shit on a guy because he made a mistake or looks different or wants something society doesn't get. And they don't let the world shit on the people they care about if they can stop it happening.

But they don't go around breaking heads. They just look like they could, and usually, that's all that's required."

"What if André isn't intimidated?"

"Then we have a good number of witnesses that we haven't broken any laws, and if Joe wants to come back with us and be left alone, there are a lot of people to back up his story. If André does something to try and stop him, we can go to the cops, and he'll have one hell of a lot of eyewitnesses to explain away."

"You...." Cam bit his lip. "You've totally done this before."

Craig shrugged. "Pip's ex got into some trouble. The guy he dumped Pip for turned out to be some sort of drug dealer or something. The ex wanted out of the relationship, but the dealer kept hauling him back, using his addiction and shit. Pip pulled him out over and over, and finally, he asked, so we went with him. He got his ex out of the rathole, and we made it clear he was not going back. The dealer was pissed, but he went away. That's just an extreme example. Pip and his brother Cage are useful when little sisters or daughters get involved with deadbeats. Or even decent guys, sometimes." He grinned wide. "That's always fun, to see some poor kid nearly wet himself promising to be a gentleman when their girl brings them to the bar and introduced them to Pip or Cage and calls them 'uncle.'"

"Cute," Cam muttered. "What happened to the ex?"

"Hmm?" Craig glanced over at him. "What ex?"

"Pip's. You got him away from his dealer, but did you save him from himself?"

Craig shrugged. "Pip's got a way bigger heart than I have. Last I heard, he wasn't an ex anymore. Maybe he'll stay that way if he stays sober. Pip's got more patience than God."

"I see."

"We can get Joe back, Cam."

"If he wants to come back."

Craig made a noise, and the cab went silent for a long time.

"We'll get him back." Craig reached over and patted Cam's knee. "He'll come back, but you have to be prepared for the possibility he won't come back to you."

"I know."

There wasn't much to talk about after that, and in a few more minutes, they were pulling onto the interstate. The rumble of motorcycles filtered through the road noise of Cam's truck, and it was a comforting sort of sound. It reminded Cam a lot of Uncle Albert's tractor returning from the fields at the end of the day, and he let it soothe his nerves in the same way. It let him believe the world wasn't a completely cold and screwed-up place and that good things happened to good people because they deserved it.

nineteen

Joe was glad of the fact that he hadn't had the truck when he lived here. Neither André nor any of their neighbors would recognize it, parked on the street outside their building. And, miracle of miracles, he did find a space, right out front. He parked, locked the truck, and then dug out his key as he headed into the building.

The doorman smiled at him and greeted him by name. "Have a nice trip, Mr. Conner?"

Joe gave him a small nod. "Thanks, Jimmy. Yeah."

"Good."

"Is Mr. Floros home?"

"I just came on shift for the night," Jimmy replied. "Sorry."

"No problem. If he comes in, just… don't let him know I'm back, okay?"

"Keeping it a surprise?"

"Something like that. He wasn't exactly expecting me tonight."

"Very good. I'll be sure not to tell him, then." He gave Joe a conspiratorial wink and waved him inside.

Joe hurried to the elevator and used his key to open the doors. He punched the button for the eighth floor and rode up. His heart pounded. If André was there, if he was up, this wouldn't work. He had to not be there.

"But if he is." Joe wiped his palms on his thighs and willed his heart to slow the fuck down. He was a grown man. André did not own him. All he had to do was tell the other man he was only here for his things. He wasn't staying. There was nothing André could do to make him stay. There was not one thing he owed the older man.

Still, his mouth was dry and his palms wet when he stepped out of the elevator on their floor. Above him the night sky and the lights of the taller buildings shone through skylights in the small elevator lobby. This top floor of the building housed only three large apartments, and André's was one of them. Joe had moved in with him just over a year before, and had been shocked by the luxury of it all.

Compared to his tiny student studio apartment he'd scrimped and saved to pay for, André lived in decadence. Joe fumbled his key ring and found the key to the door of number 801. He held his breath as he slid it in, aware André might well have changed the lock if he truly thought Joe wouldn't come back. Thankfully, he hadn't. Maybe he still believed he held that much sway, that it was only a matter of time. Joe turned the lock, and carefully pushed the door open.

"Honey," he whispered. "I'm home."

The door opened into darkness and silence. The apartment breathed with the peculiar tense waiting that Joe remembered. It settled over the place when André wasn't there, as if even the rooms awaited his return fearing the mood he'd bring with him. But for the moment, at least, there was no one there, and Joe let out a sigh of relief.

"Clothes first." Because that was easiest. He hurried to the bedroom and hauled his battered suitcase from under the bed. He didn't bother to be neat but yanked open drawers to pull out shirts and pants and toss them into the case. He grabbed slacks and button-downs from the closet and less conservative attire from the shelves there, but then decided against taking those things when the case filled up too quickly. He didn't need the school clothes or the slut wardrobe André had provided him. He took only his own things. Jeans and T-shirts, sweaters, and boots.

That done, he wheeled the case to the front hall and left it by the door, then dashed to the spare room and dug out a pile of folded file boxes from the closet. André had chided him for not throwing the boxes away, and many times, he almost had. He'd almost allowed André that much sway. Almost believed he'd wanted to stay.

He could have kissed those boxes now. But he didn't waste time, just unfolded them and began tossing in books, papers, CDs, and videos. Everything of his he could lay hands on until he had a pile of a dozen boxes filled and lidded and ready next to the suitcase.

The last box he brought to the bedroom and set on the bed. He dropped in a wooden box from the dresser top, a partially charred copy of Shakespeare's comedies, and a battered stuffed bear from a drawer on his side of the bed. The toys and cuffs he left, even though the ones in this room had been his before he'd met André. If ever he needed such things again, he wouldn't use these. He wouldn't let any facet of that life he'd shared with André converge with what he built after he left the man. He did dig through the pile for a scrap of burgundy ribbon tied to a heavy leather wrist brace, though.

For an insane moment, he was tempted to hold the leather to his nose and see if it still smelled of Cam's sweat. It hadn't in years, but the habit was a strong one, and good God, did he wish in that instant that it could again. He held it close to his face and inhaled. And wished. He closed his eyes, pressed his lips to the studded leather, and wished some more. Then he pulled himself together and dropped that into the box as well.

Next was the tall dresser in the corner. There, he found the few things that belonged to him: a gold chain Aunt Marie had given him he put on; a few photographs of his family that he tucked into the book; hankies and a hair brush, which he tossed in the box without much thought. He took them, because they were his, but he pushed aside empty jewelry boxes and odds and ends. He didn't take the trinkets or gifts André had given him He was looking for the watch Uncle Albert had gifted him when he left for school.

It wasn't there.

"Where the hell is it?" He closed the drawer and glanced around the room. Various boxes and drawers of André's dressers yielded all manner of expensive jewelry. The bedside tables, which he searched again, held only the detritus of their disastrous sex life, but the watch wasn't anywhere. He wasn't going to leave that behind. It was his.

He took the box to the living room and stood there, looking around the room, wondering if he'd set the watch down out here and forgotten it. Had he taken it off and left it sitting somewhere? It wasn't something he normally left lying around.

He went back to the spare room and glanced at the surfaces there. At the bed, at the ropes still lashed to the posts, and noted the bedspread had been changed. The pale blue one that had been there his last night here was gone, in favor of moss green suede he didn't recognize.

The ropes caught his attention again, and he rubbed at his wrists. He remembered how they felt, and how careful he'd had to be not to pull or twist so the rough material didn't burn. That memory brought back others. The feel of that missing blue bedspread on his bare skin. It had been an old spread. One Marie had given him, with nubbly texture, too thin to be warm and too rough to be cozy. Definitely, it had been agonizing, stretched out on it in such a way he couldn't shift more than a few inches, and couldn't lift off it. *Candlewick*, she had called it, and hellishly rough, but he'd kept it because she'd given it to him.

He didn't know where it was now, but he remembered lying on it, the coarse fabric abrading his stomach as André paced around the bed explaining what was to come.

"You need this, boy," he said, in that cold, uncompromising voice. "So we'll just get it over with."

Joe said nothing, but tried to focus on where André was. The carpeting didn't give much away as André wandered around the bed in bare feet. The blindfold didn't let in even a bit of light. The gag kept him from asking. So all he could do was listen and wait.

The first blow, when it came, was a shock. He hadn't been warned that was what was going to happen. He'd assumed this was going to be another of André's tormenting denial lessons. Joe hated them, but being brought to the brink of orgasm and denied was at least familiar.

The next blow was more forceful, and he cried out behind the gag, thrashing against the bonds that held his arms and legs spread apart and slightly up off the bed. He didn't even know what André was hitting him with. A crop, maybe, or a switch? He wasn't sure. He didn't have any experience to tell him how the blows should feel, but they hurt.

A third blow stung like fire over his back, and he whimpered.

"That's it, dog. Take it, because that is what you're for." Another blow.

Joe shuddered. He didn't look for the blue spread. He didn't want it back. He entered the room, though, and searched the end tables for the watch. Maybe it had been left in here when André removed it to tie him down.

He rifled through the drawer, tossing aside the toys and clamps, ignoring the clatter of them hitting the floor.

"Looking for something?"

Joe froze with André's cold voice slicing down his spine and leaving him shivering and exposed.

"Did you hope to steal in and run away while I was out, pet?"

Yes.

"I'm just picking up my things," Joe said, rising and taking the box with him as he stormed past André and out into the living room. "All I'm missing is my watch. Do you know where it is?"

He was not going to cower. André had no power over him anymore. All he needed was that watch and he would be gone.

"This watch?"

Joe turned and André held up his right arm. The watch was fastened around his wrist, looking elegant even though it was a simple black band and gold-cased white face. The fine gold roman numerals glimmered behind the crystal as André turned it to the light. He held the thing close to his face, as though listening to the faint ticking, so Joe was forced to watch his lips as he spoke.

"Do you have any idea what this beauty is worth, Joe?" André grinned, but then sighed. "No. I suppose you probably don't. You're nothing more than a hayseed, after all, aren't you? The workings, though, did you know that the self-winding workings in this particular brand and model are rare? Especially to find one this old and as well… loved, still ticking, that is."

"Give it back," Joe mumbled.

"Give it back." André sneered. "The original crystal makes it even more valuable. But you wouldn't know that."

"I don't care. It belonged to my great-grandfather, and now it's mine. Give it to me."

"Oh, sweetie, don't be like that. Call it a gift." He dropped his arm again and shrugged, settling the sleeve of his suit back in place. "A down payment, if you will. It doesn't cover all of what you owe me, but it is a good start." His arm flashed out so fast Joe didn't have time to move back. Fingers closed about Joe's wrist, a vise grinding the bones together.

Joe yanked back, but too late, and André pulled. He twisted as he did, and Joe stumbled forward and down to avoid getting his wrist broken. He landed on his knees at André's feet.

"Better," André snarled, gripping Joe's chin and lifting his face. "We can talk about how you're going to repay the rest of your debt later. Right now, I think you need a lesson in manners."

André glanced at the piles of boxes by the door. "I would tell you to unpack, but I don't see the point. None of that garbage matters." He waved negligently, and Joe took the opportunity, face released from the man's grip, to scramble free.

"Nice try." André twisted his wrist again, and Joe couldn't stop a yelp of pain. "I'll have the super by in the morning to throw that shit out. As for you—" André reached for Joe's face once more, but Joe wasn't about to put himself at this man's mercy ever again.

He struck out, with all the force he could muster, and slammed the heel of his right hand into the outside of André's left knee. André jerked, and Joe heard more than felt the crunch of bones in his wrist as it gave way before he was free and André was going down with a howled curse.

Launching backward, Joe landed on his ass, putting both hands down to catch himself. His wrist hurt then, fiery pain sheeting up his arm into his shoulder as the bones crunched again. It took him too long to blink through the agony, and a hand swam through the fog to coil around his throat.

He was hauled up and slammed against the door. His vision cleared long enough to focus on André's face twisted to a mask of fury. "A little fight will pay for itself, *dog*," he snarled. "To the right buyer. Keep it up."

Joe scrabbled at the hold around his throat as black shimmered around the edges of his vision.

André's smile lacked the arrogance Joe expected. It wasn't really even a smile, so much as a patient expression. Almost, it reminded Joe of that parental tolerance aimed at him by Marie or Albert, maybe even his own parents before…. "You have to trust me, pet," André said softly. "I know boys like you." He petted Joe's face, but the caress was distant and vague through the haze. "I train boys like you. You want a place, and I'll give you that. Just stop fighting it."

No. That wasn't right. This was not how he was going out. He lashed out with his knee, connected, and André went down with a huff. He hit the floor, bent in on himself, and Joe slumped, heaving in breath after ragged breath. The air burned like acid along his throat but sweetened as it hit his lungs, and he recovered enough to get back on his feet and ready for André's next attack.

He needn't have bothered. André was dry heaving in a tight ball at his feet, both hands cupped around his groin. His face was an alarming shade of crimson. Joe watched him for a moment, trying to find something to guide him. André was clearly in desperate pain. Joe's own wrist and neck throbbed. His head swam. His heart hammered, and his lungs were like bellows in his chest. But his mind was curiously blank.

He glanced around the room, spotted the box he'd earlier set on the coffee table, and remembered why he hadn't left already.

"I want my watch," he mumbled, reminding that distant part of him that he'd had a reason to be here. That this writhing man on the floor was… was what? He crouched and peeled André out of his fetal position until he saw the glint of gold and pearly white on his wrist. He dragged that arm out, had to use his knee to hold it still, but undid the clasp and took the watch.

"Thank you."

"Fuck. You." André clung to his ankle and glared up at him "I own you."

A surge of black fury raged through Joe, blinding him to the man's agony, and he drew a foot back, seeing nothing for a split second but his own anger and fear. André glared up at him. No fear. No sneering, now. Just the face of a man who didn't even understand why Joe was furious. A man who had no idea why what he'd done had hurt Joe so much.

Joe placed his foot carefully back down on the carpet and yanked free.

Slowly, André sat up, still cupping his crotch. "You will be punished for that," he said, the pain evident in his voice. He reached up. "Help me up."

Joe took a step away from him.

"Don't be a brat," André said, almost indulgently. "I get it. You had a taste of what your life was like before. You think you want that, but what happens when you don't get the control you need, boy?" André's gaze was cold, but not cruel. "I know what you need, so help me up. You can keep your stuff if it's so important to you. The watch, you can sell. It'll be punishment enough for you to see it go."

Clutching the watch in a tight fist, Joe shook his head. "You're wrong," he said at last.

"Sorry?" André watched him, curious. The indulgence was waning again, but Joe was no longer frightened. The man had no sway over him, and Joe wasn't so helpless he couldn't look after himself.

"I said, you're wrong. I don't need you to show me my place. I know my place."

"Well, halle-fucking-lujah. Now help me the fuck up and get me some ice."

Joe did go to the kitchen and rummage in the freezer. He found a bag of frozen peas and tossed it to André. No way was he getting within spitting distance of the man. He *could* look after himself, but violence turned his stomach. He rubbed at his neck, and his wrist throbbed at the motion, so he found another bag of corn for himself. Ass settled on the dining table, he wrapped the corn in a dish towel, then around his aching, swelling wrist. At least he could move all his fingers. Experience told him he'd dislocated something and then snapped it back into place when he'd fallen on it. He was pretty sure there was no grievous damage, but it hurt like a bitch.

He sat there, watching André gingerly fumble the peas to rest between his legs. "I don't need you to tell me what I can and can't do, André," he said.

"You don't know shit about yourself if you think that. You need a keeper."

"I need to be my own keeper," Joe corrected.

André snorted. "Good luck with that." He looked up at Joe as he flipped the corner of his suit jacket over the bag of peas, partially obscuring it from view. Vain, even through the agony of crushed balls. He didn't get up. "You think you can do this job without me to ground you? You're delusional."

Joe studied him a long moment. "You really think I'm coming back to work for you."

"You are." André shrugged. "You like it too much."

Joe narrowed his eyes. "Like what too much?"

The look André gave him was incredulous. "You won't be able to stay away from the scene, Joe. You're addicted to it."

Joe tossed his makeshift ice bag onto the table and stood straighter. "You're the one who doesn't know shit about me." He braced himself for the pain as he picked up his half-full box from the coffee table. It hurt like hellfire, but no way was he leaving the apartment without at least this pile. These were the things that mattered the most. The rest he could replace if he had to, but not these.

"You honestly think you can live without someone to tell you—"

"I don't need anyone to tell me how to live my life. Least of all you."

"You need to be under someone, Joe. You need it like you need to breathe." Still holding the bag of peas in place, André used the edge of the couch to haul himself to his feet. "I can forgive this little fiasco, because I know how bad you need it and you've been too long without. You need it now, obviously, or you wouldn't have gone so far off the deep end. Come here and let me remind you what it is that makes you a good, happy boy." He held out a hand, and Joe gazed at it.

André was a strong man. He'd done many, many things to Joe with those wide, firm hands that hadn't been violent or hurtful. Joe had learned a great deal from him, and been happy to do so. He'd thought he loved the man. He swallowed through a raw throat and took a step back. Once, he had thought he would do anything for André. Including sell himself for André's pleasure. André's profit. André's pocketbook.

Joe backed away from him toward the door as he shook his head. "Need it like I need to breathe." He echoed André's words. "You're right about that. But not from you."

The effort of getting the door open made his eyes sting with tears and his wrist scream jagged horror at him. He stumbled out into the hallway.

"Joe!" André's own voice was frayed.

Joe didn't look back. He didn't slow getting to the elevator, but pressed the button, grateful the doors opened immediately. André appeared in the door to the apartment, hobbling, but coming too fast.

Joe dropped his box and stabbed frantically at the Close Door button. The watch strap dangling from his tight grip clinked against the stainless-steel console as he poked. Not that it did any good. He knew that. But he was otherwise helpless as André bore down on him.

Thankfully, the door moved, and André arrived just in time to bang furiously on the metal as it slid shut on him.

Joe slumped against the back wall and expelled a long sigh. He hadn't even time to pull it back in before the doors opened on the lobby. He kicked the box out and scurried after it. He knew André would be riding it down as soon as it went back up. Gritting his teeth, he picked up his belongings, but it was too much. His wrist gave, and he was only halfway across the lobby when he had to concede and grip the box desperately by one handle. It was too heavy for the old, fragile cardboard, and he watched helplessly as it fell.

Only to be grabbed out of the air by a pair of quick, competent hands. "There you are, Mr. Conner," Jimmy said calmly. "You know these men, sir?"

Joe looked from the rescued box in the direction Jimmy indicated. The doorman had a seriously dangerous look on his normally friendly face.

"I daresay they aren't the type you usually associate with," he said.

Cam and Craig were standing by the front desk, looking thunderous.

"Cam."

Behind Joe, the elevator doors swooped open, but Joe was already in motion, hurrying across the lobby, launching himself, and Cam caught him.

"Okay." Cam surrounded him, fastening muscled arms around his back and waist. Joe welcomed the press of strength on the healing cuts on his back because Cam held in the pain, the hurt, the exhaustion, and everything else Joe was. Cam kept him from flying apart at the seams. "Okay. I've got you. What happened?"

"Joe!" André's harsh tone pulled Joe out of his relief, and he straightened, pushing Cam off him. Twice, since Cam kept reaching for him.

"It's over, André." He lifted his chin and took a few steps in André's direction, leaving behind Cam's comfort. "I'm done. I owe you nothing, and I don't work for you anymore."

"It isn't just the work," André said. "You know it was never just the work. We never said that's all we were."

Joe swallowed. "We never said it was anything else, either."

Somewhere behind the pain and fury of André's gaze was the man Joe had first met. The man who had wanted to give a dying old friend something to make him happy and used Joe to do it because that was all he knew. Inside the slick suit and styled hair was a kid whose sense of right and wrong had been skewed by people too selfish to know what they'd done to him. Joe shook his head. "I can't fix any of it for you."

"I don't need fixing."

Joe smiled, but it didn't reach anything inside him. He knew André really believed that. He knew that was the reason he had to leave and not look back. "Then maybe it's too late for you." Really, that hurt more than his wrist or his throat or his back. Maybe he had loved André in some way. He turned his back and motioned to Cam and Craig, who held his box of treasures.

"This it?" Craig peered at the odds and ends. "This is what we came for?"

Too tired to even think about everything left behind, Joe nodded.

"What about your clothes and your books?" Cam asked.

"Doesn't matter." Joe flexed his fingers around the watch still in his fist. "I got everything that matters."

"No." Cam stepped forward, blocking his way to the front doors. "We came to get your things, and we aren't leaving without them."

"I want to go home."

Cam tried to wrap an arm over Joe's shoulders, but Joe stepped away. "Not you, either," he said very softly.

Cam's face went soft and devastated, but he stepped back and turned his attention from Joe to Craig. "Craig?"

"Already done," Craig said, stuffing his phone into his back pocket.

An instant later, the door to the street opened and two gigantic men bustled into the vestibule.

"Who the fuck are they?" André gasped.

"Friends," Craig replied. "Joe, you remember Pip and Cage, from the bar?"

Joe nodded slowly. "They came to…."

Craig punched his shoulder. "Of course they did, brat. You're mine."

Joe flinched.

So did Cam, but Joe understood what Craig meant in the context of the crowd of men now waiting in the street.

"Let them in, Jimmy," he said quietly. "They came to help me move out."

Jimmy shot a glance at André, who sighed and nodded once, then stood off to one side as Jimmy opened the lobby door and let in the stream of men.

"Go on up," André said resignedly. "Door's open."

"Just take the boxes piled by the door," Joe instructed. "And the suitcase. Don't touch anything else."

Cage gave him a curt nod and led his friends into the elevator.

It all took only a matter of minutes. Cage's men streamed into the building and out again, each carrying a box. It all happened just as fast as the elevator could carry them up and back down. Only one trip each. Joe's life was his own in that amount of time.

The bikers loaded everything into Joe's truck, and he turned back to André, content to let men used to traveling pack his things and cover them with tarps. He lifted his gaze to meet André's.

"This is it," he said.

André studied him. "What are you going to do?"

"Not your concern," Joe told him. "But it will have nothing to do with you. You stay out of my life, and I'll stay out of yours. Come near me or my family again, and I go to the police with names, dates, places. I have enough to bury you."

André's eyes went wide. "I trusted you."

"And I trusted you." One step carried Joe into André's personal space, and he realized that at some point over the past few years, he'd grown that extra inch or two and no longer had to look up at the older man. "You broke that trust the first time you hit me with that crop."

"It was training. I—"

"It was a limit," Joe said gently. "My limit. My choice, and you took it from me. Now I'm taking it back. No one gets that amount of control over me ever again. I did learn from you that night, André. Not how to take a crop. How to protect myself. You're a predator and I won't be your prey."

"I cared about you, Joe."

"Then you should have taken better care *of* me. Now I'll do it for myself, and I have you to thank for knowing how to do that. I'm not afraid of what I am anymore, André. Thank you for that."

He turned and walked out the front doors of the building. He didn't look back or stop to thank his friends for coming to his aid. He had to be out of there. It was one thing to tell André what he had. Another to feel the ripping, gouging pain of knowing what the lesson had cost him, and what it might cost others. André was a predator. Joe should do more to stop him.

Right now, he just hurt too much.

twenty

DAWN HADN'T yet lightened the horizon as Cam followed Joe out of the apartment building and over to his truck. He'd just reached him when the sound of keys striking pavement alerted him to the fact Joe wasn't as calm as he looked.

"Babe?"

Joe shook his head sharply, but said nothing. Nor did he pick up his keys. A pocket of motionless, soundless space enveloped him, and Cam stopped a foot away.

"Talk to me," he said, keeping his voice gentle.

"Can't," Joe replied. "Not... can't."

"Okay." Taking the situation over, Cam located the keys on the street between the curb and the truck's tire. He had to prod Joe to one side in order to reach them. Once he had them, he led Joe to the passenger door and opened it.

"Get in. I'll drive."

Meek and pliant, Joe let Cam deposit him in the front seat. He carried his right arm close to his chest, and Cam noted swelling along his wrist.

"He hurt you," Cam said. With utmost care, he picked the arm up and angled it toward the light. "Broken?"

Joe shook his head. "It was dislocated, I think, but pretty sure it all popped back."

"Should take you to urgent care."

"Nah." Just as gently as Cam had manipulated the arm, Joe wiggled it free of his grip. "It isn't urgent. I just want to go home." At last, he lifted his head, and Cam caught sight of his throat.

"Joe." He ran light fingers over the bruising already evident. "Joe." Blood drained from Cam's extremities, leaving fingers and toes tingling and Cam light-headed. He watched his own fingers run over those blooming bruises without feeling the connection of skin to skin. "God, Joe, he could have killed you."

A faint smile flitted over Joe's features. "He didn't. Couldn't." He met Cam's gaze, then tripped fingertips over Cam's cheek. "I'm okay. I can look after myself."

Cam clamped his lips tight. He wanted to protest that comment. Joe had done such a crappy job of it up to now. But the way the other man was looking at him, through a roiling bank of clouded emotion, Cam managed to say nothing. He refused to add to Joe's turmoil. If he needed to believe in his own self-sufficiency, Cam would not take that from him.

"Okay. But the clinic tomorrow, Joe."

Joe nodded.

"Promise me."

"If you want me to go, I'll go. At home."

Cam nodded, moved back, and started to swing the door closed. "Just gimme a minute to go around."

But Joe barred the closing of the door. "I want Craig to drive."

The prickling nausea of realizing he could have been too late to help Joe seemed suddenly insignificant to how he felt under this rejection. Having been prepared to fight for him, and enduring the blow of realizing he'd been too late, too slow, again, he'd thought he was rolling with the punches pretty well so far. Still, nothing prepared him for Joe turning him away. If every nerve ending sparked him to refuse, every bit of knowledge he had about his position in Joe's life told him to back the fuck off. It was near impossible to close that door and go to Craig. Worse still to surrender the keys.

"Cam, I—"

"He wants you. Go."

Cam snatched the keys to his own truck from Craig's fingers and stalked across the street to where they had parked. He was climbing in, refusing to look back in Joe's direction when a deep voice caught him, like a hand to the scruff of his neck.

"You all right?"

Cam stopped, door hanging out into the street as Pip trotted up.

"Fine." He growled and reached for the handle, but Pip was already in the way of the door's swing.

"You ain't."

Sullen, Cam offered only a curt shrug. "He asked for Craig."

"I don't know about you and him, but I knew about him and Craig back in the day."

Fucking hell, was everyone going to slice at Cam's heart tonight? "So?"

"Craig always said he was stronger than he thought he was. A good kid." His hand was huge, and he cupped it over Cam's thick shoulder, engulfing it. "He ain't a kid anymore. What he just did, that was a big deal. Don't undermine it by trying to coddle him. Let him look out for himself until he comes to you. He likely asked for Craig because that's safe. Platonic. But still sheltering. A friend who knows what he just left and understands what he still needs is better for him than a lover who might not be able to step out of his way."

"I only want to help. Protect him."

"What's going on might be inside him, and you can't help with that."

"And if he goes back to Craig?"

Pip crushed his shoulder with that grip. "That's between them and that baker of Craig's. You have to give him his space."

Not what Cam wanted to hear. But then, what could he expect from a stranger with only third-party knowledge? "What would you know about it?" It was unfair to lash out. This man, kind as he was to come all this way to back up a claim that wasn't really his, was only trying to help.

"I know about being the dominant half when the submissive half has to be his own man. It's fuckin' miserable. It hurts. But you don't want to be his keeper forever. A man who can't keep himself can't give himself, either."

Conflicting impulses raced through Cam. He wanted to tell the man to fuck off and not tell him how to run his life or figure out his relationship. Pip didn't know either him, or Joe. And yet, he wanted to beg the guy to tell him it got better. That it worked out. That all it would take was the drive back home for Joe to realize what he actually needed was Cam's guidance.

"He don't need you to tell him how to live or what to do. He needs you to be his safe place. He needs you to be his shelter. He needs you to trust him."

Aching with the effort of holding back the anger and frustration, Cam nodded. "Yeah. Whatever."

Pip squeezed his shoulder again. "I know it ain't what you want to hear, but I hope you take my advice. It might feel like daggers in your heart now, but he'll be the man you need when he's strong, not the man you have to take care of because he never had to be strong and so never learned how. You'd resent him for that, eventually."

It was worse that everything Pip said made sense. Cam might have been able to shrug off his unasked-for advice if it didn't make so much goddamned sense.

"If you need to talk, I'm at Reilly's most weekends. Eat there most nights. Just come. Sit. Brood."

"I don't brood."

Pip chuckled. "We all do." His voice grew serious almost immediately, though. "We need shelter sometimes too, Cameron. You can't be strong every second of every day, and that's part of the reason you have to give him space to find his own strength. And have people who don't need you to be strong. People who can hold you up when he gets heavy." His fingers dug deep, and finally, Cam had to look at him. "You got people, yeah?"

Cam shrugged under that heavy comfort.

"You got people," Pip said again, and waved an arm back across the street to where his brother sat astride his bike. "Don't be too proud to let us help. It won't do your boy any favors if he does come to you and you're too inside your own head freaking out to be what he needs."

"I am what he needs."

"You can't tell him that. He has to come to it on his own."

Cam wanted to look away, but he couldn't. He needed reassurance, and Pip only warned him he might never get what he'd been waiting nearly a decade to have. He wanted to hate the man. He wanted to rail and bitch, and then Pip slapped his shoulder.

"I know. It sucks. But one thing you can never do is lie to yourself, or you risk being the same thing he's just left."

"An abusive bastard?"

"The worst thing a Dom can do is let their sub believe in a lie. And convincing him he doesn't have to be strong just so that you can be his strength is letting him believe he can always count on you. No one can sustain that level of dominance forever. When you break, when you fall, you'll crush him."

"Unless he can hold himself up. Yeah. I get it."

"Let him find his strength, and he'll be able to hold you up too. There's nothing sweeter than a sub who can carry you when you're done and can't stand for another moment."

"You have that?" Cam asked, transfixed by the glow of pride emanating from Pip as he spoke.

"I have a guy who was in so many pieces I thought he'd never be whole again. He could carry the world on his shoulders now. He carries mine. He carries *me*. But I didn't put him back together. I let him go, and it was the hardest thing I ever did. I thought I'd condemned him to death, really. Drugs and pimps and guns and… shit." His voice shook, and his grip, tight again, wasn't comforting Cam this time, but taking comfort, and Cam squared his shoulders and offered what he could. "He came back. Cleaned up. Got strong, and never doubt, he is the strong one. When he needs me to hold him down, it isn't because he's weak. It's because he needs connection. He needs to know where he belongs. That he's got a place. That the pieces can come loose and not be lost. It reminds him that he can put himself back together, and I don't mind holding on to him when he needs, because he carries me all the rest of the time."

"You make it sound like Doms aren't all that strong."

Pip grinned and shook his head. "We aren't. You really doubt that?"

Cam considered the nausea roiling in his gut, the way his fingers still tingled, the way he wanted to climb into a dark corner and hide away the hurt of Joe's rejection. He felt weak. Useless. He had nothing if Joe gave him nothing. He was nothing without Joe.

With a sigh, he rested his head against the back rest of his seat. "I don't know."

"Shelter," Pip said. "Safety. Trust. Peace. Those aren't easy things to give. But they are mostly what a sub needs. Any gift of compliance and obedience you get in return is just that—a gift."

"That I know," Cam assured him.

"So build him a safe haven. When he's strong enough to accept the risk of taking the invitation, you'll be ready."

"I could wait another decade."

"You might. Or you won't. But is he worth the risk?"

"He's worth everything."

"Then that's your answer, isn't it?"

"It fucking hurts," Cam ground out, admitting to a near stranger what he might not tell another soul. What might be too raw a truth to offer anyone else.

"Yeah. It fucking does. Nobody said it would be easy loving a man who hasn't figured out how to love himself, but he left a bad situation tonight. He set himself on the path to a better place. You can't know how long it'll take him to get there, but you can try and be there when he arrives."

"Does it ever get easier?"

"Not really."

"You're a great advocate."

"I've built this life on truth. Honesty. There's no other way to do it right. My sub needs it, and I don't treat any other person with less. It isn't worth the lie in the long run. You know, his belief in me makes it imperative that I always live up to it. It sucks. It's next to impossible to always be that honest. And that's why I need him to hold me up. You see how that works?"

"Maybe I can't do this." Cam whispered the frightening idea out into the velvety night. It wove into the sounds of street noise and city. It vanished through the cracks of pavement and melted against the orange of the streetlights' glow. Disappeared. The very real thing he'd been carrying in his soul since Joe had come home bled into the night and left him empty.

"If you'd said it was no problem, I'd have worried, actually," Pip said. "You've got the right end of the stick, though."

"It's shitty."

Pip barked out a short laugh. "Yeah, well, the other end is a barbed hook, so there you go."

"Why live like this if it's so impossible?"

Pip clapped his shoulder one last time, then drew back. "Try living any other way. If you can, then the best thing you can do for that man is walk the hell out of his life."

Cam rolled his head around until he was looking at Pip. "Is it worth it?"

Pip's grin said all he needed to know.

As the admission of weakness drifted off into the slowly growing grayness of a weak dawn, he realized there was room in him now for something else. Dragging in a deep breath, he sat up straight and slid his keys into the ignition. "Fuck my life."

Pip laughed again. "I expect you'll be saying that a lot more in the next while. But you got people, yeah?"

Cam glanced to the empty curb where Craig had already driven off, then gave Pip a grateful nod. "Yeah. Thanks."

HE CAUGHT up to them at a rest stop about halfway between the city limits sign and the turn off of the interstate toward their hometown. Cam parked in front of the dust-covered white clapboard building. Next to the door, a wooden cutout of an ice cream cone canted to the side, and the ice freezer, rusted out in one corner, supported its lean.

Inside, white paint sported a film of time on every yellowed surface, and it had built up in the corners of the linoleum-covered floor. Off-white tiles interspersed with the odd red square were partially obscured by the splayed metal legs of chairs and tables right out of the sixties. Along the window wall, a row of booths in red vinyl and dark, lacquered wood gathered to collect the first streams of early-morning sun and hoard it for the patrons crammed onto their narrow benches.

Joe sat hunched and silent at a booth, both hands wrapped around a steaming white ceramic mug. He stared at the scarred wood under it. Pip and Cage and two other bikers occupied a nearby table. Craig was at the counter talking to the waitress. She nodded, glanced at Cam, and Craig lifted one eyebrow at him.

"Yeah," Cam said, "whatever you're having is fine." He was distracted by the pensive look on Joe's face.

Craig nodded, told her to make it three, and she poured another cup of coffee, which Craig brought over and placed on the table across from Joe. He slid into the seat next to the quiet man and bumped his shoulder.

"You okay?" Craig asked.

Joe nodded without looking up.

"Can I sit?" Cam asked.

Again, that miniscule, abbreviated nod. Cam slipped onto the bench opposite Joe and Craig.

"You think he'll stay away?" he asked, directing the question at both of them, and at no one. It floated there with the steam from their coffees for a few minutes, then dissipated into nothing.

Cam dragged his gaze from Joe's bruised, slightly swollen wrist to the window and past the sheer pane of ghosts and reflections to the lot outside. There were another half-dozen bikes and riders out there, smoking, drinking from to-go cups, and basking in the coolness of early-summer sun. Leather jackets draped over seats and helmets hung on handlebars. Shards of light glinted off chrome. Teeth flashed through thick beards, tattoos glowed with color in the morning light. The melee of life, easy friendship, patience, fierce loyalty broke apart the rigid shell of illusion around what a bike gang *should* look like and showed him what it really was.

"How can I thank them?" Cam asked, turning his gaze to Craig.

Morning sunshine flung an arm in through the window, across the table and painted a patina of gold and rose over Craig's cheek. The pocked network of acne scars there writhed up into the folds of a habitual smile. Imperfection disappeared behind the expression. The image of biker and barman and rival vanished into the face of a friend.

Cam swallowed, dropped his gaze to the burnt umber ripples marring the surface of his coffee, and realized he was shaking. Good God, what was wrong with him?

Movement from across the table and fingers forming a cuff of reassurance around his wrist caught Cam's notice. Strength fused fingers to arm, arm to table, and pressed warmth into his skin.

He looked up.

The small hairs on his forearm rippled up to stand on end. Joe gazed at him from the depths of sleepless bruising and pale exhaustion. His fingers, clamped so tightly around Cam's wrist, squeezed yet more calm into him, and Cam swallowed again, unable to figure out what to say.

Fearful of Joe's reaction, still, Cam let go of his mug and turned his palm up under Joe's grip. His fingertips tingled, as before, as his heart clamored and climbed his rib cage to his throat, pumping all his blood from his extremities to God only knew where. His head swam, but Joe's face remained the center of the maelstrom. Calm, despite Cam's imploding universe, Joe watched him from dark, glittering depths.

Slowly, the pressure of Joe's encompassing grip brought Cam's attention back to the physical, to the connection, and he looked down at their joined hands.

The swelling in Joe's wrist had gone down considerably. Bruising mottled the skin to tones of livid purple and angry blue with wavering borders fading away into newly tanned skin. Sinews stood out along the backs of his hands, and the wristbones were prominent, sharp, and casting distinct shadows in the slanted sunshine. A darker mark of a horseshoe inked on Joe's inner wrist caught Cam's fancy and seemed to wink remembrance at him. Cam didn't see weakness in the injuries, though. He didn't see the limitation of malnutrition or the paleness of years spent away in the city, in a life too precarious. He saw Joe. He saw the way he manipulated strength and tenderness into one motion, and felt the incredible reach of that combination as it wove tendrils up his arm and over his chest.

Cam's heart pumped heavy but stable, and slipped back into its cavern where it belonged. He found the will to move at last. With a featherlight grip, he closed his fingers over Joe's bruises.

"Hold on," Joe whispered.

"I am." Cam looked from the miracle of clasped hands to Joe's face, to his lips, a thin line of concentration, and to his eyes, still deep and unreadable.

"Tighter." The lips moved. The fingers cemented, and Joe blinked, slow and deliberate. "Hold tighter."

"I don't want to hurt you."

Joe dug his fingers into the muscles of Cam's forearm.

"I won't let you," he said, and the words carried the promise of truth and protection. "I won't let you. Hold on to me."

Cam forced his fingers to ignore the plea in his heart to tread lightly and crushed the bruises under them until Joe's jaw locked and his teeth ground.

"Yes," Joe hissed. "Like that."

The sting of tears was so fast and sharp Cam had no way to defend against it save to blink, and that sent them over the edge and down his cheeks.

"Joe...."

Joe responded to the plea by pulling their connection across the table, inexorable, until Cam had to lift his ass off his seat and lean, or let go. Joe had asked him to hang on, so he did, and rose for Joe to take whatever it was he needed.

Joe's mouth on his was hot, wet, consuming, but so brief it tore a strip from Cam's being when it left.

"Oh God." He heard himself say it. He closed his eyes, shutting away any more wetness behind the lids. "Joe."

But Joe was releasing him already, making him blink back to the moment and the sunlit space. His attention caught on the white finger marks next to the bruises, slowly filling in with color. They distorted the marks already there and left an imprint of Cam's presence on Joe's skin.

As he watched, Joe lifted the arm and examined the results "There." He set his arm back across the table in satisfaction. "You over him," Joe said. "You on my skin. How it should be."

The waitress appeared before Cam could think what to say to that, and Joe picked up his fork. He ate awkwardly with his left hand the moment she set his plate down, leaving his bruised and battered arm on the table like a trophy.

"Eat," Craig said after a few moments, shocking Cam into remembering he was even there. "Going to need your strength." Craig winked. His wry tone made Joe chuckle, but he didn't look up from his food.

Cam picked up his own fork, but his fascination with Joe's methodical cleaning of his plate and requesting more kept him from emptying his own until the eggs had cooled and the bacon congealed. Joe was polishing off his second round by the time Cam had finished the first.

twenty-one

JOE GAVE Cam the list he'd asked for. Not folded into an envelope and left on his pillow, but in person, kneeling at Cam's feet, three weeks after they arrived back at the farm.

He intoned acts he'd submitted to and acts he'd tolerated. Cam had expected the list to be ripped from Joe's soul and left, bloody and gutted, for Cam to figure out how to clean it all off and restore Joe's confidence. It wasn't.

Every item on it was polished clean of connotation and laid at Cam's feet as fact and not broken shards of Joe's soul. Just a list. Words. Acts of sex he'd performed for men who were willing to pay for the privilege. When he was done, and it took eons, Cam was the one feeling lacerated and feeble.

"What about André?"

And Joe gave him that too. In a wavering voice, he offered the acts he'd despised. The times he'd been with André that hadn't been horrible as well as the last night when André had crossed the line Joe couldn't forgive. Even that, now, was given up with a steady gaze and the certainty that it was behind him.

"And that's everything?" Cam asked.

Joe nodded. "All of it."

Cam itched to touch, but he couldn't. Not yet. Joe had given the list of what he'd done, how he'd felt about it. It was left to Cam to decipher the meaning. What had Joe not said? Cam studied the top of his bowed head, the curve of his shoulders, and the lax position of his hands at the small of his back. What had he left to interpretation?

"No impact play," Cam said, finally. That was easy enough, given the shudder and the bandages and the tightness with which he had delivered the acts of his last scene with André.

Joe agreed, without looking up.

"And no humiliation."

Now he did look up, flushed scarlet, but he nodded once more. "I've done that to myself enough. I won't allow it anymore. I can't."

With a nod and a relieved sigh, Cam agreed to the limits. "Anything else?"

"Every waking moment, I spent wondering if what I was doing would please André."

Cam nodded, but Joe wasn't looking at him.

"I didn't take time to find out what pleased me."

"And?"

"This is my home. I want to learn to work and run it. I need a mentor." He caught Cam's eye then. "Not a Master. Not like him." He tipped his head toward the bed. "There, I surrender. Outside?" He shook his head and kept a steady gaze directed at Cam. "I won't."

"Fair enough."

"Is it?" It was plaintive. Scared.

Cam nodded and bit his lip. "Yeah, Joe. It is. You run your own life. I don't have to do that for you. You don't need it."

"You don't want it."

"I wouldn't be good at it. Not now. You've gone through so much. I'm not equipped to give you that kind of guidance."

Joe looked up at him when long minutes had passed in silence. A hesitant smile softened his face. He opened his mouth, but Cam found he had one more question. The thing he needed the most to know.

"You ran from me and that clearing, what we did, and not from any of that?" he asked, unable to see the logic.

Joe's smile slowly faded to serious contemplation. "I walked away from André and his manipulations with my head up, and my back straight," he said finally. And then he looked Cam in the eye, and the smile was back, only sadder now. "I ran from you because you *touched* me."

Cam knew his face sharpened to frowning impatience. "And they didn't? How many men had their hands on you for pay? All I did was love you!"

Joe said nothing. He stared Cam down. Placid brown eyes locked with his as he waited.

"I loved you. Still love you. I—"

He'd lifted a hand toward Joe's face, but Joe leaned back, away from the outstretched fingers, breaking Cam's protest off like a snapped twig.

"You come to me like this"—Cam sliced the air in front of Joe's naked body—"and I can't touch?"

Still slightly discolored skin adorned Joe at neck, wrist, knees, and hips. He bore the marks of the life he'd left behind. His wrist sported the woven indentation of a brace he'd removed, and he carried that arm delicately, but with no less strength because it was tender. He was careful with his tender parts.

Cam watched him. "I don't know what to do," he confessed at last, when Joe had said nothing and hadn't moved. "What do you want me to do?"

Joe rose, fluid and agile, and eliminated the space between them with one long stride. He looked into Cam's eyes, petted his cheek, studied him.

"I thought I wouldn't be able to do this," he whispered. "Be like this with you."

"Like what?" Because Cam didn't know what *this* was. He only knew he'd waited for so long, so many years, then more weeks since Joe had left André, until he was sure he was going to burst into a million pieces from the strain of not speaking. Not touching. Not revealing how much he wanted.

"I was going to wait until every mark of his was gone. Faded."

Cam traced the edge of the decayed brown bruise just above Joe's collarbone. When Joe trembled, but didn't move away, he removed his fingers and replaced them with lips.

Joe lifted his head, sighed. His fingers closing about Cam's biceps were warm and unsurprisingly strong. The grip imprinted points of electric shock on Cam's flesh through the flannel of his shirt. It grounded Cam, and he focused on Joe's mouth and the heat of his skin under his lips.

He didn't remember Joe being as tall as he. But then, when he'd left, he hadn't been. Now, when he lifted his chin, Cam didn't have to bend much to inflict sweet agony on Joe. The sounds he made, soft groans and sighs, tingled along Cam's nerves. When Cam backed off for a moment, and saw the sight of the man, head back, Adam's apple working, eyes closed so his lashes brushed soft against his cheeks, it went straight to Cam's heart, then flashed deeper and heated his belly.

"Fucking hell, Joe."

Joe lowered his chin slightly so he could get a clear view of Cam. "Kiss me like that some more."

Cam gently extricated himself from Joe's grip. With deliberate care, he pressed a thumb under Joe's chin and lifted before echoing the hold Joe had taken of him and clasping his arms. He pressed them tight to Joe's rib cage as he slicked his throat with tongue and lips, then offered the sharp prick of teeth.

Joe jumped in his hands, surprised. His breath caught, he groaned, and finally let out a breath.

It was Cam's signal. He eased off. "My mark over his, you said." Cam recalled their conversation from the trip home.

"Only your mark from now on," Joe corrected in a whisper. "Only you."

"My touch doesn't frighten you anymore?"

Joe leaned against Cam's hold on his arms, pulling back, but not free.

Cam straightened to wait as Joe's eyes once more glazed and his focus turned inward. "I was afraid of how it made me feel," he said at last. "Not of you. Craig...." He flicked a gaze at Cam, and there was uncertainty there. Because he feared mentioning another man now? Cam wasn't sure, but he gave a slight nod, and Joe continued. "He didn't touch me the way you did. What he taught me was incredible. It was intense and physical, but not... like you? Not inside."

Allowing animal instinct to drive him for the instant, Cam yanked Joe against him. He fastened lips to Joe's skin just in the dip above his collarbone and sucked adamantly until Joe squirmed and whispered affirmation of the possession. Baring his teeth, Cam nipped, fed on the yip of surprise from Joe, and bit down, a pinch of skin between his teeth.

Joe's reaction was instant and as animal as Cam's attack. He swayed, gave guttural, approving acceptance, and turned his head so Cam had unfettered access to the spot.

Consent received, Cam released him, laved the spot with his tongue, and left a butterfly touch of a kiss over it.

"I want…."

The air around them crystallized. Joe's waiting stillness was brittle. Breakable.

I don't want to hurt you.

I won't let you.

He remembered the words. He didn't know how to apply them.

"Joe?"

Was it wrong to ask guidance from the one he was meant to direct? Joe's head came to rest on his shoulder. He could feel warm breath drop on his neck and shoulder, bubbles of promise popping open on contact.

"Joe, talk."

"I want you to want me. Like I am. Not perfect. Battered."

"Beautiful," Cam corrected.

Another puff of air, this one pushed out along with a small huff of sound. "Only to you."

"Who else matters?"

"Me?"

Cam stood back, hands still gripping Joe's arms. "Yes," he agreed. "How you see yourself matters. You think you're less than beautiful?"

"Been bruised and pulled apart and stretched thin." Joe's voice was low, abraded, and weak. His gaze skittered and danced. He was too tentative, as if the list he had just delivered with so much equanimity had been the extent of the power he'd managed to muster over the weeks since he'd left André. Now he swayed in the least breeze of Cam's breath, and Cam feared to let go of him.

But he did.

Releasing Joe's arms, he took a step back, crossed his arms, and tipped his head to one side.

Joe watched him, the edges of his clear, crystalline walls crazing and glittering with cracks. The least pressure would shatter his self-protective husk. Cam leaned the full weight of his dominance against it.

"A lot of the things I want to do to you require you to be fit."

Joe's throat worked.

"And since you aren't, yet"—he ran a single finger up the side of Joe's hand, over the protrusion of his wristbone, and back down the outside of his thumb—"that limits my options."

More swallowing precluded Joe speaking. Cam didn't give him time to unjam his thoughts or form them into anything more than the flickering motion of lashes and fidgeting of his hands. He dragged one over the back of his neck as Cam watched, then dropped it when Cam frowned.

"Restless?"

Joe shuffled his feet, shifted his weight, and gave a tiny shrug.

"Kneel."

Joe did. There was no hesitation in the move, but he remained behind that sparkling wall just the same. Cam leaned harder. He undid his zipper, and there, behind Joe's eyes, came the first flicker of reality: trepidation.

Joe fixated on Cam's hands, on his cock, less hard than Cam needed it to be for this, so he stroked, and Joe watched. Cam took no pleasure in scaring his lover. His lack of enthusiasm showed, and Joe's eyes flicked up to meet his.

"Help me with my jeans," Cam said, and Joe moved, mechanically assisting Cam to pull down his jeans and toss them out of the way. In the process, Cam touched Joe, raking a hand through his hair, leaning on his shoulder for support as he lifted first one foot, then the other, and cupping Joe's cheek when Joe didn't immediately move away from him once he was bare.

"That's it," Cam soothed, concentrating on the scrape of stubble under fingertips.

Joe huffed out a soft breath over the base of Cam's cock and nuzzled close. His nose prodded Cam's groin through the thicket of hair, and he flitted his fingertips ever so lightly over Cam's thighs.

"Behind your back," Cam said gently. "When your wrist is fully healed, I'll tie them there, but for now, you have to do the work."

Joe stopped his hesitant exploration and looked up at Cam through his lashes. Slowly, he moved his arms behind his back and clasped his left hand around his right forearm. The question was in his eyes, and Cam nodded.

"Like that, yes." He caressed Joe's cheek again, touched his thumb to his lower lip, just enough space between Joe's mouth and Cam's hip for the contact. "Good boy."

Under his thumb, Joe's lips twitched. They puckered and kissed, quick, darting, as if he might be reprimanded for the effort, and he closed his eyes, hiding.

Cam shifted just enough to rest his now hard cock against Joe's cheek. "Does that feel like I'm displeased?"

Joe shook his head.

"Pardon?"

"No."

"Good." He rocked his hips a bit, the prickle of stubble on the velvety skin of his cock a rush of exquisite sensation. "Because I'm very pleased so far." He pulled back enough to trail the head of his cock along Joe's cheek. It left a line of precome in its wake, and this time when Joe's eyes closed, it was accompanied by a hitch of breath and a sigh.

"You want it?" Cam asked. The hand he had been combing through Joe's hair tingled, and he stopped to crook his fingers into the strands. It kept Joe from moving his head. His answer had to be audible, and he cleared his throat to make it.

"Yes. Please, Cam."

Cam traced Joe's lips with the head of his cock. The hot breath emanating from his partially open mouth sent another deep shiver through Cam.

"Taste that," Cam ordered, and Joe licked his lips.

"Good?"

"God, yes." Joe opened his mouth wider, reached blindly, like a baby bird, for more.

Instead of offering his cock, though, Cam caressed Joe's bottom lip with his thumb again.

Joe sucked the digit into his mouth and swirled his tongue around it.

"Talented," Cam observed.

Joe's eyes opened, and the look he shot at Cam was all flash and heat and defiance.

"You've had practice," Cam said gently, sliding the finger along the same path on Joe's cheek his cock had recently made. He sucked the tip of his thumb into his mouth and smiled as he pulled it out with a small smack of his lips. "That's okay. Because I want you to pleasure me, and I want it to be good."

Joe said nothing. His gaze didn't waver.

"And you want me to accept who you are."

Joe dropped his gaze, dipped his chin in a small nod, and replied with soft, assured tones. "Yes."

Cam stroked himself lazily and began combing Joe's hair again. "Everything that came before is going to make everything that comes after this better, Joe. That's a promise." He rested the tip of his prick against Joe's now closed mouth. "You want this?"

Joe watched him, unmoving, for a heartbeat, then another. Slowly, finally, he opened his mouth and took Cam in, working his way forward with slow, torturous attention to detail. His gaze never left Cam's as he worked, and when he drew back, sucking hard and applying just the suggestion of teeth, Cam groaned and fisted his hair.

"Yeah. That's perfect. God, Joe, you're perfect." He tipped his head back and closed his eyes. "I'm all yours," he promised. "All yours." He sighed heavily as Joe sucked him in again and laid hands on Joe's shoulders, for connection, not control.

For a lifetime of bliss, he let Joe suck and lick, until his lover gently released him, and Cam cupped the back of his head.

"Why you stopping?"

"Why did you?" Joe countered.

"Stop?"

"Stop holding me?"

A smile rippled through Cam, and he released a shudder as it manifested on his face. "God, you really are perfect." He tangled his fingers in Joe's hair again and jerked his head back so Joe had no choice but to look at him. "And you're mine, yes?"

"Yes." Joe whispered the assent, eyes glittering now, and Cam once more caressed his lips, his nose, the track of a tear that slipped free and coursed down Joe's cheek. "Make me come. Down your throat."

Joe nodded, very slightly because that was all Cam's grip allowed, and eagerly took Cam's cock back into his mouth. He worked hard, sucking, licking, grunting occasionally as he took Cam deep.

Cam took his measure, encouraged his efforts, and demanded more when Joe stopped short of Cam's full length. "You can do this," he whispered, and pushed in, when Joe looked up at him. His lover balked, eyes widening as Cam's cock bumped the back of his throat. He convulsed, gagging, but Cam held his head in place. He stopped pushing, but neither did he retreat. "You can take this," he said. "Show me."

Joe's eyes watered again, but he wasn't gagging anymore. He'd mastered the reflex for the moment. Still, his gaze shimmered behind tears, and Cam stroked his cheek. A tear smeared through stubble, and Cam brought the damp thumb to his lips and licked the saltiness away. "Mine," he whispered.

Joe reared back, the movement unexpected, and Cam instinctually tightened his grip in Joe's hair. He needn't have worried, because he just as quickly plunged down again, dropping his jaw and taking Cam to the base. He sputtered, but sucked and pulled back, ignoring the yank of his hair and the resistance in his throat.

The animal ferocity needed no translation. It fired heat in Cam's groin that spread up through his chest and flared hot behind his eyes. Joe became a shimmering fiend in his sight, pulling an inferno of desire out of Cam. It burned down his walls, dragged him from the place of waiting into Joe's grasp. He went up in flame.

"Joe!" The warning was pointless. Joe slammed back down, engulfing Cam in the hot slick of his mouth and sucking the orgasm to the surface, then swallowing it down.

Cam wheezed and shook as it deserted him in pulsing waves of white heat. And Joe swallowed every flame, every lick of desire and tongue of desperation built up in Cam over five years of waiting. He took it all.

The orgasm choked them both, and Joe heaved after a breath as Cam pulled free and backed up a step. Bereft of Cam's support, Joe fumbled forward, caught himself on both hands, and winced, snapping his right one off the floor even as it touched.

Cam sprang for him, grabbed him up—hauled him, really—to his feet, then tossed him, bodily, onto the bed. Joe bounced and stared up at him. There was no hint of resistance in his expression. His cheeks were wet, his lips curved and shining. Spittle and come slicked his chin.

Cam dropped to a knee on the bed at Joe's side and grabbed the hand Joe would have swiped across his face. He pinned it, along with the sore one, above Joe's head, careful in some barely rational corner of his brain not to put weight on that injured wrist.

"Leave it," he snarled.

Joe's eyes widened, but not in fright or surprise. His pupils blew, his lips parted, and he panted some sound, as animal in its surrender as the sputter and reach for breath had been a moment ago.

Cam jerked the hands, pressed them into the mattress harder. "Leave them."

Joe nodded. He squirmed, just enough to twist himself straight, but no more. His back had landed on the bed, but his hips and ass hung off, his lower half supported by the strength of his legs and feet, firmly planted on the floor.

Cam dropped to his knees between those outstretched legs and took Joe's long erection in hand.

Joe fluttered his lids and jerked his hips. He met Cam's hand stroke for stroke and groaned aloud, bucking, needing.

Cam smiled, knowing exactly what it felt like to want that release like one wanted breath and to feel the sunshine. He sank forward, mouth hot and demanding on Joe's prick.

He had only to suck once, twice, and a third time before Joe was giving all in a frenzied humping. His thighs flexed and jerked as he thrust into Cam's mouth, and his throat worked, trying to release sounds that died behind closed lips.

Cam sucked and squeezed with his fingers, and at last, Joe burst. The brittle shell around him shattered with the sound his orgasm ripped from his chest. He spilled into Cam's mouth, too much to swallow all at once, and the excess dribbled over Cam's fingers and into Joe's curls.

Beneath his touch, Joe trembled, shaking violently under the effort to remain as he was, half off the bed, and not slump to the floor. Cam crawled up, licking come from his fingers as Joe's hot gaze fixed on him.

Joe parted his lips, flicked a tongue out, and Cam brought the tangy treat to his lover's lips. Joe kissed, licked, sucked each finger into his mouth one at a time until he'd licked all of his spend from Cam's skin.

"Perfect," Cam whispered, stroking his knuckles down Joe's cheek.

Without a word, Joe heaved up, flinging an arm around Cam's shoulders and burying his head in the crook of Cam's neck. He clung, all the tensile strength in his too-slim body wrapping around Cam and holding to him.

Cam did likewise, encompassing Joe around his waist and hauling him up onto the bed properly. For some untold length of time, Joe huddled like that, face hidden, body convulsing, off and on, with shivers and uncontrolled tremors that relaxed only when Cam manipulated his limbs, gripped his hair, showed ownership of Joe's weakness as he'd accepted the strength earlier.

Eventually, Joe came down and rested, limp but sated in Cam's arms, and his lips began a new exploration of Cam's neck, his collarbone, and his chest. He moved with a lazy thoroughness that had Cam improbably hard before long.

"Roll over," Cam ordered when Joe was showing clear signs of getting ready to lower his attentions to Cam's erection again. Without a single mewl of protest, Joe did as he was told and rolled to put his back to Cam.

As he did, Cam drew his hand down Joe's shoulder, his arm, until he had his wrist in hand. He kept hold of the arm, and as Joe settled on his side, the hand came to rest at the small of his back, secure in Cam's grip. He wiggled, and a moment later, the fingers of the arm underneath him tripped at Cam's own, as if requesting admittance to the stronghold inside Cam's fingers.

Cam obliged, taking his hand and placing the back against Joe's upturned palm.

"Lift that upper leg," Cam instructed.

Joe did, and canted his hips to offer the access he intuited Cam wanted.

"Good." Cam glanced around, spotted something yellow peeking from under Joe's pillow, and he pulled it free. He chuckled and kissed Joe's shoulder. "Perfect, in fact."

He wrapped the tie loosely around Joe's wrists, mindful of his weakness, playing to the strength of his surrender, and let the token bonds suffice. He dragged a hand over Joe's flank and slipped fingers down the crease of his ass to find his hole.

With no hesitation, Joe pushed back into the touch.

"Nightstand," Joe whispered. "Lube."

Cam kissed his shoulder again and fetched it. There were no condoms. He said as much, and found Joe peering back at him. "Don't need 'em."

"Joe."

"Part of my job requirement, Cam. I was scrupulously careful. You?"

Cam laid his forehead on Joe's shoulder and let that sink in, breathed through the thick muck of acceptance. "I'm clean, remember" he said finally. "Would have had to fuck someone to not to be. Never did. No one but you." He whispered, letting Joe's heated skin soak up the words, the admission.

"Never?"

"Played. Never fucked. Never did anything but toys and bondage."

Joe groaned and squirmed, pressing his ass up against Cam's body. "Let me be your first," Joe begged.

"Already were." Cam kissed his shoulder a third time. "So long ago."

"Not like this." Joe moved again, and his hands contacted Cam's belly. "Tie me up proper and fuck me, Cam. Like we both want."

"You're still healing."

"I want this."

"It'll hurt."

"I want your pain, Cam. Your cock." He tipped back so he was almost on his back. "Do this for me. Do it to me. I won't break."

"I won't chance that wrist." Cam dropped a kiss on Joe's lips, deepened it when Joe opened for him, and thrust his tongue farther when Joe let out a groan of need and surrender.

"Will you let me be the judge of what I can take?" Joe asked. "Will you trust me?"

Cam nuzzled at his neck.

"Will you believe I won't let you hurt me?" Joe whispered.

"Promise." Cam said the word before he'd really thought it, and wished he could snatch it back. It wasn't his place, here and now, like this, to extract promises from the man he had under him. That was for before they were in this. It was for him to make the promises here. Not to ask for them.

"I promise," Joe said. Not a whisper. Not a hesitation. Nothing but the same strength with which he'd delivered that damning list of sins. "I will never let you hurt me, Cam. You have nothing to be afraid of. I'm done running from this. Trust me."

Cam curled around him, pushing him back onto his side and sweeping a hand up his stomach, chest, to his throat and cupping it there. He could feel Joe's pulse under his palm, the beat of his heart under his forearm, the heat of his skin where his back pressed to Cam's front. He could feel the offer of his body against the demand of Cam's cock. And the reassurance of his strength in the press of his palms to Cam's belly.

"Do this, Cam. You need this."

Not *I* need it. *You* need it. And he did. He needed it so badly his entire being pulsed with the rhythm of Joe's heart and breath. Gently, he released Joe's body and knelt on the bed behind him.

"Speak up if I make it too tight," he ordered, pushing his voice into the depths of his own craving.

"Of course." Joe whispered again, his voice soft and assured. Murmurs of calm acceptance of his place beneath Cam's hands.

He crossed his wrists, and Cam took his time binding them, not tight, but secure. Joe tested and gave a small nod and a deep exhalation. His body sank to the mattress in relief of tension he'd been unable to let go of before. He drew his upper leg toward his chest and rolled so his ass was as accessible to Cam as possible. He closed his eyes and began to rock.

Cam realized he was humping the bed, rubbing himself off on the sheets.

"Stop that." He drew a hand up and lowered, as if to slap, then remembered at the last instant the twisted look on Joe's face as he detailed the last time Joe had let André tie him down. He clamped a hand on Joe's hip. "You'll get yours. Once I'm done with you." Cam bent and kissed Joe's hip. "Promise."

Joe moaned softly and nodded. "Thank you." It was barely a whisper. Barely an acknowledgement of his need, but it was there. It was a clue to what he wanted that Cam had the power to give or refuse. Cam slipped a finger over Joe's hole, then down, and pressed the skin of his sac and stroked the length of his cock, drew it from between the bed and Joe's body and laid it out so it pointed toward Joe's extended foot.

Joe whimpered and tried to lift his hips enough to swing it back.

Cam held him in place. "Wait."

A soft curse dropped from Joe's lips. He struggled a bit, but Cam held firm as he popped the lube open and dribbled it, cold and wet, over Joe's crease.

"Fuck!" Joe jumped, unable to really move under Cam's restricting hand. "Cold!"

"Behave, and I'll warm it next time," Cam said, implacable. He used his restraining hand to part Joe's cheeks, drawing the top one up and away from his goal so he could easily see what Joe was offering.

He took the next few minutes to prime Joe, fingering him slow and relentless, enjoying Joe's frustrated moans and his inability to get more inside him, or more friction on his cock, still splayed for Cam to watch as it leaked on the sheets.

This was something he was good at. Something he had become known for, this drawn-out trip to ecstasy. His play partners had come to him for this slow ride, and he'd perfected the skill. Watching Joe writhe under his ministration was a kind of torture all its own for him, though, and he knew he would have to learn the skill all over again to ever be as good at it with Joe as he was with those he'd once played with.

Joe held a piece of him that pulled at his need to protect, and that included ending the torture for both of them before it really got going. This was something that might take him a lifetime to relearn with this man. Cam grinned at the prospect even as he drew his fingers free and slicked his cock.

The sigh of appreciation, of acceptance that Joe let out as Cam finally entered him echoed itself in the deepest part of Cam's being. His chest loosened, his heart stuttered, and he groped for breath. None came.

Joe's fingers twiddled against him as he thrust home, and the touch grounded him, easing him back from the edge of panic to the here and now and the perfect heat accepting him. He thrust home, listened to Joe's grunt and hiss as he eased out.

"Okay?"

Joe gave a curt nod and Cam thrust again. Again, Joe hissed, as if in discomfort, but his fingers grappled the moment Cam stopped moving, and he glanced over his shoulder.

"Take it," Joe said with a huff.

Was he telling Cam to take him? Or telling Cam he could take the burn?

Joe ground out a breath and hauled in another. "We won't break. Trust," Joe said, and heaved his hips back and his body onto Cam's shaft. His muscles clenched around Cam, and the tightness of it nearly had Cam's eyes rolling back in his head.

Who was the bound one here, anyway? Who was in charge?

Cam stilled Joe's hips with the weight of his body over him and pulled out as far as he could before thrusting home.

Joe's breath came easier this time, and his body sank into the bed once more, deeper than it had. Yes, he canted his ass upward for the taking, but his shoulders relaxed. His torso sank under Cam's weight, and his hands, at last, ceased their endless questing and stilled.

"There." Cam recognized the surrender for what it was. This wasn't Cam controlling anything. It was Joe finding the safety to give, and Cam accepted the gift as it was offered. He began to move for real, thrusting and drawing back harder, deeper, faster with each stroke until they were both panting and moaning. He didn't warn of his orgasm when it came. It was his to enjoy, the gift of Joe's giving, to take and have for his own. When he shuddered out his release, he found he wasn't there alone. Joe quivered around him, his body sweat slick and gripping and his heart pounding. His spend wet the sheets between his legs and mingled with Cam's as it leaked out and down the underside of Joe's pulsing cock.

Unable to hold his weight off Joe, and unwilling to crush his lover under it, Cam rolled back and off. He propped himself on one arm after a heartbeat and looked down on Joe. His back rose and fell in a steady rhythm, deeper than normal, and his skin, hot to the touch, was flushed. He had his eyes closed, but his lips turned in a gentle smile. Their mess, mingled and staining the bedding, leaking from Joe, offered mute evidence to their mutual enjoyment. Then Joe shifted, straightening his bent leg, and the wet spot didn't seem to bother him as he rolled into it. His fingers flexed slightly and relaxed and he lay quiet.

Cam ran a hand down his back. He traced the veins in his forearms and the uneven splotches of bruising still visible on his wrist and lower back. The bandages had been removed weeks ago, but the scars remained, and Cam traced those too.

"How bad is it?" Joe asked. His fingers were on the move again, only flexing and twitching, since he was now positioned on his stomach and Cam was out of reach.

In answer, Cam leaned over Joe and kissed and licked at each scar.

Joe sighed, visibly relaxing. When his hands were at last still, fingers slightly curled, arms resting, Cam undid the bonds and rubbed at Joe's muscles, kneading the blood back to its proper flow. Joe groaned and sighed. Cam covered him as his body heat cooled, and finally rolled him, unresisting, onto his back. They kissed, spending eons in the tender discovery of that pastime before Joe's pecks became few and far between and his eyes no longer flicked open to peer up at Cam. His breathing steadied, and Cam laid his head on Joe's chest. One lazy arm came up to circle his shoulders, and soon after, he fell asleep ensconced in Joe's fulfilled promises.

twenty-two

SOMEONE ELSE moving at his side tugged at Joe's pocket of sleepy lassitude. He smiled into the gray predawn light and burrowed closer to the warm body.

"Mmm. Cam."

"Hey, sleepyhead." Cam's arm tightened, a steel band of strength and comfort around Joe's chest. "Sleep well?"

"Perfect." Joe let his lids slip closed as he pulled in a deep breath. Cam's scent was everywhere. The faint residual odor of the night's activities permeated the room, and for a few minutes, he wished he was back in the city if only to have that Sunday morning sleep-in feeling. There was no sleeping in on a farm, though, and he wrapped his mind around the idea of getting up as slowly as he thought he could get away with.

"You snore," Cam whispered as he nuzzled at the back of Joe's neck.

"Do not." A wide grin took over Joe's lips, though, and he chuckled as Cam's rough chin ticked at his spine.

"Oh, but you do." His hold loosened, his bulk rolling away.

Without warning, the morning laziness fell away, and Joe gripped Cam's arm before it slipped off. "Wait."

"Joe?"

"Hold on to me."

Cam rolled back to press his body along Joe's, chest to knees. "I've got you. What is it?"

Joe shivered for a moment, unable to control the ripple of chill memory. The few times he'd allowed himself to hope, André had always left him to wake in a cold bed. "Don't leave." Joe clutched and whispered the plea, unable to get the words above a hoarse sound with his throat going hard and tight around them.

"I won't." Cam nuzzled again, finding skin with his lips, then his tongue, and finally, his teeth. He nipped up a pinch of the skin on Joe's shoulder and clipped it tight. Joe gasped as a tingle of lightness spread outward from the spot.

"I used to be…."

When Joe hesitated, Cam did hold him tighter.

"Stronger?"

Cam released the pinch of skin and laved the spot. "You're not sure?"

"I'm really not." Joe clamped both hands around Cam's forearm. "Do you know?"

"I'm sure the man who called me here last night and knelt at my feet is not the kid who ran from that clearing. Not even the guy who came home and didn't know which way was up."

"I had to leave him."

"Yeah."

Quiet. Pause. Cam was waiting for something, but Joe wasn't sure what. Or if he should say it, maybe.

"He took something from me," Joe said finally.

"Yeah."

"I had to get it back."

Cam squeezed him. "Did you?"

"It was mine, you know?" Joe asked, and waited again.

Finally, Cam kissed his neck and whispered, "I know."

"Not yours," Joe went on, once he'd heard that.

"I know."

"He didn't take your Joe. But I had to get that part of me back before I could come back to you. Do you understand?"

Behind him, Cam shifted, then a moment later, slipped his arm free and rolled Joe onto his back. He propped himself up and looked down on Joe. There was strength in his expression, but compassion too. And love. And fear. He dragged fingers down the side of Joe's face. "I understand you," he said. "I understand you have to stand alone."

"No—"

Cam touched his lips, held his finger there until Joe kissed it, and then went back to petting his face. "Yes, Joe, you do. You have to stand alone and be strong on your own. It's who you are. You lost everything when your family died. That fire made you this lone, solitary soul. You don't need me to stand for you, just with you. To tether you."

He moved, leaning past Joe to grab something and pull it back. Something cool and silky flowed over Joe's arm, and that damn yellow tie made another appearance. Cam kissed it and laid it gently on Joe's breast. "I'm not going to be your strength. I'm going to support your strength. I'll hold you up when you slip, but I won't carry you."

Joe remained silent, watching.

"I love you. That's enough. The rest you can do."

"You think?"

Cam's smile was radiant, if small. "I know."

"I can't believe you drove all that way after me."

"What did you think I would do?"

"But a bike gang?"

"That was all Craig."

"You went to Craig." A sharp sting prompted Joe to blink a few times. "I can't believe you went to Craig, either." Over the weeks, Joe had wanted to ask Cam about that, but he'd needed so much time. So much space to get his head together, and the opportunity never seemed to come up before now.

"I needed help." Cam dipped his head and pressed his lips to Joe's clavicle. "I needed help," he whispered again. "And I couldn't let you do that alone."

"I had to do it alone."

"I know. Now. I was… selfish."

"Because you wanted to help me?"

"Because I wanted to keep you. I wanted to be what you needed."

"You are."

"No." Cam looked into his eyes and that smile came back. "No, I'm not. I'm what you want, thank God, but you don't need me. You're strong, Joe. You always have been. It's what I first knew about you, even when we were kids, thought I didn't understand it for what it was at the time. But you are. You have to be to do all the things you did."

"You think I did all that because I was strong?"

"I think… I think you did all that because you had to believe you were being strong. I think you went back because you knew you were."

"Maybe only because I knew you had my back."

"You just said you couldn't believe I drove all that way."

"I did say that."

"You didn't mean it."

"Guess I didn't mean I couldn't believe it. More like that it was an incredible act of love." He cupped Cam's face and steadied it so he could keep that glowing gaze on him a little while longer. "And I had forgotten what that really meant. I got lost in what I had with André. When I came back here, I remembered. I woke up, I guess. And I panicked because I wondered how you could possibly still love me if you knew. But then…."

Cam waited, captured, staring. Finally, he had to prompt Joe. "Then what?"

"Then you wrapped that halter lead around my wrists."

"Stupid, that. I was way too ahead of myself there."

Joe smiled at him and lifted his head enough to kiss Cam, deep and steady. "And you took it off again. That was the thing that reminded me what was real. You tethered me, like you said, by taking it off again."

"You sometimes make absolutely no sense."

"It wasn't the strap I needed around my wrists. It was the string to my heart. The promise."

"André never made you any promises?"

"He doesn't make promises. He makes deals. You said 'not yet.' I heard 'later.'" The sting hadn't left his eyes, but he quit trying to blink it away. It didn't matter. If anyone could accept that he needed that release, it was Cam. "I heard the promise, and there was nothing attached to it. No bargain. Just a promise." He swiped at his eyes and managed a choked little laugh. "You didn't want anything from me."

"Well." Cam kissed him, pecking at his lips, at his cheeks, licking a few times and smiling all the while. "That certainly isn't true. I wanted… everything." He closed his eyes, and his head dropped to rest on Joe's chest. "So much. I didn't dare ask."

"Afraid I'd run again?" Joe asked. He drifted fingers through Cam's loose hair and kissed the top of his head.

"Yeah."

"I won't."

"I know that now."

"I know you know."

They lay quietly for a while before Cam finally lifted his head to look at Joe. "Did we just declare undying love or something?"

Joe laughed. "Or something." He took firm hold of Cam's face again and gazed into his eyes. "I declare that I love you."

Cam stared down at him, and Joe wondered why there was no queasy rolling of his gut, no tightening of his throat. Nothing of the unease he'd known when André didn't say the words in return.

Lowering himself, Cam breathed out a sigh and dropped a kiss on Joe's lips. It was nothing to catch the kiss and return it. Less still to give one of his own and allow Cam the authority to reconfigure it, weight it with what he felt. When Cam drew back, parted his lips as if still uncertain as to what to say, Joe smiled.

"You don't have to say it, Cam. I know. I've always known. I knew it that day and that was terrifying. It isn't now." He picked up the tie and popped Cam on the nose with the end of it. "You wanna tie me to the bed and fuck me before we go feed the horses?"

"Brat," Cam growled, snatching the tie from him. Abruptly, he got off the bed and held out his hand. "Get up."

"What?" Joe took the offered hand and Cam hauled him to his feet.

"Get dressed," Cam told him. "Breakfast in ten." He whirled and disappeared out the door in only his boxers.

Joe heard his tread on the steps up to his room and stood in bewildered shock in his empty room. "What did I do?"

"Hurry up!" Cam called down to him.

The command made Joe jump, then smile. Okay. So Cam was right. They had work to do, and it wasn't Joe's place to tell Cam when they'd fuck. But damn, he still had his morning wood, and the idea of being tied to the bed in his brain. "Bastard," he muttered.

Even as he jerked himself into motion to find clothes, Cam reappeared at the door. "Nice tent," he stage-whispered, and was gone again, pounding down the stairs.

"Fucking hell." Joe palmed himself and groaned at the inadequate touch. "This is how you show your undying love?" he shouted, scrambling into his jeans.

He heard Cam laugh, and the sound made him shiver, made the air around him vibrate. He grabbed socks and yanked on a T-shirt as he hurried after his lover.

Hands grabbed him the moment his feet touched cold linoleum, and he gasped as a mouth clamped over his. The gasp was sucked into the heat of the kiss, taken from him. Then the hold and the kiss, lightning quick, vanished. He hadn't even had time to reciprocate.

"Fuck me," he groaned.

"Language, Joseph," Cam teased. "Language. You don't want Marie to hear you swearing like a sailor around her baby." He had both his hands over a grinning Mindy's ears.

"Like she's never heard it before."

Mindy shoved Cam off and laughed. "Breakfast is fend for yourself today, sleepyheads. I think Mom's already gone into town for her morning coffee date, and the hands picked the table clean an hour ago."

Joe stared at her. "Hey," he said, and she grinned back.

"Hey yourself."

"I—thanks, baby girl."

Her grin turned quizzical but didn't fade. "For what?"

"I don't know." But her morning sunshine grin was nice. The way she just accepted that something had happened, something had changed, and it was a good thing, made his chest ache a bit, made him warm inside. It was somehow a big deal that she hadn't made Cam's kiss, the obviousness of the new thing between them, a big deal.

"O…kay, then." She rolled her eyes at him. "I'm off to school. Have a good one!" She waved over her shoulder as she torpedoed out the door at the sound of the school bus honking at the end of the drive.

Joe grinned. "Now you can kiss me proper." He swayed his hips as he approached Cam, but got only a hand in the center of his chest, holding him off, for his trouble. "What?"

"Morning, Joseph." Marie's prim greeting froze him, mid hip-swing.

"Auntie." His face heated and he hastily stepped back from Cam's hand. "Uh. Morning."

Marie gave him a pert smile. "Keep it clean around the children, boys, yes?"

Joe nodded vigorously and Cam made a sound deep in his throat. Joe was gratified to see the deep red patches on his cheekbones.

"Good." Marie patted first Joe's cheek, then Cameron's. "I'm going into town for coffee."

"Hey, Auntie, who do you have coffee with every day?" Joe asked, curious.

It was Marie's turn to blush slightly. "Who says I'm going to see anyone?"

"Really? We have a perfectly good coffeemaker right here." He lifted the carafe in demonstration.

"You don't know him," Marie said, gathering her keys and purse.

"In this town?" Joe poured himself coffee. "We know everyone." He took a good swallow of the heavenly brew.

"He's not from town. He lives down the highway. Rides in to have coffee with me. It doesn't mean—"

"Rides? The highway?" Cam asked.

Marie looked at him, expression blank.

"Doesn't drive? He have a bike?"

Marie frowned. "I don't see it's any of you boys' business."

"Auntie." Joe took her hand. "If he makes you happy, then it's all good. If he hurts you, we have to know whose knees to cap."

She very nearly giggled. "Oh, honey. You can't hurt him. He'd break you in half."

Joe exchanged a look with Cam, and they both shook their head. "No. You think?" Joe asked.

"Have a nice morning, boys," Marie said as she hurried out the door.

Cam shook his head. "Nah. Pip's gay. Cage is, what? Forty? Maybe? He's too young for her."

Joe shivered. "I need more coffee."

Cam held out the carafe and poured.

Joe reached for the aborted kiss, but once more Cam held him off. "You've spent the last three weeks getting back in shape. Think you're up for a day of fence riding?"

"Sure." Joe tilted his head a bit. "But what does that have to do with kissing me?"

"Nothing." Cam's gaze flicked to Joe's crotch. It was enough— just that little fleeting instant of attention—to renew his cock's interest in the whole kissing thing. "But for one, you didn't say please."

"Pl—"

Cam's finger pressed to his lips. "And for another, you want me to show you how much I love you?" He drew close and flicked Joe's earlobe with his tongue. "Believe that by the time I do fuck you? You won't doubt how I feel."

"I don't doubt it now."

Cam stepped away from him and brought his hand once more to Joe's chest. "I know that."

Joe glanced down at the fingers, blunt against his sternum, and noticed that damn yellow tie, now a bulky wrap around Cam's left wrist. "Oh." Heat flashed up to Joe's cheeks.

Cam only grinned at him. "Seán left a note to go see him about the fences that need mending. Abby has her list for the garage equipment she needs ordered. We'll go out and talk to them, first off, then see what else needs attention."

"Really?"

"Really."

The talk with Seán went fairly quickly. It was littered with knowing grins and satisfied nods.

"What?" Joe finally asked the old man. "Why do you keep doing that?"

"He's happy," Abby said, approaching and holding out her list to Cam. "We all are. It's about time."

"What's about time?"

Both Seán and Abby chuckled. "Sweetie, this has been a long time coming. I've known it since I first got here. I'm just happy you finally realized it."

"I—" Joe stared at her.

"Just accept it, son," Seán said. "We all knew the day'd come. And here 'tis. Go on, now." He gave one more self-satisfied nod. "Ain't no fences 'round 'ere need mendin'. Probly only the ones out in the middle of noplace what needs lookin' to. Best take a couple mounts and picnic basket, lads." He winked. "Make a date of it."

Joe flushed. "Seriously?" he muttered under his breath. "You all just sit around taking bets on when we'd—" He flushed deeper.

"Wouldn't put it past them," Cam said quite close to his ear. The breath on Joe's neck sent a cascade of goose bumps down his arms. "You really want to know?"

"No!" Joe stepped away from Cam and immediately missed the warmth. He blinked at his lover, who smiled rather greedily at him.

"Saddle up," Cam husked.

"Oh. Fuck my life," Joe mumbled. His cock jolted in his jeans, and he hobbled toward the stable. "This is going to be a long day, isn't it?"

epilogue

"WHAT ARE we doing here?" Joe stood at the center of the clearing.

"Definitely not picking daisies." Cam grabbed the front of his shirt and hauled him close. "Or collecting stones."

"What then?"

"I'm interested in how your ass looks all speckled with grass imprints."

"Are you?"

"Problem with that?"

Joe gazed at Cam through his lashes. A stray breeze dipped over the tops of the aspens and picked a few strands of Cam's hair. It fluttered in front of his face and stuck to the sweat at his temple. The tip flirted with his lips.

"Nope," Joe whispered.

"I brought this." Cam held up a wrinkled, stretched silk tie.

The rush of heat and desire in Joe's being was instantaneous and fierce. He stepped back and held his hands in front of himself, wrists together. "No more sprained wrist," he whispered. "No more bruises."

Cam gazed at his hands, one eyebrow cocked. "I'm going to have to take that wristband off," he said, running a finger along the worn leather. "I can't believe you still have it."

"Of course I do." Joe swallowed hard and watched Cam's face. A few weeks previous, he'd taken to wearing the wristband Cam had given him, years and lifetimes ago, to cover what he wasn't quite sure he was ready for the world to see. "Go ahead," he finally encouraged Cam when his lover hadn't moved. "You can take it off." He wasn't sure if Cam knew why he was wearing it, but it was time, he decided. What better way to reveal his new ink than for Cam to be the first to see it?

So Cam popped the snaps and let the leather band fall into his palm. Revealed was Joe's faded black horseshoe tattoo, but also a new *C* in rainbow colors, styled to match the patterns on the original horseshoe. It was linked through the old one and the whole thing was finished off with a yellow ribbon knotted and circling his wrist.

"Oh." Cam traced the lines of colorful ink, turning Joe's hand over to see the entire tattoo. "Joe." He glanced up, and the look of wonder on his face made Joe's heart trip all over itself.

Joe grinned. "You like it?"

"Like it?" Cam's throat worked and his eyes got a little too shiny. He leaned in and plastered Joe with a kiss that had Joe's breath as tangled and erratic as his heartbeat.

Without speaking further, Cam pulled away and wrapped the old tie around both Joe's outstretched wrists, making short work of the binding. He helped Joe to the ground, laying him out on his back and stretching along his side. "Can you believe it's been a year?" he asked.

Joe's gaze never wavered. "Best one of my life." He held up his hands. "That's why I got this. A year is only the beginning."

The deliberation Cam used to lift Joe's arms over his head was mesmerizing. "You sure you want to do this here?"

A sigh escaped as Joe lifted his chin, soaked in the August heat and Cam's patient control.

"Where else?"

The next few hours they spent remembering, in the flesh, what warm summer breezes felt like on skin rarely bare to it. The way it cooled sweat-slick backs, how quickly it dried spent semen, and how warm the afternoon sun could be in the lethargic aftermath of lovemaking without boundaries.

Joe was sore in places that would make riding a challenge for a few days, but sated so deep in his soul, the heartsickness he'd come home with no longer found a single dark corner to hole up in. He wiggled under the constriction of Cam's hand on his hip as Cam languidly kissed down his abdomen.

Cam's calluses ran rough over the tender skin, and he gasped. He squiggled away, but the hold only strengthened and the weight of it held him in place.

"Going somewhere?"

"Apparently not."

Cam snaked back up his body and once more pinned his tied arms over his head. "Definitely not." His body was dead weight on top of Joe, his hands viselike and immovable.

This was everything. This was the fullness of complete ownership he'd craved for so long. This was what he'd thought he'd found in a man who only wanted him so he could dole him out to the highest bidders, a piece at a time. Now, here he was, in the place where he'd first discovered he wasn't his own, and with the man who would never part with a single breath at any price.

"Cam."

"Yeah?"

"Can you hold me any tighter?"

Cam's legs squeezed both of Joe's between his. "Always."

Joe dropped his head onto the ground. The grass tickled at his ears and imprinted his back, even through the scars there. Cam's weight eased the trepidation out of him, and he fell from contained, captured, to utterly free and unfettered. He'd been so afraid the first time. He'd felt the empty air around him and had nothing to hold to and no way to get back. He hadn't understood that he could never be lost in all that space as long as Cam was there to ground him. He got it now.

"I remember how it feels," he whispered.

"How what feels?"

"Safety."

Cam kissed his cheek. "Guess André—"

"No. Not him. The fire. Never felt safe after that. Always felt like there was nothing around me to hold on to." He blinked and looked at Cam. "'Cept you. Weird, but the tighter you hold me, the freer I am. That was fucking terrifying that first time. Had no idea how to deal.

When Craig tied me up, I felt… tied up. Contained. Held in place. When you do it, I'm not. I'm free from everything. All the worries and missing Mom and Dad. Regrets. Everything falls away for a time. And it's easier to look at when I get back." He studied Cam for a while. There wasn't much to read in his lover's open, sultry expression.

"You know what I'm not sure of?" he asked finally.

"What?"

"What you get out of all this."

Cam blinked at him. "What do you mean what I get?"

"I get damage control, and freedom from all the crap I've done. All the icky stuff. You get… what? A messed-up boyfriend you have to take care of every time we make love."

Cam smiled. Not the reaction Joe expected. "I get you, dumbass."

"That's no prize"

"Mmm." Cam's smile grew sly and he dipped his head. He planted a soft kiss on Joe's lips, but didn't linger. "I get your sweet sounds." He licked at Joe's throat. "I get that arch you do when you come, the way you throw your head back and hum a tiny bit." He sucked up a patch of skin on Joe's pec. "I get to mark you however I want. See the mark." He licked the spot as he let it go and smiled smugly. "Any time I want." He crawled lower and nuzzled at Joe's abdomen. "I get a warm body in my bed."

"Oh good God, Cam, I don't think I have another in me," Joe whispered as Cam huffed warm breath over his pubes and soft cock.

"I get to see you undone." He kissed Joe's cock and reversed the path he'd taken, more leisurely, and with more marks left behind, until he was once more astride Joe, clamped down tight. "I get to see you remake yourself into this bright, beautiful thing that I can call my own."

"My precioussss."

Cam snarled and closed teeth over the side of Joe's neck. The blunt pressure made Joe squirm and break into laughter.

"I get that," Cam said breathlessly as he reared up and watched him convulse. "Joe, I get this. You. All I ever thought I could want."

"And it's enough?"

"More than."

"Swear?"

Cam confirmed his truth with a kiss that left Joe weak and breathless and sated. They lay for a while in the grass, ignoring the itch and the dampness of the little field that never quite dried completely, and breathed summer air, sweet memory, a million possible future joys.

Strands of hair loosed from Cam's ponytail fluttered across Joe's chest, stroking the love bites with flighty fingers, and he smiled. The sun warmed his closed eyelids. "When we get married, let's do it here, okay?" he whispered.

Beside him, Cam stirred. "That was the lamest proposal ever."

Joe chuckled. "We can wear yellow ties."

"Okay." Cam kissed his bicep, because that was where his lips were closest, and he didn't have to move. "I take it back. Best proposal ever."

Joe held his breath.

"Stop it." Cam thumped his belly, and he let out his air in a whoosh. "You know I'll say yes."

"So say it."

Cam did move, then, enough to look Joe in the eye. "Yes. Of course yes, a thousand times, yes. I will wear a yellow tie."

Joe snorted. "You're an ass."

"Mmmm. But I'm your ass." He snugged an arm around Joe's waist and laid his head on Joe's stomach. "And your ass is mine."

"And this grass is soggy. Can we go home and finish this in bed?"

Cam sat up. "Thought you didn't have another one in you." He stood and helped Joe to his feet, though.

"I have whatever my master commands of me." Joe caught Cam's gaze and held it.

"Turn around," Cam ordered, and Joe did. A moment later, he felt fingers trace over his buttocks. "I was so right about that."

Maybe it was a ridiculous thing to be proud of, but Joe was. It warmed him to his core, and he smiled as he let Cam help him into his jeans. He somehow knew his lover was going to sneak him into the foreman's quarters they had moved into still bound, and it was too delicious a thought not to begin a new, heavy stirring in his groin.

"Good?" Cam asked, once his jeans were fastened.

"Very."

"Excellent. Let's go. Home. Bed." He spun Joe around and took a heady kiss. "Fucking. Yes?"

"A thousand times yes," Joe muttered.

"That's my boy," Cam said with an indulgent smile. "God, I fucking love you, Joe. So much."

Joe would have replied, but he was too busy being kissed.

JAIME SAMMS has been writing her stories between men long enough to know better but not nearly long enough to have told all the tales she has to tell. She splits her time between a day job that pays the bills and her writing that feeds her soul. She's also a mom with a saint of a husband, who keeps the kids fed and clothed and homeschooled and herself on a schedule that keeps her sane. She also reviews yaoi novels for Kuriousity, http://www.kuri-ousity.com/. The three cats in residence seem to approve of this arrangement enough to warm her toes at night and keep up a supply of mice from the backyard they think the family needs for survival. Who are we to argue?

Visit her website: http://www.jaime-samms.com,

her blog: http://jaimesamms.blogspot.com,

and her LiveJournal: http://dontkickmycane.livejournal.com/.

Jaime Samms

OFF STAGE: IN THE WINGS

http://www.dreamspinnerpress.com

Off Stage from JAIME SAMMS

Jaime Samms

OFF
STAGE:
RIGHT

http://www.dreamspinnerpress.com

Also from JAIME SAMMS

Better

Jaime Samms

http://www.dreamspinnerpress.com

Also from JAIME SAMMS

THE
FOSTER FAMILY

JAIME SAMMS

Also from JAIME SAMMS

Also from JAIME SAMMS

Also from JAIME SAMMS

http://www.dreamspinnerpress.com

Still Life

JAIME SAMMS

http://www.dreamspinnerpress.com

Read more from this author in

http://www.dreamspinnerpress.com

Also from Dreamspinner Press

http://www.dreamspinnerpress.com